PERVERSIONS

and

INFIDELITIES

by

Eve St. Albert

Fossil Cove Publishing

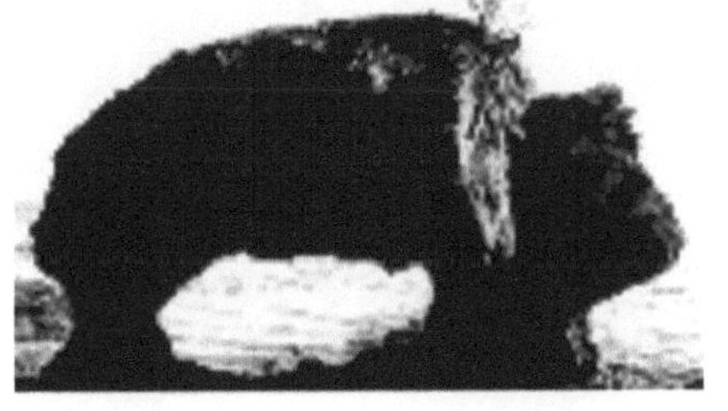

Winnipeg, Manitoba

PERVERSIONS AND INFIDELITIES

By Eve St. Albert

Fossil Cove Publishing, 1301 - 90 Garry Street, Wpg, Man, Can, R3C 4J4

EBook - ISBN: 978-1-998453-07-8

Print Book - ISBN: 978-1-998453-08-5 (IngramSpark)

Cover design by Dawne Dominique

Published by D.G. Valdron, Fossil Cove Publishing,

Text set in Garamond

PERVERSIONS

and

INFIDELITIES

THE TALES

<u>Dedication</u>

You know who you are

To everyone else

A mystery

CUFFED

She never thought of herself as kinky.

Kinky, to her was an ungainly combination of the appalling and the ridiculous. Pretentious youths with too much make up, blotchy tattoos and too many piercings, or dumpy self-absorbed people, pushing middle age. She didn't see herself in there, the rope bondage seemed pointless and uncomfortable, the role play demeaning. Floggers and paddles and clamps... That all looked like it would hurt. It didn't appeal to her at all.

She was, when she bothered to think of herself, quite conservative. She was from a large farming family, full of brothers and sisters. The recklessness that had accompanied puberty had been closely monitored by the elders and busybodies of her small village. Rebellion was little tolerated, and there had been too many chores and too much babysitting to get into much trouble. She'd gotten better marks than her peers in school. This had led to college, and a career in accounting, a job in the city.

She never felt really comfortable with her peers though. Shaped by an odd mixture of small town values, family responsibility and the demands of single urban life, she found herself mostly alone. Not a virgin by any means. That had been dispensed with at university in the aftermath of too much drinking. It had been a perfunctory and unsatisfying act. She'd had sex a few times, found masturbation to be superior, had learned to suck a cock not for any particular enthusiasm but because everyone was doing it and it simplified things. There'd been a few boyfriends, even a relationship or two, but nothing that had lasted.

In reflective moments, she thought that she was one of those self-contained people that didn't need someone in her life to complete her. Growing up in a crowded household, she relished the privacy of her own apartment. At times, she worried about growing old, a childless spinster, but she was only in her thirties, there was still time.

It was late September, she was shopping for the twins' birthday. The twins were a nephew and niece, she had a lot of nephews and nieces. They all had birthdays and Christmases and Easters and Halloweens, it added up. So she ended up in the Halloween section, looking for gifts which would be cheap and unique.

A pair of trick handcuffs caught her eye. Perhaps the nephew would like it? Boys always wanted to be cops, or secret agents, or cowboys. She picked up the package and hefted it. To her surprise, there was a bit of weight, they were real handcuffs, steel, with keys and everything.

A closer look showed that they were trick handcuffs, each cuff had a little release latch so that you didn't actually need a key.

Silly thing, she thought. If it's got a release, why would you even bother with a key? And why handcuffs that you could release so easily? For children's games, she thought....

Or adult games...

Her nephew probably wouldn't like it, and even if he did, his parents probably wouldn't approve. Perhaps she should go looking for a Nerf pack.

But still, less than ten dollars? Why not? She tossed it into her cart.

Later that evening, after supper, she wrapped the twins' presents. The handcuffs? Definitely not included. They didn't go with the other purchases, unisex sets of Nerf toys. Maybe she'd pass them on to some other relative? Perhaps in a bridal shower?

She poured herself a glass of wine, carried them to the couch with her, and clicked the television on.

"Made in china."

Well, that was why they were so cheap. She handled them, weighing them in her hand, there was a surprising heft to them. They seemed well made. She played with them absently, running the clasp all the way through, listening to and feeling the click, click, click as it ran through the teeth and then swung free.

Really, if they opened so freely, what good were they? But then, she thought, if there's something in there, then it can't go through all the way, it would catch.

Experimentally, she stretched out her wrist. Let the cuff slip on, felt the click, click, click as it ratcheted closed around her wrist.

Her heart beat a little faster.

The metal was cold against her wrist. The other cuff dangled free at the end of the chain, a pendulum weight tugging at her arm. She stared at the shining steel locked around her wrist, silver plated and

Perversions and Infidelities / Page 2

catching the light. There was something ... remorseless, about it, relentless. She shivered.

They put these on bad people, she thought. To hold them, keep them. She'd seen enough cop shows and movies to know the combinations. Wrists in front, the prisoner, helpless in the dock. Cuffed to another person or a piece of furniture, enforcing immobility, or forcing them to follow. Or behind the back, to render somconc powerless.

What would the real ones be like? She'd never thought of what it might be to be a criminal.... Or a prisoner. Would there be a feeling of helplessness as they went on? A loss of freedom? What went through their minds?

Humiliation? Submission? Surrender?

The metal was hard and cold and heavy on her wrist. Was it like that for them? For someone being cuffed, to hear every click, to know that freedom was vanishing in the bites of hidden metal jaws.

Carefully, she slipped her other wrist under the second cuff. Turning her other hand, to ratchet it shut. It was harder, the links between the cuffs limited her mobility. As it bit tight against her wrist, she realized she was caught - her world now defined by the space between three silver chain links and to pieces of ratcheted chrome plated steel.

Her heart skipped a beat.

Deep in her stomach, butterflies launched and batted themselves against her chest. The cuffs were cold on her wrists, she could feel their slight weight..

Take them off, she thought. Right now. She got up to retrieve the keys from the kitchen table. But they were too tight, there was no room for her wrists to twist inside them. The cuffs were facing with the keyholes the wrong way. She couldn't quite get the keys in.

That was okay, they had quick release levers. She'd worked them several times, as she'd played with them. A cold thought struck her, the release levers had worked, except that they hadn't been encircling anything then. Her breath caught just a tiny bit, a gasp so subtle that no one else would have heard it. Her hands trembled just slightly as she tried to work her fingers around to the release catch.

She found it, the tight steel ring loosened, and she opened it up completely, freeing her wrist and then undoing the other. She laid it on the kitchen table. What a silly thing, she thought. Not so silly if she hadn't been able to open it though. She wondered, out of the blue, if 911 got a lot of calls from people who'd accidentally handcuffed themselves like that and couldn't get out. What a thing to have to explain.

Leaving the cuffs on the kitchen table, she went to the bathroom, then back to the living room, settled on the couch, and channel flicked until she found a decent movie.

About an hour in, she paused to go to the kitchen, make a cold plate of cheeses and pickles. Distracted, she picked up the cuffs again, and absently played with them, as she watched the rest of the movie, listening to the click of the ratchets, the play of weight from one cuff to the other, the shaping of the hinged jaw. Once in a while, she'd slip it around one wrist, ratchet it closed, and then release it again, but only one wrist. A friend called, she chatted, casually dangling it from a fingertip, watching the light play off the chromed surface.

Eventually it was late. She went into the bedroom and undressed, dropping her clothes in separate adjacent laundry bins, one for underwear, one for whites, for colours, for darks. She was always vaguely pleased at how organized and tidy she was. It was an instinct.

The bathrobe was plucked from the bedroom door hook. Into the bathroom, hang up the bathrobe, turn on the shower, and when the temperature was just right, step in. She enjoyed showers, there was a casual sensuality to it. She liked the needles of hot water jetting against her skin, liked the private exhibition of her nudity. Sometimes, in the right mood, she played with herself in the shower, occasionally to orgasm.

Bathrobe on, hair toweled, moisturizer applied to face and body

After that, she proceeded through her apartment, shutting off the lights. It was a ritual, start with the kitchen, check to make sure all the appliances are off, then the lights, then the doorway and hall, around to the living room, lamps off, television off and so on....

As she reached for the last remaining lamp by the couch, she noticed the handcuffs again on the coffee table, ratchet jaws open, catching the soft light on the chrome surface and throwing it back.

She sat back on the couch, picked them up. They seemed heavier in the low light, more ... potent? More.... Sinister? She flashed back on the awkward moment when for a second she thought she'd been trapped. Not really, of course, but there'd been a moment... of helplessness.

Her heart beat a little faster.

They put these on bad people... she thought. Naughty people, wicked people, people who committed crimes, broke the law, robbers, drug dealers, hookers... Dirty people.

To make them helpless.

Her heart was beating just fast enough for her to be aware of it. Her stomach felt light. Did she feel a tingle?

Not this toy of course, this one was safe, easy to get out of.

But, still....

Abruptly, she stood and slipped out of her robe. Naked she laid back on the couch, reclining up against the arm.

She watched the ratchet jaw close, felt the vibration as the teeth rotated through, capturing one wrist.

Then the other.

She was naked wearing nothing but handcuffs. It made her tingle. In the low light, the metal seemed to shine bright. It wasn't as tight as before, she could move her wrists a little. She pulled her hands apart, feeling the millimeters of slack vanish against the clinking of the chain links. Caught, she thought. Helpless. Anything could happen to her, someone who cuffed her could do anything they wanted, and she'd have to submit.

She pulled one leg up on the couch, knee bending, thighs opening up.

Heart pounding, she lowered her cuffed wrists to her pubic mound, letting her fingers crawl through the black thatch of pubic hair. She touched her lips. She was already wet. She could feel the cold metal against her pubic mound, as she rested her wrists between her legs, fingers opening herself, thumb rubbing against her clit with a fierce urgency. She arched her back.

"Fuck!" she whispered, and kept whispering it louder and louder, pulling against the chains, feeling the cuffs, the captivity, the constrained mobility, her excitement building and building.

Until she came. The orgasm was a blinding rush, like a landslide falling on her, a sense of impact striking her and just surging up and through her body, leaving her breathless....

The handcuffs were a fascinating new toy. She hadn't expected the effect on her, and couldn't adequately explain it to herself.

Was she a masochist? She didn't think so. She felt no urge to be whipped, to wear a collar, dress up in a leather harness. Calling someone 'Master' just seemed silly.

And yet, there was an allure. Somehow, it made things more intense. Maybe it was the restriction on mobility, the fact that she could not move her wrists freely, it meant her hands were like a pair of horses in tandem harness, working together. That was certainly part of it, it seemed to focus her more when she masturbated it.

But there was more. There was just a ...sexiness to them. She liked the way they shone in candle light. She used her silver polish to make it shine and catch the light, it worked best in low lights, under a single lamp, or in front of candles.

Sometimes, she'd carefully wrap it in a tea-towel and leave it in the fridge while she went to work, so that when it went around her wrists it was bracing cold, the iciness making the metal ruthlessness more emphatic. Chilled handcuffs, she thought, there was something sexy there. It was hard to ignore or overlook chilled metal binding your wrists, it focussed your attention...

There was something about looking down at her body, especially her naked body, and seeing the arc of her arms, drawn together, the unforgiving shining metal binding her, shaping her posture. There was a fascination to it, it was almost hypnotic.

For the first time in her life, she would watch herself intently as she masturbated.

It was a wonderful toy. Sometimes she'd carry it in her purse, shopping, or to work. She'd never wear them outside of course. But just knowing they were in her purse, that secret naughtiness. It was a thrill.

Perhaps, she thought, it was like the earnestness of teenage boys carrying a condom around, sometimes for months or years, never using it, never having even a chance, but just having it. It was the signifier of sex, of naughtiness.

She wondered sometimes about why it affected her? A signifier of sex? Perhaps.

A signifier of ... badness, wantonness, of criminality and rule breaking. Did it excite her because it made her think of herself as a bad girl, a naughty girl, the sort that broke the law... There was that, definitely, she'd feel oddly wicked and powerful, liberated, when she wore them. The sort of girl that does sexy nasty things and doesn't care what anyone thinks.

But there was also surrender, submission, and helplessness. Yes, that was there too. It occurred to her, when she thought of it, that the feelings wearing the handcuffs were contradictory. That it didn't make sense to feel both liberated and surrendered, nasty and helpless at once. But she was smart enough not to worry about it, and just revel in the sensations.

Exploration came slowly. She wore them in the kitchen, in the bedroom. Once, she spent a whole evening naked in cuffs, watching TV, fumbling as she made a meal, masturbating repeatedly and touching herself. She wanted to wear them in the shower, by candle light, but was afraid that the water might damage the inner mechanism.

Once on the bed, she knelt, ass up in the air, face down on a pillow, gasping as she struggled awkwardly to a shivering orgasm. Another time, leaning against the bedroom, legs spread, face and shoulders pressing against the wood grain, as close to a police pat down as she could get, hands between her legs, leading her to an orgasm that made her knees tremble.

Mostly, she liked to watch. She liked a comfortable position on the couch, something where she could sit up and look down, knees up, legs spread, steel glinting against the black pubic hair of her mound.

But of course, she couldn't really see that much. She'd never been one of these feminists who got to know their vaginas with mirrors and speculums. She'd always thought that was vaguely disgusting, there's nothing special about knobby toes, or flabby skin, or the odd places of anatomy. She'd seen cats' assholes, she'd never felt an urge to get a look at her own.

But now? The cuffs made things different, she wanted to see herself framed by the cuffs. It started with awkwardly trying to use a hand mirror at the same time, which gave her shaking views of the insides of her thighs and rushed glimpses of pubic curls. Then a stationary mirror.

Then on the couch, hips elevated on pillows, a mirror propped up on a kitchen chair placed carefully.

It was a revelation. Her hands, cuffed at the wrists, joined by silver links, seemed almost things of their own, pink butterfly wings, fluttering, joined by chrome. Between the pairs of slender fingers, the black pubic hair, the pink slit. She saw herself wet for the first time, saw not just her pinkness but the shining shimmer between her lips.

Mirrors became a part of it, not always, but often enough. She watched herself in different positions, different postures as she masturbated in handcuffs. Watched a vibrator slip inside. She tried masturbating in different ways. Sometimes she watched her whole body, her pussy hidden between her legs. She stared in fascination at the signs of her own arousal, watched her lips as she gasped, stared at nipples hard and rigid as the glass, noticed the sweat, gazed at the trembling of muscles. It was as if she was seeing herself naked for the first time, seeing her own body, appreciating it, enjoying it rather than simply living in it.

She cropped her pubic hair, something that she had very consciously avoided. She wasn't a model, why not let it grow. But messy bush clashed with the elegance of steel, the shapeliness of fingers and hands like butterfly wings. Butterfly wings, she liked that image, sometimes handcuffed, she let her hands flutter between her, imagining a bird or butterfly in flight. From a cropped bush, then to a bikini line.

One night, she shaved it off completely, just to stare at it in the mirror, before sending the butterfly to flutter her to orgasm.

Shaving brought a new self-awareness. Panties felt differently. Not just utilitarian, she was more aware, lace was different, satin was different, a thong stretched over her hips, silk worked its way between her lips. Underwear was now an adventure, even if she was the only one to ever see her in it, it was still something.

Lingerie interested her. She bought a garter belt, spent nights of frustration cursing clips that didn't seem to hold, discovered stay ups and never looked back. She visited La Senza and Vieux en Rose and Victoria's Secret, pored among bustiers and teddys, slips and robes. It was a little too much though, too over the top. She bought a long silk robe, and then on another occasion, a short silk top.

But really, her favourite lingerie was her hand cuffs, there was nothing like the elegant symmetry of its shape, the shine and weight and chill of its steel, the implacability of it all. No push up bra, it seemed, could shape her body, could pose so sexily and elegantly as her wrists joined together.

It was such an odd small thing, but somehow, she felt more alive, more sexual than she ever had before. It became a game, an exciting game. Sometimes at work, she'd think of some new thing to do with the handcuffs, a new position, or with the mirror, or wearing Cuban heels. The decision to shave away the last of her pubic hair had come during an appallingly dull teleconference, had livened the rest of the day, added a spark of anticipation.

It was better than a vibrator, she thought, since the cuffs inspired infinitely more variation. It didn't hammer her clit, but somehow, it allowed her, invited her to do more things. It was better than a boyfriend, much as she loved the feel of a live hard man inside her, it was a lot less maintenance, available at her whim, receptive to her impulses.

Her fantasies ran riot, there were men in them of course, sometimes two, sometimes a black man or a Chinese man, sometimes a tattooed Goth. There were fantasies of being handcuffed to a tree, or a desk at the office, or a chain link fence, there were scenarios of arrest and captivity where she was feared, too dangerous to be loose. In her mind the links between the cuffs seized with a brutal hand, arms yanked away from her pussy, above her head, her body roughly claimed. Or she would be straddling a hairy chest, wrists joined, palms flat, supporting her weight as she impaled herself. There were arrests, kidnappings, hostage crises, romances, astonishing things that had the common thread that as satisfying, as exciting as they were, she'd never do them in real life.

But it did kind of draw her. She had a vibrator, and used it. She had a dildo and used it. But it was her using it. The thought of a live man, a body above her, a hard cock that throbbed in her, that moved by someone else's will.... At some point, she knew she was going to wear handcuffs to bed with a man, the thought excited her as she masturbated.

Of course, at times the idea seemed freakish. What would he think? Would he laugh? That would be unbearable. Would he think she was some kinky sex freak? She wasn't really. Sometimes the idea of wearing them to bed seemed like such a horrible misjudgement. Fated to be a disastrous embarrassment.

As it turned out, when it did happen, it was quite unexpected.

It was a Saturday, she was at the mall, her feet were getting a little sore from walking around so much in heels. She decided to stop in the food court for an Orange Julius.

As she sat and sipped the thickened orange juice, a couple of security guards sat at the table next to her. She glanced at them. Young men both, in their early twenties. They wore faux police uniforms, and bulky vests. Were those really bullet proof vests? She wondered. Or fake - designed to look like Kevlar in the way that the security uniforms were designed to look like law enforcement? They wore utility belts - flashlights on loops, unidentifiable pouches, handcuffs, pepper spray? No guns of course. The handcuffs were black.

The two men chatted briefly, then one walked away, leaving the other to sip his coffee.

"Excuse me," she said suddenly, "are those real handcuffs?"

"What?"

He looked at her. He was unshaven in a hipster sort of way, short brown hair, thick eyebrows, but large expressive eyes. He was very tall, at least a head taller than her, but with an average, unassuming build.

She blushed. The words had escaped her, a throw away impulse. Perhaps her own handcuffs, carried now in her purse, had pushed her, put the thought in her head, or gave her the little extra impulse to ask.

"Oh," she said, "nothing, I'm sorry."

"These?" he said, patting them and lifting it off the belt clasp. "They're not police issue or anything like that. But they're real. I mean, they work. The company pays enough money for them."

"Oh, I see," she said. "I guess that you don't get police issue gear."

He smiled. "Not for what they pay us, no. But it all works, mostly. It's for show, but it has to work, obviously."

"Have you ever needed it?"

"Mostly no, people are cooperative. I had to pepper spray a drunk fighting with his girlfriend in the parking lot once."

"Really?"

"It was terrible. He threatened to sue. I got written up six different ways for it. It went on forever."

"I'm sorry," she said. "Have you used the other stuff?"

"Sometimes. Ninety per cent of the time, all I use is a notebook. I've had to handcuff a few people. Mostly if they're being belligerent. Just to keep them from hurting anyone."

"Not shoplifters," she smiled.

"No, shoplifters usually just come along quietly," he said. "I've never had a problem with a shoplifter."

"Good to know," she hesitated, and then cautioned, "Not that I plan on shoplifting or anything."

He laughed. "You don't look like a shoplifter."

"Thanks."

"Though you never know."

"Maybe you should keep an eye on me."

"Maybe I should," he laughed. They smiled at each other.

Ask, she told herself. It was a sudden impulse. Go ahead and ask.

"Can I see?" She asked, breaking the silence.

"What?"

"The handcuffs, can I see them?"

He hesitated for a second, surprised by the request, not sure if he should agree, but seeing no clear way to refuse.

"Oh sure," he took them off his belt again, and placed them in her outstretched hand.

They were a bit heavier than her own handcuffs. Cool, but without the chill that she liked on her own. There were four chain links, forged. The cuffs were matte black, not chromed. No quick release lever. She'd gotten so used to her own release levers that half the time she forgot where her keys were. They seemed slightly larger than her own. But on the whole, she was struck by how similar they were.

"What's the difference between this and police issue?" She asked.

"I have no idea. I think these are actually used by some police forces, just not the ones in town."

She didn't want to hold them too long, didn't want him to think she was kinky or anything like that. He seemed edgy, probably wasn't used to people handling his gear. She gave them back.

"Very nice," she told him, she needed to cover herself a bit, "I won't ask to see your pepper spray."

He laughed. "That would be a little much."

She nodded.

"Well, Josh," she said, it was on his nameplate. "It's been a pleasure. Thanks for being patient with me."

"Likewise." He fidgeted as if to leave, shifted in his seat, half stood. "So..." he said, "you're meeting your husband here?"

"I'm not married," she replied, and then added, "I'm single."

"That's surprising," he told her, "you're very nice."

"Nice," she smiled. "Never tell a woman she's 'nice', Josh, it's a backhanded compliment."

"Sorry," he said awkwardly. He moved as if to stand up.

"It's all right," she told him. She watched him fidget. Her fingers slipped into her purse, fondled the ratcheted steel jaw.

"Josh," she said, "are you working up to asking me out?"

"No...."

"Because I don't mind."

"Sort of... yes."

"I wouldn't mind going out for a drink sometime," she said. Some part of her was screaming 'What are you doing? He's at least ten years younger than you are. More than ten years.'

"Good," he said, "That would be fun."

"Do you have a car?" She asked. That was sort of a minimum standard. A man without a car... Well, what was the point? What kind of man was that? Probably still living with his mother.

"What? Yes? Sure!"

"Good," she said. "Then you can pick me up tonight."

They exchanged phone numbers, addresses. She watched him walk off. Nice ass, she thought.

Then, she thought, I've done a very stupid thing. The sensible part of herself was appalled. Dating a security guard? Why not a parking lot attendant? She was a professional. And he was so much younger. What the hell was she doing?

But then again, when was the last time she'd gone on a date with anyone? Why not? It would be good to just get out and do something. It didn't have to go anywhere. She wasn't shopping for a husband. What's the harm of going out? Worse come to worse, she'd just beg off and call it a night.

Unconsciously, she took the handcuffs out of her purse, and rotated the jaw over and over, fingers sliding against the smoothed metal, with the ritual insistence of a devout stroking prayer beads.

The rest of the day passed in a blur. She got home, she practically tore her clothes off, threw herself on the couch, masturbated in steel shackles, her fingers blurring inside her. She felt elated, almost wanting to laugh spontaneously. It was so different, so bold, she was so timid usually, so bland, she felt as if she'd stepped into a free fall. She liked this new self, this little bit of adventurousness in her.

What would it be like, she thought to herself, as she cleaned up the apartment, to just meet him at the door naked? To just say to hell with drinks and just fuck him right then and there? She'd never do that of course, but she could imagine the look on his face. She couldn't imagine actually being that bold. But it was exciting to think.

He arrived on time. The apartment buzzer went off. She almost jumped out of her skin. She wasn't quite ready, so she invited him up to wait.

A moment or two later, there was a knock at the door. She opened it, there he was standing there, looming over her, no longer dressed like a pretend cop, but still well dressed, clean and casual, male and youthful. She invited him in, offered him coffee. He didn't try to kiss her, which she was glad of. Aggressiveness might have been scary. He was polite.

She excused herself to go to the bedroom and finish getting dressed.

Once the door closed, she sat heavily on the bed. Her heart was starting to pound forcefully, beating away. She took a deep breath.

What am I doing? She asked herself.

They could go out for drinks, and then they'd talk and tell each other things about themselves, then they might ... what.... go dancing, go for a walk, go for ice cream... And then maybe her place, or his place, getting naked and sweaty, or maybe they'd find it wasn't really working and he'd drop her off and that would be that. That's how it would go.

Or....

Her heart started to pound even harder, her breath caught in her throat and butterflies exploded, battering and fluttering against her insides, her hands shook.

Or....

He looked up as the bedroom door opened, and she stepped out... Not quite naked, smooth shaven pussy glistening, nipples hard, wearing nothing but black stay ups on her legs and shining chromed shackles around her wrists. For a second, they stood there, him just staring at her naked flushed body, her shivering and blushing, her eyes dropping, half in submission, half in embarrassment.

Then he was on her, his hand on her shoulder, the other seizing the chain between her wrists. He marched her backwards, towards the door, lifting her wrists up over her head. She felt her back slam lightly against the wall, the cold solid flatness of the wall pressing against her back. He lifted her wrist higher, forcing her up on tip toes, pulling the cuffs hard against the edges of her wrist. The chain slid up and over a door hook at the top, trapping her.

His mouth descended on hers. One hand, a large hand, grabbed her breast. He had such big hands, his palms were cold. She moaned, her lips parting under his, his tongue pushing into her mouth. His free hand shoved up between her legs. She was already wet, she was dripping, she could feel how wet she was. It shocked her how sudden and intense her arousal was.

Fingers entered her, she spread her legs for him, her weight dragging her wrists down on the cuffs, the steel biting into her in a way it never had before. He thrust deep, fingers opening her, the heel of his hand hard against her clit and all of a sudden she was coming, instantly, as fast and hard as an express train.

Bound by the handcuffs, wrists pulled almost painfully tight above her, hanging from the door hook, the orgasm that erupted from his hand gripping her pussy took her by surprise. She had never come so fast or so hard. She arched her back and thrust, pushing her hips down on his fingers, forcing them up against her pussy with a ferocity that surprised her.

She felt his mouth cover hers, opened her jaws wide, swallowing his tongue, pushing hers into his mouth, barely aware of his hand squeezing her breast.

He pulled back for a moment, his hand leaving her pussy. She felt her hips roll, trying to follow the hand. She knew his fingers were slick. He was grabbing at his pants, unzipping.

"Yes!" Some part of her screamed. He was going to fuck her. She couldn't wait, she wanted it. It was all she could think of. Her urgency, her heat, was like a runaway train.

"Wait," she said, "do you have a condom? Put it on."

She was almost disappointed when he stepped back, fumbling it from his pocket, his pants falling around his knees. His erection was huge, already thrusting between the part at the bottom of his shirt. His hands were shaking, she saw, as he tore the wrapper, rolled it on.

Then he stepped forward. She lifted up her knees, letting her wrists and the handcuff chain take her full weight for a moment. He stepped between her legs, she wrapped them around him, locking her ankles, as he reached down. They seemed to shift together, finding each other, his cock sliding against her pubic mound, the inside of her thigh....

Then suddenly, she felt him at her lips. She tried to arch her hips, lift her legs a little higher, one heel digging into the small of his back. Suddenly, he surged deep, all the way up her in an instant. Her legs loosened and she felt the weight of her body settle around the base of his cock, pushing it deeper up inside her. No man had ever been so deep, had ever had so much of himself in her. They were so deep, so tight together, she felt the imprint of his pubic hair pressed into her labia.

He kissed her again, his mouth ravenous against hers. His hands grabbed for her breasts, squeezed and then caressed, he lifted them, as if to memorize the shape and weigh them. Finger pinched her nipples, as she worked her thighs up and down, humping herself against him. He reached down, grabbed her ass lifting some of her weight and began to thrust savagely in her, long deep thrusts that had her screaming with pleasure.

Her back and ass were slammed against the door, banging in its frame with each heave of his body. She was already drenched with sweat and excitement, could feel it running down her spine, trickling between her breasts. All she wanted was him inside her fucking harder and deeper.

He let go one ass cheek to grab her breast, mashing it almost painfully between his fingers. With only one cheek held, her weight shifted, she felt him move differently inside her body, the angle of penetration changed a few degrees. Her legs kicked up, wrapped around him, fell, kicked and wrapped, she tried to climb up his cock with her thighs, her hips grinding down against his cock.

The long thrusts rapidly gave way, becoming shorter and faster, each lunge of his hips slamming her against the doorframe harder and louder. They were both loud, screaming, grunting, moaning. She was coming again, and she could feel him, his thrusts going frantic and brutal, pounding up into her and she knew he was coming too. She wanted to come first, could feel the rushing surge of pleasure.

And then it hit, she arched her back, her legs dropping, wrapping around his thighs, pushing herself down on him, she shrieked. She could feel him thrusting harder and faster up into him, pounding, his orgasm exploding even as hers went on and on. He stiffened inside her and against her, pushing mindlessly, and then slowly relaxed.

Finally, it ebbed. The pleasure was still so intense, that even after orgasm, her skin tingled. It was almost too much pleasure.

He stepped back, his cock falling out of her.

"Holy shit," he whispered. He seemed almost deflated, as if coming had emptied him out physically. "That was intense."

"Uh huh," she didn't trust herself to say anything more complicated. She just leaned back against the door, feeling the smooth panel slick with her sweat. Letting her cuffs take the weight, it hurt a little, but she didn't care. Her legs felt too wobbly and weak to support her weight.

He stepped forward, reaching between her legs, and she felt a tiny pull, a slick movement. The condom came away in his hand, he let it fall to the ground, making a tiny plop. It had come off his cock half in her, she thought, after he came. As he'd lost his erection, she'd been squeezing, and her pussy had stolen it.

She took deep shuddering breath and tried to straighten her wobbly legs. Her chain rattled against the door hook. She couldn't quite pull it off herself.

"Help me to the couch," she asked him. She felt his strong arms wrap around her, easing her weight up briefly. Her cuffs came off the hook, and the relief in her arms and shoulders was exquisite. Together, they staggered to the couch and flopped on it, still panting with relief.

"Holy shit," he said again, "this was like something out of a porno. I never imagined anything like this. It's like the stories you hear about."

At his words, she felt this strange flush of pride. She was like something out of a porno, out of stories. It made her feel special. Powerful in a strange way.

"It was pretty amazing," she said. "I've never done anything like this before."

"You're kidding!" His amazement was in his voice, and obvious on his face. "You've got to be kidding?"

"No," she laughed. "First time."

"Wow." He laid his head back. "Well, if that's a first for you, then you got it right in one. My God. Why me?"

She laid her head on his chest, listening to his heart beat. His shirt was half undone, the lower buttons opened. She could see a hairy belly, and bare thighs. She reached down, finding his cock, even limp, she wanted to feel it, to squeeze it in her hand.

"I don't know," she replied. "Right time, right place, I guess."

"Oh," he said. He sounded a little disappointed. She wondered if she hurt his feelings.

The handcuffs had served their purpose. Rather than triggering the release latches, as she usually did, she had him get the keys from their little bowl in the kitchen. There was an intimacy in having him unlock her, even if it was unnecessary, she still enjoyed it. Her wrists were bruised, red welts in the flesh where the handcuffs had bitten into it. She allowed him to massage her wrists.

Afterwards though, neither of them found that they had much to say to each other. He was at least a decade younger. She didn't feel like she wanted to talk to him. After-sex conversation, the idea of it seemed exhausting. She felt him grow restless as well. When he made some excuse she was all too willing to let him leave, his presence now unwelcome and unnecessary.

Once he was out the door, she simply relaxed for a while. At length, she made herself a hot cup of coffee, and sat back on the couch. The handcuffs, opened and harmless were on the floor. She picked them up and put them on the coffee table. She couldn't help smiling at them.

It was a satisfying, amazing experience.

Brief. Had it only been ten or fifteen minutes? Amazing.

Finishing the coffee, she went for a shower, luxuriating in the feel of the hot water on her skin. She didn't scrub, just let the water wash over her in hot rippling sheets, carrying away the sweat and smell of sex. And yet, there was something so sensuous about the shower, the glow of the sex had never left her. Her fingers slipped down, feeling hard nipples, teasing them, pinching them. One hand slipped lower, spreading her lips apart, stroking her clit gently.

Closing her eyes, leaning against the side of the shower, she could feel the heat, the lust building up again. She reached for the memories, concentrated on them, the feel of him, the wet sounds of his cock thrusting into her pussy, the feel of the cuffs, the way her legs wrapped around him. The frenzied passion.

Abruptly, she stopped and turned off the water. She put her hands up flat against the shower stall, panting. She wanted to touch herself.

Not yet, she told herself, not now.

It would be better in cuffs. It would be so much better, wearing the cuffs.

She toweled off roughly, her body still half wet, droplets clinging to her skin everywhere, her hair heavy and limp.

The cuffs were on the coffee table in the living room. Reaching for them, she noticed a text. It was from him. "Had a wonderful time, would love to do it again."

She almost laughed, it was so carefully neutral. "Fucked you like a slut, can't wait to pound you all over." Would have been better.

"Are you hard?" She texted back.

The answer was instant.

"Yes."

"Then come back and fuck me again."

"10 minutes!"

She laughed at this eagerness.

She hoped that he'd last longer this time.

"The door will be unlocked."

With her knee, she pushed the coffee table away from the couch. Her heart was pounding all over again. The first time, that had been a wild wanton impulse, but this was deliberate, this was calculated. It excited her, made her feel bad.

The lights were too bright. She turned them down, and lit a couple of candles. She moved the coffee table further out, making sure that it would not obstruct the view of the couch from the doorway.

She wanted him to open the door, and see her right there on the couch, legs spread. She leaned back, the cuffs in her hands, assuming the position. Back elevated on cushions, so she could look right at him. Carefully she spread her legs wide, one knee lifted, foot on the seat cushion, the other leg sprawled off the couch.

She was wet all over again. This is how he would see her when he came in. He'd stand there in the doorway and look, staring at her naked body draped over the couch, at her wet pussy waiting to be fucked.

At the glint of steel between her wrists. She ratcheted one of the cuffs closed.

And below them, her fingers opening her.... The other cuff closed.

She stretched her arms down between her legs, letting the cuffed wrists rest on her lower belly.

Gentle fingertips teased her clit....

Opening herself for him.

She blinked slowly, playing with herself, watching the door.

By the time he arrived, she had almost come two or three times, had brought herself up to the edge of orgasm, but held it back. She didn't want to come until she felt a hard cock inside her, until she felt a male body on top of her. She wanted to feel him between her legs, to listen to him grunt, to touch him, smell him, lick him.

The door opened, spilling light into the living room, overwhelming the candles. She blinked. He was silhouetted, frozen, staring as she had imagined. She writhed, half in pleasure, half in performance for him. Long fingers reaching between her lips, she slid them against the labial folds and pulled apart, opening her wetness.

She imagined he might simply drop his pants and rush upon her, fucking her with the furious urgency of the last time. Instead, he stepped in, and closed the door, locking it.

"Fuck," was all he said, half prayer, half amazement.

He approached slowly, unbuttoning his shirt, staring at her as if afraid to look away, as if he was afraid that she might vanish if his gaze wavered. She shifted her hips as he moved into the room, keeping her opened wetness facing him. She watched him, enjoying his hypnotized fascination.

He's hard already, she thought. He was hard before he got here. But when he opened that door, it was as if he hadn't had anything, all of a sudden all he could think about was how hard he was for her, how badly he wanted her again, she thought. She loved the effect on him, loved the sense of power and excitement.

Still watching her, he slid his pants down to his ankles, kicked awkwardly out of shoes, and stepped toward her.

He did not immediately lunge to mount her, lift her legs and push his cock hard into her with one brutal, exciting thrust. Instead, he circled the coffee table, moving towards her, his erection bobbing between his legs, until he was near her head. His cock was inches from her face.

He reached between her legs, pulling her chained wrists away from her pussy, up towards his cock. Linked by the cuffs and the narrow chain, her hands were almost in the position of prayer. Guided by him, they curled around both sides of his cock, her little fingers brushing the soft sack of his scrotum.

"You wanna suck my cock?" he whispered. Half a request, half an order. Or was it simply a statement. She had never cared much one way or the other before, but at that moment she wanted to suck this cock. To taste it, to feel the shape of it against her lips, under her finger tips.

She ran her bound hands along the shaft, enjoying the hardness of it, the hotness, the texture of the skin and the feel of the veins. It curved a little she noticed. He was uncircumcised. She peeled the foreskin back gently, staring at the graceful curve of the glans. There was already a bead of pre-cum. She stuck her tongue out, licked the tip lightly, harvesting the wet pearl of semen. He pushed forward gently. Abruptly, she opened her mouth, took the head in, squeezing with her lips just past the glans.

He moaned. It thrilled her to know she had made him do that. Was there a trembling in his thighs? She felt him move, balancing his weight with one arm over her, on the back of the couch. His cock bobbed gently between her lips. She felt his other hand on her belly, spread her legs a little wider, arched her hips until she felt his fingers curling into her pussy. It was her turn to moan.

He let her suck his cock for a while, sometimes her mouth pulling off, to lick and lap its length with her tongue. Sometimes she cradled his balls in her cupped hands, as she worked the head. She tried to get that moan out of him again, the sound of helpless pleasure, and was gratified every time he gasped.

Finally, he pulled his hand from her sopping pussy, she felt his weight shift as he stood upright, the cock pulling away from her lips. For a second, there was a long thread of drool joining his glans and her tongue. A condom was pressed into her cupped, cuffed palms.

"Put it on," he ordered.

"Oh yes," she whispered.

She hadn't put many condoms on. Mostly, men just did that for themselves. But she wanted to do it now, it was like a new adventure, an action. Opening it, placing, rolling it down his length.

She gave a chaste quick kiss to the tip of his glistening, latex member, tasting a hint of lubricant oil.

"Time to fuck me now," she whispered. He pulled her cuffed wrists back, until her arms were straight out, above her head, out of the way. It wasn't uncomfortable, but it left her whole body open for his gaze, his touch, his cock.

"Oh yeah, I'm going to fuck you," he said, moving to straddle her, one knee sinking down into the couch cushion. His hand moved from her pussy, the knuckles parting her lips, up her belly, up her ribs to close around one breast.

"Fuck me good," she told him, bending her knees back. Looking down, she could see his erection hovering over her belly, could see her pussy lips. He reached down, moved his cock. She felt the head of it slide over her clit, down between the lips.

Her breath froze as she watched it enter her, watched and felt it at the same time. This time, there was no instant orgasm, no explosion, no runaway freight train. This time, it was a steadily mounting excitement, a heaviness and lightness within her, a feeling of accumulating tension and desire, that built and built.

He sank in her up to the hilt. His body pressed down against hers, one hand still clutching her breast, the other forcing her bound wrists above her head, his weight partially on her. She loved the feel of him, the way the couch seemed to creak and shift under them.

He began to fuck her. Not like before, not in the frantic out of control way, as if he had been racing to stay one step ahead of his orgasm. No, this was a good fucking, a hard fucking a steady rhythm that built and built up inside her. It took ten minutes to reach her first orgasm, and then only a moment after that for her second, and she loved every moment of it.

His passion built. His hand left her breast, his entire weight pushing her down into the couch. His mouth found hers, his free hand cupping her face.

She came as they kissed.

Abruptly, he pulled out. She floundered awkwardly, as he turned her over, moved her into position on all fours, her upper body straddling the arm of the couch. He thrust into her from behind, fucking her doggy style, pulling her hair, making her back arch as she came, her ass thrusting, pushing back onto his hips.

Later again, she turned, onto her back, legs wrapping around him, him lifting her half off the couch, only her shoulders touching it, as he pushed in and out of her until finally her grip broke and she fell back, only to come as he plunged into her.

By the time he came, she'd lost count of her orgasms, was drenched with sweat, the couch soaked with their fluids, her whole body ached and felt hot and feverish. It was wonderful.

After sex, after they had fucked into aching, sweat drenched satisfaction, once again, he'd released her from the cuffs, and then in the ensuing awkwardness, he'd once again made his excuses, and she'd patiently waited him out the door. She hadn't bothered to shower, just crawled into bed, wrapping herself in sheets, and drifted off happily.

Lying in bed, she thought about the night. A smile crept over her features. Her shoulders ached a little, but she didn't mind. It was like a reminder, it brought her back, made memories flash, images and sensations. What she'd done to get that ache.... soooo satisfying. She stretched her arms out into the air, waving them around unselfconsciously. There were red marks around her wrists. Not too bad, she stretched an arm out above her, looking up its length appraising, as if examining a bracelet or piece of jewelry.

The next day, she woke refreshed. There was no gradual transition at all. She simply woke, consciousness switching on like turning on a light. Her first thought was what she'd done the night before. She grinned.

Get up, shower, coffee, breakfast, get dressed up, go to work.

On the way out, she stopped at the door. There was an imprint of her butt on the door. It was barely visible, the light had to catch it just the right way. But yes, there it was, painted in sweat and skin oils, the smeared shape of her ass against the veneer of the door, from where she'd been fucked up against it. She knelt, staring at it, tracing it upwards with her fingers. There was her back. She remembered sweat running down the small of her back, the pull in her shoulders from the weight of her body on her wrists, his cock thrusting up inside her, the door shaking in its frame with each thrust. Yes, the shape of her ass and back, and right above, two smears that marked her shoulder blades.

She was entranced, a physical image of her fucking. She glanced at the floor below the door, but the carpet was clean. The leather of the couch seemed unmarred. There was just this marvellous image of her on the door, round ass cheeks and sharp shoulder blades, the narrow smear of her back connecting them. Like the Shroud of Turin, she thought, the Shroud of Fucking Turin.

For a second, she thought of getting a j-cloth from the kitchen, a bit of spray, and washing it off. But she didn't really want to. Instead, she reached for the doorknob. Time to go. It would be here when she returned, waiting for her, the thought sank down into her, a warm little secret.

Work was a breeze. She smiled, she sparkled, everything just seemed to go perfectly. She waited for anyone to notice the red marks circling her wrists. She had a terrific lie all ready to go - something about heavy grocery bags, plastic wrapping around her wrists, having to wait in line... But no one asked. It was a little disappointing. They remarked on her cheerful mood, she just smiled. Laughed. The day flew by as if it had wings.

Buoyant. That was it, she thought, that was the word. This light, floaty almost weightless feeling. She thought perhaps she should feel guilty. But she didn't. Or ashamed, but she didn't. She didn't feel particularly kinky. She just felt good, liberated.

She felt completely and absolutely unapologetic. It was almost as if she wanted to go to Church, to enter a confessional, to divulge in graphic detail every nasty moment, to relive each image, the flash of chrome around her wrists, the shape of his cock in vivid detail, the way the underside of it had tasted as it lay on top of her extended tongue, the way his hands had felt cupping her ass and lifting her, the way her weight had shifted back and forth from hanging from her wrists, to pressed against the door, to her ass lifting under his grip.

She wanted to tell that to a priest, and then say "I'm not sorry at all! He hung me from a hook and fucked me and I loved every minute of it! No Hail Marys! I want to do it again, I want to do it and do it, until every part of me aches!"

It was personal, it was hers, it was just for her and no one else. It was a step outside the world, outside responsibilities and duties and all the routine and necessity of life.

In hindsight, the only surprise was that she waited so long to call him back that next evening.

He found her waiting on her bed, on knees and elbows, wrists chained, the lights dim, the room smelling of scented candles. She'd been waiting for fifteen minutes, slowly growing wetter and wetter. When he stood in the doorway, she was so aroused her pussy lips had parted of their own accord. She imagined what she must look like to him. She was dripping...

She loved being on all fours, presented for mounting, wrists bound in the cold unyielding cuffs beneath her gaze, her elbows splayed for balance. She loved the moment when his hands clamped on both sides of her ass. The way the mattress shifted and bounced slightly as his knees settled behind her. It was as if she was hyper aware, aware of her heart beating, aware of the air moving across the fine hairs on the back of her neck. The moment when he entered her, filling her with one thrust, made her cry out with pleasure. She gathered the sheets in her fists, pulling them from the bed, the force of his thrusts pushing her cheek against the mattress.

After a while, the handcuffs became a bother. She had him use the keys to remove them, she never told him about the release latch, that was always her secret. Although he was always gracious and obedient to her wishes, it still made her feel more confident. It meant the real power over her bondage was with her, no matter what he decided, she was cuffed only as long as she wanted to be. It didn't matter, they fucked hard, her legs wrapping around his hips, her butt off the bed every time he pulled back for another thrust.

Later on, she had him put them back on her, chaining her wrists behind her, taking her bent over the kitchen table, as she came continuously, over and over.

And of course, afterwards he left.

She was slightly embarrassed to admit to herself, that was one of the best parts. She revelled in being alone with her satisfaction, did not want to share the blissful feeling of satiation.

The next night, she hung from the door, grunting like an animal, her legs suspended in the air, knees dangling over crooked elbows, the door smashing again. The next morning, she took a moment to stare at the shape of smeared in skin oils on the door. She reached up, toggled the hook, it was loose in its screws. That probably wasn't good. An awkward image of it letting go during wanton sex flickered through her mind.

Her shoulders ached again, worse. There was a particularly sharp pain under her left shoulder blade. It occurred to her that maybe it wasn't a good idea to hang from a hook while fucking. The red marks dug into her wrists were particularly livid. Ligature marks, he'd told her they were called "ligature marks" between bouts of sweaty sex. There'd been a small satisfaction in learning it, of course there had to be a name for it, once you thought about it.

Maybe a table then, or a counter or something. Something to support her weight. She thought about it off and on during the working day. Nothing she had seemed to do. Perhaps she would shop.

Fucking continued. Not every night. But again, and again. Never at quite the same times. There was a lack of routine in their couplings. A hungry unpredictable eagerness. He told her once, that he would get hard randomly, just thinking about hrt. Watching television, out with friends, patrolling the mall, he'd think of her, of their hungry intense couplings and his cock would go rigid.

Once, he'd texted her at her work, offering, demanding. She'd immediately taken the afternoon off sick, had gone to his place, showed up at the door with her panties peeping lazily from her purse. He'd seized her wrist, bent her over in his hallway, her legs spread, his black security issue handcuff dangling from one wrist, her other hand braced up against the wall as he pounded into her.

Oh god, that had been so good.

She had been reluctant to allow him to put his own security guard handcuffs on her. There was an extra threshold of real-ness. Those were real cuffs, slightly heavier, more substantial, the ratchet had more teeth. And there was no latch, no release catch.

The first time he had put them on her, there had been a shiver, a frisson of genuine fear and nervousness. She'd stood it as long as she could, and had asked him to take them off. And he had. That made it easier, knowing that the minute she asked they would come off.

Still, she preferred her own, she decided, one night, playing with them on the couch. It wasn't just that they could release with the touch of a latch. It was that they were hers. They were the symbol, the device, not just of her submission, but of her power, her wantonness. Wearing someone else's handcuffs undermined that power a little, she decided. And then she decided she was over-thinking it.

Perhaps it was simply that they were more convenient. Convenient? No, that wasn't quite right. They were more accessible to her. She didn't need him around, to put them on, to wear them.

Casually, she fitted one of the steel rings around her wrist, ratcheted it close.

She liked putting them on. Wearing them before he came over. It was a process. A wickedness. It was like foreplay, except not quite. She rolled her tongue around in her mouth, tickling the metal of the dangling cuff with her fingernail. It wasn't foreplay. It was arousal... Yes, that was the word.

The handcuffs were about arousal, and that was sex, but it was also something else. She let the second cuff close around her other wrist, feeling the cold steel, listening to the now familiar ratcheting. Bent one knee, lifting her foot up on the couch, letting the chain lay across the knee, the weight of her hands dangling the wrists on either side.

Arousal.

Very slowly, very deliberately she drew her other foot up onto the couch, bent knee high in the air. She spread her legs. Her heart started to beat, just a little more rapidly.

Arousal.

She thought about calling him. But then decided that the thought of him was enough for now. What they had done. What they might do. Would do.

Arousal.

Her hands slid down her thighs, the metal links connecting the cuffs clinking slightly, the cold metal brushing lightly against the smooth skin, of her inner thigh. She made it slow, slower, and slower. When her fingers finally parted her lips, she was already wet.

She came to enjoy his handcuffs. It was different from her own. There was more surrender in it. But more abandonment, more liberation, more freedom to simply be. They were more about the sex, when he put them on her, she was moments from being fucked.

She wore his for shorter times though, sometimes on one wrist, his hand wrapped around the other cuff like the handle of a leash. Often taking it off during sex, putting it on again, as positions changed. Sometimes the cuffs were threaded through a pipe or a piece of furniture. Once she let him handcuff her to the toilet, but it hadn't been a turn on.

Another time, her hands were cuffed behind her, and he had her on her back. But the cuffs bit into her tailbone, hurting her. They tried a cushion between the cuffs and her ass, but it didn't quite work. Finally wrapping a towel around the cuffs under her did the trick, she could just feel the cuffs against the small of her back, there but not hurting.

Absolutely aware of her helplessness she looked up at him, looming above her as he grabbed her ankles, lifted them, and parted her legs. She felt her lips part, opening, felt a sudden exquisite rush

Perversions and Infidelities / Page 23

of wetness, a tightening up deep inside her. Her hips elevated by the cuffed wrists allowed him to plunge deeper, making her gasp at the bottom each stroke. In that position, they could only manage sex for twenty minutes before the stress on her shoulders got too much. But what a fucking it was.

When she couldn't take it any more, instead of releasing her, he'd flipped her over. Used the cuffs behind her back to pull her to her knees and thrust his cock hard and fast into her, rushing towards a grinding roaring orgasm. He left her in that position, ass up in the air, her pussy drenched, sweat covering her body, panting, face pressed against the mattress, just fucked and incomplete.

She remained in position, listening to him go to the bathroom, listening to the sound of him pissing, the sizzle of the piss striking the toilet bowl, the sound of the flush, of him padding around the apartment. Helpless, waiting, she began to drip, she could feel it, could feel her pussy squeezing.

He went into the kitchen. She couldn't see him, just a flash of movement around her peripheral vision. She could hear the sound of his footsteps padding into the kitchen. There was the sound of the fridge door opening. Him drinking. A cupboard, clatter of a cup or dish. The fridge again.

She waited.

He padded back, his footsteps more felt than heard. The mattress surged as his weight settled behind her.

She waited.

An exquisite wet coldness touched her clit. She gasped loudly back arched, she pushed forward. Was that an ice cube? Cold fingers? She could not tell. The touch returned, sending a shiver all the way through her. His fingers slid down, cold chilled fingers, between her lips. They slid inside, two fingers curling up inside her, cold cold cold, she was breathless. They began to move back and forth, her mouth opened soundless and wide, her toes curled, she squirmed and wriggled. But the fingers kept moving, and moving, thumb stroking her clit until she came.

Her next sex toy was from Ikea.

When she saw it, her pussy tightened, she felt a sudden wet surge, and went red from top to bottom. The people around her noticed nothing. The voice of the sales clerk faded away, and although she could see his lips moving she couldn't hear a word he was saying. She swallowed, and swallowed again, almost shaken by images, carnal couplings, sweating bodies, cocks and pussies, naked legs curling around his ass, a deep sexual grunting.

"That looks nice," she said finally, her voice almost breaking. "I'll take it."

Just like that, she was the owner of a hall table, a credenza.

It was perfect, shallow, just wide enough for her to perch her ass on. The legs were sturdy to take her weight, the forward edge was curved for ease of fucking, and bevelled so the corner wouldn't bite into her ass. Even the height was perfect. Perfect for fucking, perfect for a cock to slide into her pussy.

She stared at it, and all she could think of was about fucking on it, being naked on it, spreading her legs and resting her heels against the table legs. Maybe tie her ankles to those table legs, so she was spread helpless, lips parted and dripping. Maybe she could turn around, press up against the wall, the table pushing her ass out just enough to be taken from behind? She'd probably have to wear high heels.

Note to self she thought, shop for heels, not to wear, but to be fucked in. The thought made her shiver.

The thought of selecting shoes, not for walking, not for any normal purpose, not even for display, but for the sole purpose of fucking, of raising her heels on stilettos, altering her posture, thrusting her ass out for fucking... It was utterly, deliriously wanton.

Better than wanton, it was deliciously insane.

She imagined going to a shoe store, addressing staff. "I want shoes to be fucked in."

All through the purchase, the taking it to the checkout, having it loaded in her car, she kept blushing red, her thoughts going to what she would do on the table.

She'd never thought about things like this before. But now, it crept into her mind. Standing in the subway, packed with people, thinking about a short skirt, 'accidental' exposure.

At her workplace, she sat at a boardroom table and gave her report, but in the back of her mind, images of being bent over the table, straddling the table like a stripper, fucking in the huge plush leather office chairs. Furniture had always been furniture, but now, it seethed with carnal possibilities. Everything seethed with carnal possibilities.

Even a park bench took on a new excitement.

It was liberating, it was liberation. Like being awake for the first time. Like looking at the world with new eyes, seeing things in ways she never had before. It was like being alive.

Along the way, she bought a wall mounted coat rack.

At home she assembled the credenza herself with breathless excitement, planning the night before her.

Later on, she drove her building supervisor nearly mad with her insistence on the placement of the wall coat rack, far higher and too inconveniently placed to be of any use. And then there was her insistence on extra deep screws, to make sure it wouldn't come loose this time.

She texted Josh, set a time for him to come over.

The rest of the evening flew by. There was something deliriously delicious about the anticipation. Sex was a certainty, by now, she had played enough with him that she had absolute confidence as to what would happen, how it would happen.

But that wasn't dull, not at all. It just made the anticipation excruciating.

Getting ready, was so much fun, she had to resist touching herself in the shower. There was so much process, it felt like everything was foreplay and arousal. Shaving her legs. The 'oh so careful' and meticulous process of shaving her pussy, clearing away stubble.

She liked to have a mirror in front of her so she could watch, could both see and feel her growing wetness. This was a thing that had come with the cuffs. Before that, she would have been aghast at looking at her pussy in a mirror. Now she couldn't stop watching. She ran a finger along velvet smoothness, and allowed one exquisite circle of her clitoris.

Lipstick! She'd almost forgot that. She tried several, settled on one that seemed to make her lips pert. Make up, not too heavy. A bit of blush, a hint of eyeliner.

The hallway was too bright. She hunted around until she replaced it with a 25 watt bulb. Note to self, she thought: candles, wall mounted. Candle light was so much nicer. But the dim light of the 25 watt bulb made an acceptable substitute for now.

Experimentally, she slipped up onto the table, easing her back against the wall. She let her butt rest on the table's edge, bracing her heels against the table's legs. She could feel her lips part, sense her wetness.

She reached up with both hands over her head, crossing her wrists, feeling the coat hook against her skin. She felt a slight twinge of pain just under her shoulder blade. Maybe not that, not yet. Disappointment.

She parted her hands, reached for the coat hooks at the far sides. Not quite. She got off, moved the table a couple of inches to the left, and found she could stretch out and grab them easily. It was too bad she didn't have two pairs of trick handcuffs. Perhaps she could improvise a tie? But she immediately discounted that. It was a little too scary, the thought of being tied so she couldn't easily get out in an instant.

This was good. She looked up and down the hallway. Looked down at herself. Her tummy stuck out a little too much. She sucked it in, and then left it. Even with that, this was hot. This was going to be so hot. He was going to come in his pants!

She swung her legs girlishly, sitting on the table. There was still time. What to do? She really didn't fancy sitting here for a half an hour. She looked around. The light wasn't right. It needed more shine.

She went to the bathroom, picked up some lotion, and rubbed it across her breasts. Padding into the hallway, she admired the way her breasts shone in the dim hall light.

In the end, she let the chromed cuff dangle from one risk, and reached up, wrapping her hands on separate coat hooks widely separated. She let her ass ease forward, dangling from the edge of the credenza, so she could feel the tug of her weight in her shoulders. She spread her legs as wantonly wide as they could go.

Perfect.

She wished she could take a picture.

There was a fleeting impulse to ask Josh to take a picture when he arrived.

Of course, he'd fuck her immediately. After sex then? But she found herself shying at the thought of giving up the camera to someone else. These adventures were all about her, they were her creations, her possession. She could imagine taking pictures of herself, but not someone else taking them.

The weight was a little much, she eased her ass back onto the credenza, and was immediately comfortable. She let go the coat hooks, letting her hands fall to her knees, and swung her legs girlishly. Yes, this was perfect.

When she heard Josh arriving, all she had to do was reach for the hooks, scoot her ass forward. He was still dressed in Security Guard uniform, his own cuffs at his side. As the door opened, she realized that anyone passing in the hall could see her, if there had been anyone, and that spurred a flash of excitement.

Josh walked through the door rock hard, and immediately grabbed and lifted her knees, his hands dropping to his ankles. She saw that he was already wearing a condom. How long? When had he put it on? Had he been hard all the way over here? Since her call? Had he worn it all this time?

This evidence of rampant, relentless lust, her effect on him, her power over him delighted her. Almost before the door closed, he was thrusting deep inside her. She gripped the coat hooks with all her strength and wrapped her legs around him, welcoming him.

The sex was everything she wanted, and more. Frenzied, furious, weirdly spontaneous despite her planning and posing. A wanton animal act that left them both sweat drenched and panting.

Afterwards, he carried her to the bedroom, where they fucked the evening away. And as always, he pleased her by leaving, so she could revel in the experience by herself.

Was she selfish? Cold. She wondered about that. But she had affection for Josh. They liked each other. If either had reached out for a further intimacy, neither would have denied the other.

But this way added to the fun. There was something raunchy and liberating about "Come and fuck me, then go away." It felt free, and harmless.

She played with herself idly. His Security Guard shirt was sweat stained when he'd left. She hoped he had a spare. Or would he have to launder it tonight when he got back to his apartment?

Should she have offered to launder it for him? She made a face - too domestic.

Instead, she arched her back, squirming on the messy bed. The cuff was still dangling from one wrist. It felt a little sensitive. Maybe she should take it off.

Instead, she raised her arms straight up above her and fastened the other wrist. For a moment, her hands fluttered like butterflies. She stretched her hands above her head, to the headboard.

He'd had his own cuffs with him, she could have worn both, she thought. She imagined being chained spread eagled on the bed, captive and helpless, and felt a wet surge. But there was no place on the headboard to fix cuffs. And black and chrome, they wouldn't match, they wouldn't feel the same, it would be distracting.

Still, the fantasy made her breathe harder. Slowly she drew her cuffed hands down, pressing the back of her hand against her cheek.

"Oh please, Monsieur, I'll do anything! Anything at all!" she whispered. "Take mercy on your helpless captive."

She pulled up her knees, and spread her legs.

"This, Monsieur?" she whispered. "But I can't, I mustn't. I am pure, I promise. Oh please."

She let her hands slide down across a breast, pinching a nipple.

"Ow, Monsieur! You take such liberties. I am chaste, truly. You do not believe me?"

Then down between her legs.

"You want me to part my lips for your inspection! You wish to see? To examine me? You are a devil, Monsieur. But I must obey."

The touch.

"Oh Monsieur, you have found me out. You have exposed my lie. I am not chaste... but wanton. Take me now, for I cannot conceal my hunger for the touch of a man such as yourself!!!"

It was very satisfying, although her wrist ached in the morning.

The next day, she bought a four post bedframe.

And another pair of trick handcuffs.

She practised first with one cuff attached to a bedpost, until she was sure she could work the latch. It was harder, but manageable.

Then she tried both, with some trepidation. If she couldn't work the latches spread like that, it would be awkward. The experience wasn't quite satisfactory. Her arms were pulled too far, the cuffs bit awkwardly into her wrists. Her head was too close to the top of the bed, touching the headboard. It was difficult to work the latches. She'd need to add chains or ropes or something, to lengthen it and make it more comfortable.

The most awkward thing was that with both arms stretched out, she couldn't masturbate. As potentially exciting as it was, she'd need to free at least one wrist to play, or she'd need Josh.

More shopping, and more experiments, until she found something satisfactory.

Along the way, she discovered Velcro cuffs. They were so bleah, completely without the exciting sensuality, the coldness, the weight, the hardness, the delicious clicking sound of the ratcheting mechanism. Everything about her chrome cuffs was exciting. Nothing about the Velcro cuffs was the least bit arousing, particularly the sound of Velcro unzipping. But they made good ankle cuffs. She bought four - two for the bedroom, two for the credenza.

When everything was finally ready, she called Josh. Forty minutes later, he found her, naked and blindfolded, spread eagle to the four posts of the bed. The first she knew that he was there was his cold hand cupping her pubic mound, fingers flattening against her clit and spreading her soaked lips.

Her body practically levitated off the bed and she came instantly.

Afterwards, there was more of course. The blindfold came away. The ankle cuffs proved a bother and were released. Deliberately helpless, she could only spread her legs, lifting her knees to accept his thrusts deep into her.

It was absolutely satisfying.

Josh was absolutely satisfying, and though their relationship was almost purely sexual, she felt a deep appreciation and affection for him.

Josh was her very best toy!

But most of her sex life was masturbation, an ongoing exploration of herself and her toys. She played with bondage, drenching herself in scenarios of submission and captivity. Yet there was power in the submission.

In her fantasies, she was a helpless captive. But she was captive because she was dangerous, rebellious, wanton. She was a spy, a femme fatale, a police woman, an executive, her fantasy roles were powerful women who could not be tamed, only restrained. So dangerous that restraints were vital, the only way to contain them.

She explored, buying more exotic toys. Not all of them worked, an experiment with nipple clamps ended with them being thrown across the room, and then consigned to the trash bin. A ball gag was used once, found pointless, and ended up forgotten at the back of a drawer. Other items, vibrators, butt plugs, lingerie, worked out better.

She experimented with taking pictures, a project which she found excessively complicated and arduous. She didn't like the pictures, they were flat, not reflecting the adventurous and sexual creature she had become. She deleted them without showing any of them to Josh.

The most successful, and the most difficult step, was sharing her fantasy scenarios with Josh. After all, he himself was one of her fantasy scenarios. It felt like admitting to cheating to reveal that there were others.

"I'm a wanton French schoolgirl at a convent," she said. "Like Madeline, in a uniform, I look like butter wouldn't melt in my mouth. We aren't even supposed to touch ourselves. But I have this secret life where I pursue every boy... and girl that catches my fancy. Of course the Monsignor is on to me, and so he ties me in place to investigate whether I am a virtuous girl or a wanton..."

There are long heartbeats where she waited for him to laugh.

Instead, he said "Cool."

And a moment later, in the worst fake French accent she's ever heard, heavily laden with Spanish.

"Young lady, some very disturbing reports have come to my ears!"

"Monsieur!" she whispered. "I have no idea what you could mean. I am a good girl!"

It proceeded wonderfully, except for the moments when one or both of them would break down in giggles. But somehow, that made it better. She enjoyed herself thoroughly. And she enjoyed him, definitely.

She felt sensitive about it. Immensely silly and self-conscious afterwards when normal life intruded. But he was non-judgmental and accepting. He made it safe. She found she wanted to do it again.

Carefully, she shared a few more - an underworld assassin, a jewel thief, a spy, a private eye. Tentatively, they worked out role plays, sometimes awkward, but mostly satisfying. They didn't do them often, they weren't really needed, the actual sex and bondage remained volcanic in itself. But she shared a little bit.

"Here's one," she whispered following a drenching, exhausting, satisfying sexual encounter, where she'd been bent over the couch, tied and spread, and taken from behind until muscle strain caused her to call time out.

"I'm tied to the Credenza, naked, blindfolded, and a pizza guy comes to deliver an order. He takes one look, fucks me hard, and leaves. A total stranger, I never see him, never know who. He comes, he goes. That's hot."

"I could do that," Josh's arms were around her as they sprawled on the couch, spooning on the precarious lack of space on the cushions.

"No," she told him. "It wouldn't work if it's you. We've already done it. The thrill is the idea of having a complete stranger. A zipless fuck. Completely anonymous."

He thought about it.

"I could set it up," he said. "I know some pizza delivery guys."

She laughed.

"Horny pizza delivery guys?"

"Is there any other kind?"

But then, a few days later, she asked him to set it up.

For the next few days, the idea of the zipless, anonymous fuck drove her wild. She masturbated constantly, even sneaking into the bathroom at work to quietly bring herself off. She felt weightless, she literally flew through each day. The next two encounters with Josh were incandescent.

The day came. She had a phone number for a particular pizza place, a particular order that would alert a particular driver. She almost danced with excitement in the shower, washing, working lotion into her skin, shaving her legs and pubic mound. The afternoon came. She started to get cold feet.

The time to make the call approached. She got cold feet, butterflies in her stomach. This seemed like a ridiculously bad idea. The sex would probably be awful. Porn aside, how capable were Pizza guys anyway? They were probably minute men, with shrivelled dicks. What if he took pictures? What if he decided to get rough?

She should call it off. Nervously, she chewed her lip. Stomach doing flip flops. Then she called Josh.

"I don't know if I can do it like this," she said.

"I understand."

"No," she explained. "I want to, but I'm kind of scared of it going wrong. I want you here."

"To do it."

"No," she said. "I just want you in the apartment, just in case anything goes bad."

"So keep an eye on it."

"Not to watch. I don't want him to know you're there. Just hide in the bedroom, just in case. And after, if everything's okay, you can leave."

There was a long silence on the phone.

"Okay," he said finally. "I'll be right over."

They disconnected.

Staring at the phone, she felt herself blushing, ashamed of the weakness that led her to call him, appalled at her own recklessness in going through. Was she crazy? Had this wild ride gone too far?

Waiting for him to come over, she busied herself with preparations, writing post it notes, making sure the apartment was properly presentable, any loose bondage gear carefully hidden away, nothing untoward. No easily pocketable goods in evidence, to the extent possible. The stranger would have the run of her apartment, she didn't want them walking off with her laptop.

When Josh arrived, she made the call, annoyed at the way her voice shook.

"It should be about fifteen minutes," Josh told her.

Her stomach did flip flops.

"Good. I think."

"We can cancel."

She thought about it.

"No."

Josh was banished to the bedroom. She didn't really want him to see what she was doing, although he could probably guess. She got into position. The cuffs were already in place, ends clamped tightly around the base of two coat hooks above her. She was naked, except for her special red 'fuck-me' shoes with their stiletto heels. She fastened her blindfold in place, an act both scary and exhilarating.

Then carefully, she reached up with one hand, feeling around, until she found the dangling cuff. She clamped it tight around her wrist with her free hand. The ratcheting sound was insanely loud, insanely exciting, and she almost made it too tight. She'd have trouble springing it, she knew. But decided not to adjust it.

Instead, she felt around with her free hand for the other cuff. Her heart skipped a beat, as she made a spear of her fingers and slipped her hand through it until she felt it around her wrist. Then she pushed it against the wall slowly and carefully, listening to the measured clicks of the ratchet, making sure it was tight, but with enough room she could spring it easily.

She'd practised a lot the previous days, with and without blind folds, punctuated by masturbation, denying orgasms for the anticipation, She was satisfied that she could get in and out of the cuffs fairly easily, even up on the credenza.

Except now it was the real thing, and she was a lot less confident. The uncertainty made her pussy spasm with wetness, she could almost feel her clit throb. This was the real thing, not play, not pretend, it was going to happen.

She sat on the edge of the credenza, letting it bear her weight, her legs spread.

Nothing happened. She couldn't even hear Josh in the bedroom. Time ticked on. She shifted and squirmed. It felt like it was dragging on. Had he chickened out? Was it going to happen at all? Was he delayed? She realized there was no way to judge time.

How long should she wait? Maybe she should get out of the cuffs, prepare a little more? But what if he, whoever he was, arrived then. The adventure would be ruined. Should she call for Josh? What would she say?

In the end, despite endless doubts, she remained silent, waiting, listening to the sound of her own breathing and heart beating, of her blood rushing through her ears, feeling the faint breezes of her apartment against her nipples, occasionally squirming within her bonds.

There was a knock at the door.

Her heart skipped a beat, it was like a jolt of lightning went through her whole body, she almost jumped within her bonds, her muscles twitching.

Another knock.

Couldn't they see the post-it note on the door that read, "I may not hear you. Just come in, the money is on the Credenza"?

She heard the doorknob turning.

"Hello!" A voice, a male voice, a stranger. She felt the electrical jolt of excitement go through her, and experienced an intense rush that was almost, but not quite, an orgasm.

"Hello? I'm here? Pizza?"

The voice trailed off. Was that a gasp? She imagined him catching site of her.

There were tentative footsteps, approaching her. Indrawn breath, coarse with excitement. She waited patiently, her pussy getting wetter by the moment. Her nipples felt so achingly hard they could cut class.

On the edge of the credenza was a twenty dollar bill, a condom, and another post it note. "Don't speak. She is your tip. Help yourself. Do anything you want, but wear the condom."

There was a sucked intake of breath. A rustle, but she couldn't tell of what. She remained still, blindly staring straight ahead. Her heart was racing.

A whiff of the pizza. Footsteps. And then... nothing. Had he chickened out? Had he left? Was he standing there taking pictures? Just looking at her? Planning his next move? What was he doing?

The touch of a hand against her left breast, her nipple, brought a loud gasp from her. Her body convulsed, back arching. Her body's reaction shocked her almost as much as the touch, it was so extreme and unforced, a spontaneous jerk. The hand vanished, and she relaxed letting out an equally loud, equally unforced sigh.

She quieted, waiting for his next move. It came again, the hand against her left breast, finger stroking the nipple. Again, she gasped and jerked, but more modestly this time, the gasp evolving into a sigh. The hand did not withdraw this time, but cupped her breast, tracing the nipple. She sighed again. Another hand on her other breast, and she sighed in response, her back arching slightly.

For long moments, she was held there, splayed and immobile as a complete stranger felt her breasts, fondling and exploring, bringing soft sighs and sinuous movement from her. Gentle pinches of nipple brought gasps and mews, quick twitches. Her shoulders shifted within the confines of her captivity. Her legs free, remained spread. She thought she felt a brief light brush of fabric of a pants leg.

The fondling became an exploration, the hands roved over her body, bringing more sighs from her.

The touches moved along her collarbones, up the side of her neck and then along the line of her jaw. Two fingers traced her lips, and then intruded into her mouth, where she sucked them, flicking her tongue against him.

He didn't speak, but she could hear his coarse breathing.

The hands traced her shoulders and arms, teased down her rib cage, palm against her belly, but always returned to her breasts, again and again. Her sighs turned to moans, she writhed, her body rising into each touch, thrusting itself into the stranger's hands, and falling back with disappointment when those hands lifted.

Finally, the hands slid down along her thighs, pushing gently. Obediently, with a murmur, she submitted, spreading wider, her back arching to push her hips further to the edge of the credenza. Her blindfolded head tossed and then inclined, dipping as a further gesture of surrender to the stranger's imminent possession.

His hands moved to the insides of her thighs, and she felt them tremble helplessly. She could feel her labia part of their own accord, her pussy dilating with uncontrollable arousal. She was unbelievably wet, she could literally feel it flowing from her in slow pulses.

The fingertips against her pussy brought another loud gasp, a spasm of her hips. The fingers vanished, and then almost immediately returned to an equal reaction. And again, she bit her lip and whined at the teasing.

Then a firm grip on her thigh, something poking at her vagina, sliding against her lips. She moaned with hunger, raising up her knees to give access, and then the stranger slid his cock deep inside her. She grunted at the penetration, moaning and gasping openly, her legs lifting in random uncoordinated motions.

The stranger thrust wildly into her, without finesse or control. A dozen hard thrusts, shoving up inside her. Hands grabbing at her, her breasts, her thighs. She almost spoke words. But his pace was already accelerating, like a runner reaching the finishing line. The thrusts grew rapid. Then he moaned loudly, his hands tightening on her thighs, his cock pushing deep in her. His urgent thrusts became weightless. And then he was panting.

She knew the stranger had come.

That's it? She thought.

She was panting as well, breasts heaving with arousal, but nowhere close to orgasm. She tried to push her mound onto his deflating cock, but he pulled back and fell out of her.

She went quiet, panting softly, waiting to see what the stranger would do next. Her body longed for more touches, fingers, hands, his cock. She waited, legs splayed wide, freshly used vagina waiting for him to slide fingers. She could hear him panting.

She waited.

After a moment or so, she heard the door open and close.

She waited another moment or two, but the silence was total.

He'd left.

The wild excitement of the experience was followed by an intense deflation.

This was it?

After all this anticipation, the preparation, the fantasies, the fear and cold feet, the almost surreal intensity, the crackling electricity of the beginning... it had wilted.

She worked her left hand around to release the catch and spring the cuff. Pulling the blindfold off, she looked around. Gone. The place was empty. The pizza was sitting in the living room. The twenty dollar bill was gone, so was the condom. She hoped the stranger had actually used it, she couldn't really tell. The post-it note was on the floor beside the credenza. Frustrated, she freed her other wrist, massaging it.

Well, she thought to herself. That happened.

Was Josh still here? Or had he left too. Maybe he'd watched? Maybe they'd left together?

"Josh?"

"I'm here," from the bedroom. "How was it?"

She hesitated. Her feelings, when she examined them, were too complicated to articulate easily. She settled for something superficial.

"It was hot," she said. But it still felt inconclusive, she wanted more, her body wanted more. "You want a turn?"

"Oh yeah!" He came out without pants, and they fucked on the Credenza, and then on the couch.

The handcuffs were left behind, still fixed to the coat hooks. She missed them, crossing her wrists above her head as he fucked her on the couch, but it wasn't the same. She described an embellished version of events, as he pounded into her, and they both came.

Afterwards, she laid her head against his chest, cuddling on the couch, feeling the first twinges of guilt she'd ever had with him. She'd fucked him, thinking of the encounter, reliving, embroidering it, using him to deliver the orgasm the stranger had denied her. It was the first time she'd fucked him thinking of someone else.

For all the intensity, she'd found the experience deeply unsatisfying. It had come and gone much too fast, without her satisfaction. The stranger's ejaculation had felt altogether premature, something that neither of them had been ready for.

Perhaps somewhere, the stranger felt as dissatisfied as she did?

The dissatisfaction was compounded by her sense of her own cowardice, calling Josh in to stand guard. As if she couldn't handle it on her own.

Of course, Josh had set it up for her, and he'd come when called, and it had been completely sensible to have him here. But it still rankled. The fantasy was compromised, the thrill flattened.

She didn't discuss this with Josh, or give him any sign of it. But it got under her skin, and she chewed on it. Perhaps try again? Ridiculous. Perhaps try again? Why? Perhaps try again? Well...maybe. Try again?

Try again without Josh, just to show herself that she was brave, that she was in charge.

After a week or so, she called up the Pizza Place.

"Hello," she gave her address. "I had a pizza delivered here last week. I think the driver accidentally left something behind?"

"What is it?"

"A set of keys. It doesn't belong to anyone here, and we think maybe the driver dropped them when he was delivering."

"Hold on, I'll check the logs."

"Thank you."

"I haven't heard anyone mentioning losing keys or anything, but we've got the same guy on shift today. I can ask him if he lost something."

"Oh sorry. I just realized where the keys must have come from. I'm sorry, false alarm."

"No problem. Will that be all?"

"Actually, you know what? Since I have you on the phone, I might as well order a pizza. I really enjoyed the delivery last time. Now, about these toppings, I want..."

She hung up, heart pounding. What the hell was she doing? This was insane. She was totally working without a net.

It was exhilarating.

How much time did she have? Fifteen minutes? Twenty? She needed to scramble. Shower quickly, write post-it notes, get the apartment ready.

This time, she waited blindfolded, bound and spread, genuinely nervous and twitching. She was very conscious of flying without blind, and yet that added to the excitement. Time had dragged out the first time, but on this occasion it went quickly. It felt like she was only in position for a few minutes before the knock came at the door.

As before it inflicted an electric thrill. Her body jolted. She turned her head automatically to the door, despite the blindfold. There was another knock, and again, she jolted, her heart racing. She could feel spreading warmth, a flush of hotness. Her pussy clenched wetly.

This time there was no voice calling. Instead, she could hear the doorknob turning, the door opening, deliberate steps.

The sound of the lock clicking shut. Her heart skipped a beat at that. There was something ominous about locking the door, a mute declaration of her captivity. No one else would be coming through that door, the stranger had just made sure he had her body to himself.

She couldn't help it, she squirmed, on her seat, shifting her weight from one ass cheek to the other, her knees involuntarily moving together. She stilled herself and waited.

The whiff of pizza, like before. Probably depositing it in the living room. Was he reading the post it note? Did he need to read it this time?

She'd left an extra message on the post-its, both an accusation and a request: "I want to come this time."

She strained to hear. Taking the cash? Unwrapping the condom? She heard soft footsteps. Was he walking away from her? There was a creek of a door. Again, her heart skipped a beat. This was different from last time. He was exploring the apartment. Her stomach knotted with tension. She heard a drawer open and close, other sounds. This was more of an intrusion, a deeper penetration of her space than she expected or wanted. She had a sense of violation, of intrusion, that both excited and scared here.

What was he doing? What was he going to do? She started to worry. Maybe it wasn't the same person? Maybe it was someone else with different motivations or purposes? Maybe he wasn't pizza delivery at all, but some burglar here to clean out the place?

No wait, she'd smelled pizza.

In her mind, a series of panicky scenarios flashed through, a burglar intercepting the pizza guy, the pizza guy deciding to toss the place, mistaken identity, intrusion.

The footsteps returned. She turned her head left and right, trying to track it, feeling appallingly vulnerable. Tension and trepidation and arousal warred within her, the feelings far stronger than before.

This time there was no Josh waiting in case she needed saving. She'd made herself helpless and served herself up, bound, blindfolded, naked and spread to a stranger. Anything could go wrong. It was terrifying and wonderful.

She found she was panting lightly, squirming, unable to keep still.

What was he doing? Taking pictures? What if he was? What could she do?

What if there was more than one? What if he'd brought a friend? The thought made her pussy spasm, she gasped spontaneously, without being touched. Only sheer will kept her from grinding her thighs together.

Hands on her breasts, first her left, and then an instant later, the right. Rigid nipples trapped between fingers, squeezing lightly. Her back arched in response. As before, she gasped loudly, the sound shifting to a moan. Now that the stranger's hands on her body seemed to signal desire, an intent to possess her body, to have her sexually, the fears and wild thoughts seemed to ebb. Her head shifted from side to side before bowing in surrender, acquiescing to possession. She was in free fall, events out of her control.

This time, the hands on her body were more deliberate, far less tentative. More confident in their exploration of her body. The stranger seemed to stand closer this time, she had more of a sense of looming presence, her thighs and calves as they shifted seemed to brush up against legs.

She wondered if it was the same stranger? Perhaps someone else had come, utterly unaware of what had gone before, and was simply taking advantage. Or maybe the first one had shared the story of the encounter, handed her off.

Her lips formed words, but she held back from asking, as if words would break the spell. Instead, she listened intently to the sound of his breathing, focussed on the touches, the hands exploring her body, trying to determine if it was the same man. Maybe? She couldn't be sure. As vivid as the first experience had been, it had been too new, too fast, to get a sense.

A hand travelled up between her breasts, circled her throat but did not choke. Fingers touched her lips, pulling her lower lip down. Obediently, she opened her mouth. But this time, fingers didn't immediately enter, rather they teased her, running along the fatness of her lower lip, drawing her tongue to flicker out, before finally sliding two digits into her mouth.

She closed her lips around the fingers as before, her tongue flexing against them, cheeks hollowing as she sucked on them. This time, the fingers lingered, sliding in and out in a vivid simulation of fucking. She concentrated on the false blow job, whining a little in the back of her throat.

His free hand, whoever he was, explored the rest of her body, cupping a breast, squeezing a nipple. The hand slid down below, stroking her clit suddenly, making her body writhe. She sucked hard then on the fingers, feeling them slide deeper between her lips. Her body writhed, and again she moaned around them.

Two fingers slid inside her from below, pushing her lips apart to smoothly invade her wet folds. It sent shivers of pleasure through her, causing her back to arch and offering her pussy up to his invasion, her thighs clenched, closing and opening, closing and opening, indifferent to her will, seeking only the best way to accommodate this new intrusion. Every time her body brushed against some part of him it was like an electric jolt, a shock out of shadow.

The sensual sensation of the fingers in her mouth, as she sucked them, and of the fingers in her pussy, was almost overwhelming. She visualized him outside her, his arms outstretched, points of contact from pole to pole, with a kind of sensual magnetic field radiating between them.

The fingers left her mouth, leaving her gasping. She felt a mouth settling on her left nipple, and twisted to the side to thrust it forward, offer her body up even as she rode the fingers still anchored inside her, stroking her G-spot. The mouth shifted to her other nipple, and again, she twisted her shoulder to offer up her body to pleasure. Teeth bit down lightly, nibbling with increasing pressure, the bites coming in tandem with the motion between her legs.

By the time the stranger left off her breasts, her nipples were raw and drenched with saliva. The fingers left her pussy, to explore again, hands firm. There were no limits this time, the touches ranged from her neck and jaw to the inside of her thighs. Her mouth and pussy were teased again and again, stoking her desire, but slipping in possessively only at her unknown master's will. The touches were far less tentative than the first time, there was a patience now, a sense of control.

Was it the same stranger as before, now used to her? Or perhaps regretting the hastiness of the last encounter and bent on taking his time? Or was it someone new and different? Try as she might, she couldn't tell, she could only surrender and offer her body up in submission to an unseen captor.

Her body was awash with sensuality, she had made herself helpless, presented herself blind, bound, naked and spread for him, and with each touch, the stranger enforced his possession. She was almost delirious with the sensual and psychological intensity.

The stranger lifted her knees up with bare touches, her body moving on its own to silent commands, beyond her control, eager to obey its new master and consecrate the change of ownership.

He stepped away then, leaving her conscious of how she was opened before him, offered up like a sacrifice on an altar, waiting to be taken.

Then she gasped loudly, her body convulsing, as she felt his mouth on her vagina, tongue sliding up between her labia, tasting her wetness, and then lapping at her clit. She knew in that instant, it was not Josh. She could feel the brush of facial hair against her smooth shaven mound, the texture of hair different, the movement of the tongue and lips unique.

The orgasm was almost instantaneous.

Almost beyond her control, her legs swung inwards, clamping around his head. She could visualize his exact posture, kneeling in front of her, licking her pussy, teasing her clit. Her hips bucked, and he reached up, bare hands clamping on her thighs, as he captured her. His tongue descended to torment her deliriously, teasing her, until she was ready to beg for release.

And when he finally let her release, she gushed so hard and wet it was like a flood. So hard, she could feel her abdominal muscles ache.

His face vanished from between her legs, but her stomach continued to spasm, the muscles aching, the insides of her thighs felt like they were fluttering.

He waited until she was spent, limp and breathless at the unexpected surge.

Her thighs were dripping, she could feel the wetness trickling down. Her heart was pounding.

Then she felt his cock at her vaginal lips, probing an instant before it slid smoothly up inside her, bringing a deep gasp of capitulation, her mouth opening wide. As the cock slid its full length inside her, two fingers slid into her mouth, her lips closing instinctively, sucking on them willingly.

Fleetingly, she hoped he was wearing the condom. Then she realized it didn't matter. She'd surrendered that choice, surrendered that decision, when she'd given up ownership of her body to his hands, his mouth, his cock. She was property now, without will or volition, to use as he pleased, and whether he used it or not, whether he ejaculated inside her, was his decision, not hers. She could only accept his will, her body now his compliant property.

It didn't even matter if this stranger was the same as the previous one, or if this was someone new. She was property now, nothing more than a possession, her will irrelevant, her identity erased, her body dedicated to the service of this unknown master.

Her new master fucked her relentlessly with powerful strokes, moving her yielding pliable body like a rag doll. She moaned and gasped continuously, and any time she felt the impulse to form words, the fingers invaded her mouth and she sucked on them eagerly, lost in a haze of obedience.

Another drenching orgasm rolled over her helpless form, leaving her quivering, but her master's steady thrusting did not alter. She realized the consequences of her surrender and his ownership, that her body was for his use now, not her own. And yet, that understanding, of being property now on some deep primordial level, triggered an abandonment, a relinquishment of will and a chain of orgasms ripped through her, leaving her utterly helpless, as they built one after the other, until she couldn't breathe, until her stomach tensed and her thighs were literally vibrating. Again, for the first times in her life, she squirted, liquid streaming from between her legs, her muscles turned to water, leaving her helpless and trembling.

She was barely aware when her master finished using her, her body obedient and compliant, her will and identity long dissipated. She accepted his convulsive thrusts as he rammed into her with all his force, again shaking her like a rag doll. He came, and she neither knew nor cared whether he came in a condom or spilled inside her body. There was a sense of regret and emptiness as his cock fell from her pussy. His hand seized her jaw, opening it, and she accepted his lips pressing against hers, his tongue in her mouth.

Then moments later, he was gone.

She didn't move, she sat there, hanging exhausted, her body tingling, feeling boneless as rubber, her lips, fingertips and toes numb to sensation. She had no will left, only exhaustion. She was a thing, waiting for an owner to return and resume his possession.

Only the mounting pain in her shoulders eventually drove her to free herself. Half dazed, she made sure to lock the door, and then staggered to her bedroom, falling on the bed and immediately entering a deep sleep. It wasn't until she awoke the next day, that she felt returned to herself.

Afterwards, she found herself dwelling on the experience, returning to it again and again, over the next few days, reliving the blinding sensual intensity, and the feelings of deep abject surrender and submission.

In hindsight, she found herself a bit shocked and disturbed by her own recklessness, the danger she'd put herself in, the risk she'd taken. What if there'd been two of them? What if he'd been rough? What if he had a disease? A complete stranger had walked into her home and slid his cock up inside her, she had no idea who.

She found herself being very careful to lock her doors, being extra attentive in her comings and goings. But nothing happened, no one seemed to be watching her, or stalking her. Slowly she relaxed.

In one sense, that was exciting, the notion of stranger sex was primal and exciting. But it was also disquieting. The intensity of her self-abandonment shocked her. She wondered if she was truly submissive, or perhaps as to the degree of her submissiveness.

Now, with some distance, with her self-possession, she could regard the event with some degree of clinical reflection, the nature of her feelings, their depth and intensity had been a product of the circumstances, and not truly innate. She did not crave slavery, certainly many of the inherent tropes of sadism and masochism left her indifferent. Her responses had been genuine, but not the core of who she was.

Still, she decided, she needed to manage her risk better. No more fucking pizza boys in her own home. At least, not while blindfolded. It had gone well both times, gone spectacularly the second, but she was well aware of the fears she'd experienced, and of the genuine potential for danger.

Sometimes, working without a net, you simply crash.

She chose not to tell Josh about this second encounter, partly out of the twinge of guilt she'd felt about excluding him, partly out of her mixed feelings of the first encounter, partly fearing his disapproval. But mainly out of wanting to selfishly treasure the adventure and keep it to herself. Sharing, disclosing it would make it less hers in some way.

There was one thing from the encounter that she did disclose to Josh in her bedroom games. On reflection, the thought that there could have been two of them became tremendously exciting.

It wasn't that she had never thought of or masturbated to the idea of a threesome or foursome before.

But while it was happening, the thought that there could be two of them, that they would collaborate, take turns using her, was exciting. There had been so much going on, and the real experiences had been so intense, this idea had occupied little space in the swirl of terrors and cravings.

But now that it was over and she had distance, the idea took on a new intensity. It was the unturned stone of the encounter, the thing that hadn't been, and therefore intriguing in its mystery.

So she talked about it now and then, without revealing why she talked about it. Sometimes, during sex with Josh she voiced fantasies of them being watched, sometimes spied upon unaware, sometimes deliberately performing to some audience. She talked about other men joining them, or having her in succession. Sometimes, she even pointed out someone on television or walking down the street, a flickering fantasy "If he was available..."

Despite this, their trysts remained exclusive.

Talking about it was one thing, doing it was another. The one genuine suggestion from Josh, bringing in the Pizza guy, that faceless, nameless stranger or strangers, that suggestion she shut down hard and immediately. He was a little confused, but didn't press it.

She liked that about him. If she said something, he simply accepted it. No questions.

Apart from that, her fantasies and scenarios continued, the encounters with Josh remained steady but unpredictable and intense, like two random orbits intersecting. She remained thrilled with her sex life, more vivid and satisfying than she could have imagined.

Her regular life continued normally, except, of course, when stray thoughts or random images or some passing comment triggered a flush of arousal. But she loved those, it made her feel alive and vital. She was confident that barring a few odd trips to the bathroom, which she tried to keep to a minimum, no one noticed anything out of the ordinary.

But the truth was that it was noticed: She had more verve, more confidence. She strode rather than walked, her smile had flash. She was more open with her opinions, her wit quicker, but without harshness. The people around her found her more cheerful, more vivacious and energetic. She had a zest for life. They wondered if she'd found a lover, even as she parried their discrete inquiries.

There was Josh of course, athletic, able and substantially younger. If her peers had known, they would have chalked it up to the liaison, even while disapproving of the relationship.

But Josh was just a small part of what was going on with her. The truth was that somehow with this sexual exploration, she felt more like herself, more fully complete than she'd ever had before, and it gifted her with the confidence to sail through her days.

The truth was, that her life was simply better. Even when consumed by her newfound sexuality, she was happier, more satisfied. She felt like herself, more herself than she'd ever felt, it felt like she'd finally gotten being herself right.

So of course, she wanted more. She made out with Josh in her car in a semi-public location. He fingered her to orgasm, and she masturbated him. The awkward interior and bucket seats making anything more too awkward to attempt.

She dressed more sharply, particularly away from work. Tighter fitting clothes, shorter skirts with slits, heels, plunging necklines. For the first time in her life, she paid attention to men and even women noticing her, seeing her as a sexual being, and it made her glow.

This sexual awareness, this sexual expression slipped into her taste. When she shopped, she found herself attracted to mirrored chrome, to curves. She found she loved bold colours, strong but subtle contrasts. Minor items of furniture were discarded, replaced by a new and bolder sensibility. Her taste in clothes and make up shifted, not dramatically, it was definitely, masked by the fact that she retained much of her old wardrobe. Although she used that older wardrobe less.

To the outside world, she was just somehow, indefinably bolder and more striking. But not in any overt way you could put your finger on.

The real changes weren't visible to outsiders. Her underwear had transformed completely, old panties and bras, all but discarded. Now it was colors and silks, there were corsets and bustiers, garter belts. Some of it was uncomfortable, to be worn alone at home. An awareness of comfort drove her to search out more expensive bras that fit comfortably. No one, except Josh, saw her underwear, it was all for her, a secret self-expression that made her smile.

Ropes and cuffs hung from the four poster bed, and a growing assortment of toys occupied a drawer next to it. Additional sets of cuffs, both chrome and Velcro, along with a few condoms, were tucked in box in the credenza, because you just never knew.

The apartment sparkled for her, she'd fucked or masturbated in literally every room, on or with every piece of furniture and fixture, she'd posed and explored in front of every mirror.

But her true sexual odyssey was in her own mind, a revelation of herself as a dynamic sexual being, and an endless flood of fantasies, scenarios and images.

"You know what would be hot," she whispered one night, in the middle of sex, as she raked fingernails down his back, feeling him thrusting deep inside her. "Getting arrested."

"Arrested?" Josh asked. He was used to these sudden strange eruptions of fantasy from her. Some were volcanic, mind blowing, a series of words that made him rigid as a steel bar. Others were entirely bemusing, the product of strange processes he could not follow. It didn't really matter, mostly they came to nothing, spinning out in the air and evaporating way before the tangible intensity of actual fucking and playing.

Whatever they were, he went along with them, it excited her to talk about her fantasies, and her excitement and enthusiasm was captivating, part of the wellspring of sexual energy he rode.

"Not arrested for real," she whispered, her legs wrapped around his hips, pulling him deeper. "Play arresting. Like you could arrest me at the mall."

"For shoplifting?"

"No. Something good. I could be an international jewel thief or something. You could stop me, arrest me as I was setting up a job."

"Uh huh?"

"You could take me to the security office, where I'd seduce you into letting me go."

"I could handcuff you right there in the store," Josh whispered back. He'd come to know some of her fetishes. "Perp walk you through the mall, right in front of everyone. They'd be looking at you, wondering what you'd done."

"Oh yes!" she cried out with sudden enthusiasm, rocking her hips hard against him. Josh could feel her sparking, some image or idea lifting her up, sending her hurtling to orgasm. He picked up his pace, thrusting harder and faster, matching her building urgency.

He looked down, she was luminous.

A week later, she was examining jewelry at the mall, her hair meticulously coiffed, her make-up perfect, dressed expensively and elegantly, browsing among different pieces, while the sales girl, Helen, graciously removed utterly expensive rings and broaches and necklaces from locked display cases, and discussed the merits of different pieces.

She'd been there half an hour, enjoying herself thoroughly, when Josh walked in.

"Hands in the air," he barked harshly. "You're under arrest."

Helen was shocked, eyes wide, mouth gaping like a fish.

She looked up, the amethyst broach Helen had been showing her still in her hand, turned to Josh, radiating confused innocence, and perhaps, a hint of malicious confidence.

"Excuse me?" she asked.

"Put down the broach," Josh ordered. "I'm serious."

"What's going on," Helen asked, her voice trembling on the edge of panic.

She put down the broach, standing up to face him. Josh stepped forward, seizing her wrist, he slapped a cuff on.

"Hey!" she protested, outraged.

Josh turned her around, drawing her hands behind her back, cuffing her other wrist.

"Wait! What? What's the meaning of this," she snapped angrily. "Take these things off. What the hell are you doing? Who's your boss? I'll have you fired. Let go!"

"I said you were under arrest," he told her. "There are warrants for you."

The sales girl, Helen, stared wide eyed.

"She... she wasn't doing anything," Helen protested. The store manager, an older, slender woman was coming over, along with another sales girl.

"Helen," she called struggling with her cuffs. "Call the police. I'm being assaulted by this security guard. False arrest. I'll sue the entire mall."

"What's going on," the store manager demanded.

"I was showing Amy... Ms Cohen, some pieces and this Mall security guy walked in out of nowhere and arrested her."

"I'm a customer!" she snarled. "These cuffs hurt, loosen them! I'm going to sue."

"Are you sure there isn't some mistake?" the store manager asked. Her name tag read 'Eleanor.'

"Amy Cohen," Josh recited. "Stephanie Del Mar. Victoria Santorini. Magdalene Pollard. Sylvia St. James. All false names."

She seemed to deflate in front of the uncomprehending sales staff, going passive in the cuffs, defeated. Her head slumped.

Josh spoke the sales staff. "She's got warrants out right across the country. High end professional thief. She was casing you. Those are her aliases."

At that moment, she lifted her head, looking directly at the Jewelry sales women. Her eyes narrowed, her features set in feral cunning. She chuckled, a low evil sound.

"He missed a few."

Unconsciously, the three women behind the sales counter seemed to turn pale. They took an involuntary step back, as if she'd turned into a cobra in front of them. Their reaction thrilled her. She'd never in her life felt so poised, so powerful.

"You have nothing," she sneered at Josh, giving him a contemptuous side eye. "I'll be free before you finish your paperwork."

"Not this time," Josh said righteously. "We've got you."

"Big talk little man," she spat, and then pretended to look him over. "Not so little though, are you? Tell me does the length match the height?"

The sales women watched this exchange wide eyed, like three deer caught in headlights. She smiled at them.

"Ladies, my apologies for this interruption. It seems that the law here is a little bit faster than I thought. And we were having such a good time. You were so... easy. I was really looking forward to picking up a few things."

She glanced at Josh mockingly. Her voice turned sarcastic.

"Which reminds me, I have to ask. Are you fast in other ways? That might be disappointing, a strapping young thing like you. Tell you what, let's call this a misunderstanding, take these cuffs off, let me go, and I'll just disappear. No harm done... yet."

"The cuffs stay on," Josh told her. "We have you dead to rights. This time, whatever your name is, you're going down. I'll make sure of it."

She sneered, her voice laden with contempt. "You're not the first lawman to say that."

"This time..."

"We'll see."

Josh took her by the shoulders, turning her away. He glanced at the sales staff.

"Ladies, thank you for your cooperation. I would suggest you conduct an immediate audit of your inventory, just in case. I think we caught her in time, but…"

She turned to look at them.

"Oh yes," she said her voice dripping with sarcasm. "Please do. Helen, Eleanor, I am so sorry that we were interrupted, it was going so well. But don't worry, I'll be back. You'll see me again."

She winked. They looked terrified.

"Or may you won't." She grinned at them. "But regardless, I always finish what I start."

She clicked her tongue.

"That's enough," Josh told her, as he marched her out of the store.

"Where are you taking me?" she demanded angrily, as they exited the store. Inside, she was walking on air, giddy with elation. This was perfect!

"Security office," he said loudly. "It's on the other side of the mall, lower level, we'll have to pass through the food court. Once we get there, I'll process you and hand you over to the police. I'll warn you, don't make a scene or try anything funny."

She scoffed, dismissively.

Actually, the security office was straight downstairs, in the basement, literally off the fire stairs, next to the jewelry store. But this way, she'd be marched, an exquisitely elegant prisoner in cuffs, all over the mall. She was so excited she could hardly wait.

The walk was wonderful. She strode, absolutely poised and confident, a secret smile on her lips. Her pussy clenching so hard she could feel her inner thighs going slick, her nipples pushing stiffly against her padded bra.

Josh marched her at a measured pace. Everyone looked, some stopped and stared. She smirked, catching eyes boldly, sometimes making people look away. He made a point of never deviating, having people step out of the way with a curt "Excuse me, make way. Extremely dangerous prisoner coming through."

A few people, particularly teenagers in the food court, asked what she'd done. Josh would recite that she was a high end thief caught red handed cleaning out the Jeweler. International warrants were mentioned. Occasionally, she'd interrupt with some defiant remark or sarcastic innuendo.

Another security guard approached. She'd seen him previously at the mall, but seldom paid attention. Who pays attention to security guards? She knew his name was Clark, because Josh had told her.

Shorter, than Josh, but then everyone was shorter than Josh. Thicker in body, but not fat, with a shock of blonde hair and a goatee.

"What have you got?"

"Major catch," Josh said. "High end thief, major warrants all over the place. Multiple identities. I spotted her casing the Jeweler."

She shrugged.

"I was just having a little fun," she explained confidently. "A diversion while setting up the big job."

"The big job?" Clark asked.

She winked, improvising. "Sure. What was I going to clear from a shopping mall Jeweler? A few hundred thousand? That was just a sideshow. The main one is millions... minimum."

"You need any help?" Clark directed his question to Josh.

Josh looked at her, Clark following the direction of his eyes. Clark was in on it, of course. Not the details really, but he knew Josh was doing some sort of role play sex thing in the security office, and he'd had to be told and agree to it. Otherwise, he might accidentally walk in.

Josh had proposed Clark as a second, a suggestion she'd automatically rejected, but then waffled. Provisionally, the answer had been a soft no. But Clark had agreed to keep the security office clear and run interference if they needed it. He did have some hope...

She looked him over, playing the role, smiling arrogantly. Why not? Spur of the moment, she decided to go with it. She nodded carefully, meeting Josh's eyes.

"Even handcuffed, two of you might not be enough to handle me."

"Yeah," Josh said. "This is a big one. I think I need help."

Clark fell in with them, walking on the opposite side of her from Josh and taking her other arm. Bordered on both sides by security, her arms held, her wrists cuffed, she'd never felt so powerful, so dangerous. She felt like a character out of James Bond.

They walked the lower floor, into the service corridor and stepped into the battered old freight elevator, finally ending up in the basement.

The security office, when they arrived was wonderfully dingy. A bank of monitors, the security cam system, radio dock. A table, a desk, both battered. Assorted bits of old padded office furniture, their vinyl surfaces split in places.

"Can you take the cuffs off now?" she asked. "I promise I won't beat you both up and get away in my helicopter."

She was still playing the role, Josh noted, so the answer was obvious.

"Sorry. Policy."

"Well," she said. "At least switch them to the front, they're hurting my shoulders."

Josh stared. She nodded slightly.

"All right."

He produced his key and uncuffed one wrist, loosening the other so he could rotate the cuff, and then fastened her wrists in front of her.

"Thank you," she said.

Josh pulled out a chair beside the desk.

"Sit there, we'll take your information. The police are already on their way."

"Aren't you going to search me?" she asked. "Who knows what I might have concealed."

Josh raised an eyebrow. They'd done the 'up against the wall, pat down' routine many times as foreplay in her home. It had slipped his mind in the role play.

"I'll do it," Clark said, quickly.

Josh glanced at her, she hesitated, seemed intrigued but pensive nodded slightly. Josh understood the meaning, she wasn't entirely sure of Clark. She wanted to see how he behaved, if he came on too rough or too strong, Josh could pull him back before it got too out of hand, and if necessary, they could end it. Easier now than later when things had advanced.

"All right," Josh said.

Clark took her by the arm.

"This way, Ma'am," he said, as he led her towards the wall. "I'm going to pat you down for weapons or contraband. Have you ever been patted down before? I can explain the process before we start."

"Many times," she said. "I know the drill. I've had it. I guess you can say I've been drilled a lot."

She leaned forward into the wall, bracing her elbows against it, arching her back.

"I know how it goes. Bend over and spread wide," she purred. She looked over her shoulder at him and winked. "Ready when you are, officer."

Clark's pat down was careful and professional, pulling the tails of her blouse out of waistband of her skirt, checking pockets and seams. Despite that, she mewed and squirmed under his touch and pushed her bottom out into his hand.

"All clear."

That was disappointing, she thought.

"But officer," she called. "Are you sure?"

Josh frowned slightly. Officer felt like his name, in their bedroom games. It felt odd to hear her use it on someone else, even Clark.

"Officer," she called again, still up against the wall, looking over her shoulder at Clark. She wore a half smile. "Officer, come here. I want to make a confession."

Clark looked to Josh uncertainly. Josh nodded.

Clark stepped close. "Yes?"

"Officer, it's a very important confession," she whispered. "Vital even."

She paused, her voice dropped an octave going moist and husky.

"I'm not wearing any panties. Not a thing. Did you notice that when you patted me down?"

"No." Clark was blushing furiously. She enjoyed his reaction, it made her playful.

"It's true! I was so busy this morning, I completely forgot about them. Isn't that terrible?" She giggled. "Of course I hardly ever wear them anyway. I find they only get in the way. And it's not as if I need them, I'm smooth down there, completely smooth. Like satin. You didn't notice?"

"No."

"Well, I think that just shows that you weren't very thorough. I must say, I expect more ... diligence from my law enforcement. What are my tax dollars paying for? After all, I could be concealing... all sorts of things... in all sorts of places."

"I should check again?"

"Well, I certainly wouldn't tell you what to do. But maybe you should? Just to be safe? You wouldn't want any surprises?"

"All right."

"Take your time," she husked, rolling her hips slowly in a figure eight. "But be careful, I am a very (bump), very (bump) dangerous criminal."

This pat down began as professionally as the first, but more thoroughly. She felt hands on stockinged legs moving up and down. She pressed back against hands on her ass, rolled her body to his touches. By stages he grew bolder, at first circling the bare flesh along her skirt's waist feeling her belly. He cupped her breasts over her blouse, and then with encouragement, slid his hands under to cup her bra.

He pulled her skirt up, exposing the tops of stockings and garters and beyond. His hand reached between her legs, making her shiver with delight as it tentatively stroked her lips. She moaned slightly, rocking her hips.

But that was the limit of Clark's boldness, his hand withdrew.

"She's clean," Clark announced, his voice unsteady. She could tell without looking that his hands must be shaking.

"Oh no I'm not," she called over her shoulder. "I'm not clean at all. I'm dirty! Very dirty! Why, I'm positively... filthy!"

"If you can bring her over here," Josh called. "We'll take down her information."

She turned around, and with Clark's hand on her arm, and his other finding her ass, he lead her the few steps to the table where she primly took a seat, crossing her legs in a ladylike pose, cuffed hands on her knee, her shoulders swinging slightly..

Clark pulled up a chair facing her, so close she could stretch out a foot to caress his calf. He was desperately trying to conceal a raging erection. His face was red with exertion and his hands trembled. His eyes were glassy. She loved the intensity of his reaction, but worried that he might blow just sitting there.

"I'll keep an eye on her," Clark said.

"Yes," she agreed, leaning back in the chair, her knees parted, heels pointing inward, head tilted. "You should definitely keep an eye on me."

"In case..." she continued.

She casually undid a button on her already low cut blouse, exposing her bra. Carefully putting on her most innocent expression.

"...I try something."

If anything, he got even redder.

"Name?"

"Santeria Sebastian."

Josh looked up, momentarily confused.

"Santeria... that's voodoo?"

"My mother was a witch," she teased. "She could put a spell on men. So can I. Perhaps I'm casting a spell on you now? Do you feel yourself falling under my power?"

"That's not one of your aliases," Josh's brows knit.

"It's my real name, Santeria Sebastian of San Salvador. You can call me Santa," she paused and stretched luxuriously. "My friends call me Christmas."

"Well," Josh said, uncertainly, "Miss Sebastian... Santeria... Santa? I have to warn you, you're in a great deal of trouble, and it's in your own interests to cooperate. Now-"

"Pooh!" she said. Casually she undid another button. Leaning on the arm of her chair towards Josh, her knees parting further apart with the movement, the skirt riding further up her thighs.

Clark was staring with feverish intensity at the shadow between her thighs, unable to really see anything, but entranced by the possibility. All he could think of was the feel of her pussy against his fingertips, the amazing softness, the mysterious folds, when he'd reached between her legs.

She squirmed in her seat.

"Gentlemen. Boys. I have a proposition. Surely you know that my associates have already sent for my lawyers. They'll arrive here before the police. You have nothing on me. We both know it. All you will accomplish is to ... inconvenience me. Slightly."

She was deliberately ignoring them, playfully undoing another button. She shifted in her seat once again.

"But I do hate to be inconvenienced. It would be unfortunate for you. I think, you should let me go, instead. Do not trouble yourself with all this fuss or bother. That's a job for someone else far away. They're paid for it. You are not. Do your duty? You will see nothing, no money, someone else will take all the credit. You win nothing but my displeasure."

"Instead, let us forget all this unpleasantness. There is no need to involve the police. Call it a misunderstanding..."

Her blouse now fully opened, she began toying with her left bra cup, lifting a breast from it, letting it settle against the folded cup. Her nipple poked out proudly.

"Do me this favor," she told them, "and that will allow you to ... convenience me."

Her attention drifted away from the two men, as she stared down at her breast.

"Hmmm..."

She toyed with her nipple, pressing her fingernail into the aureole and making a circle that seemed to occupy her attention completely. She shifted again in her seat, the movement of her thighs causing the skirt to ride up completely, exposing the tops of stockings and beyond.

She looked up innocently from her nipple, her gaze flickering back and forth between the two men.

"Oh! I think this is hard!"

She seemed to dismiss the thought, and smiled a wanton smile, turning her attention clearly upon the fascinated men. She crossed her legs.

"What do you say to my proposition, Officers? Will Christmas come early this year?"

"Uh," Clark began.

"I think we're out of our league," Josh said. "This case is too big for us. Too hard."

"Much too hard," Clark agreed. "I think we should do what she says."

"Yes," Josh agreed.

"Then it is settled," She said, pulling her skirt up to her hips, sliding her ass forward on the chair. "Come, unwrap me so I can receive your presents."

Josh rose, coming around the table to her side. As he reached her, she twisted, bringing her cuffed wrists up to his crotch, feeling him already hard in his pants. He bent down to kiss her on the mouth,

deep and hungry. With one hand, he reached into her almost
completely undone blouse, freeing her other breast from its cup.

She couldn't see Clark, but she could feel him, spreading her legs
apart. She hooked one knee over the arm of the chair and felt his
hands, strong but shaking, against the insides of stockinged thighs.
His mouth was on her vulva, licking with wounded urgency,
frantically lapping from her asshole to her clit.

The sensation was amazing, like that time on the credenza, with
fingers from the stranger invading her mouth and vagina. Except
these were mouths, tongues, moving and wet against her,
accompanied by hands. There was no coordination, instead they both
acted out of synch with each other, and her attention was drawn back
and forth. It was exciting but distracting, she found she couldn't
focus. Her hips lifted, she squirmed in the seat held in place by
Clark's grip, and from above by Josh's hand, she was trapped,
helpless and rolling on waves of sensation.

She broke off the kiss, half breathless already. Without his
distraction, she could squeeze his cock in his pants. She stared down
at Clark's head, bobbing between her thighs.

"You should keep the cuffs on me, at least until you have had
your pleasure. Or I might overpower you both."

"Yes," Josh said, standing. "She's dangerous. Treacherous."

"I am," she pronounced. "I am the very definition of treachery.
Even together, you would be no match if I were freed. But..."

She kissed his cock, taking the head in her mouth for a moment,
and letting it out. She bared her lips, looking at it, and snapped her
teeth at it, as if to bite it

"... my danger is what you love!"

She took it back in her mouth again, her cheeks hollowing as she
sucked on its length. Josh let his hands drift to her head, moving her
back and forth. This was easier now. It was hard to concentrate on
sucking Josh's cock with Clark's frantic licking. But at least now she
wasn't floundering back and forth helplessly.

Her knee, straining, fell from the chair's arm, and Clark simply
pushed it back up, causing her body to slide down further. The cock
fell from her lips, and she felt herself bent around like a pretzel.

"This is getting awkward," she said as his cock slid against her
nose.

"Let's get you on the desk. I want to fuck you."

She stood long enough for her skirt to come off. Josh tugged at
her blouse and jacket, but her cuffed wrists prevented removal.
Instead, he bent her forward across the desk. For a moment, she felt
four hands all over her ass, two sets of fingers probing her vagina and
beating against her clit. It was a bizarre sensation, almost impossible

to describe. The one set withdrew and the others clamped around her hips, pulling her back and into position.

With a grunt of desire, she spread her legs as wide as she could and raised her ass, arching her back to present her wet pussy for mounting. Josh, she could tell it was Josh, entered her with the hard readiness of a cock that knew her intimately. She lifted up, gasping, as it slid inside her. He pushed down on her hips, holding her in place and began to pound. She was sweating in her blouse and jacket, hands forward.

"Oh god yes," she cried out. "Fuck me."

From peripheral vision, she sensed Clark on the side of the desk, he reached for her, running fingers through her hair, twining the locks between thumb and digits. He lifted her head, pushing two and then three fingers in her mouth. She heard him ordering her to suck and obeyed willingly, sucking two or three fingers alternately, licking his palm. She had the vaguest sense of his pink erection protruding from his pants, bobbing unused.

Again, there was that weird doubling, the splitting of attention that left her floundering and divided. The mouth wasn't an erogenous zone, not in the same way that her pussy was. A kiss, or finger blow job didn't have the same intensity as Josh's pounding cock. But still, it was there, demanding her awareness, pulling her in separate directions.

Spastically, her legs kicked almost randomly as Josh pounded fiercely into her. The impact of his thrusts mashing her flat on the desk, shoving her hips so hard into the edge of the desk it was almost bruising.

"Want a turn?" she heard Josh say. For a moment, she had no idea what he was talking about, or who he was addressing, the words being only a third level of distraction.

"Yeah," Clark said. The fingers left her mouth, leaving trails of drool as he moved out of her line of sight. "Do I need a condom?"

"Are you clean?" Josh demanded, still ramming into her with bruising force.

"Oh yeah, I'm clean. But what about her?"

Some tiny part of her that was listening to the conversation felt itself offended.

"You have to be sure you're clean," Josh ordered. "No fucking around."

"I don't want to get her pregnant."

Oh, that's what he meant. Offense not taken.

That struck her as senseless though. She was on birth control. She was paying for a prescription to have occasional sex with one man. At that moment, it seemed to her that it would just make more sense if the prescription was justified by two men having sex with her.

Amortizing the investment. But before she could say that, Clark spoke, "I'm going to use a condom."

"Jesus Dude. Whatever!" she snapped, annoyed by his waffling. When you're fucking a dangerous international jewel thief in handcuffs, commit to it!

Moments later, Josh froze. He pulled back and slammed one more time in a thrust so ferocious that the desk rocked, and her thighs and hips were momentarily crushed. Then just as quickly, he pulled out leaving her suddenly empty.

"All yours!"

One of Clark's hands was on her ass, she felt the tremble of it, the style of grip completely different from Josh's. His cock, when it entered felt completely different, thick and ramrod straight. Clark thrust hard several times, bringing cries of pleasure from her, and then fell out. He slid in again, this time gently, moving forward with short pumps, then going still.

Without the forceful ramming, she could push back onto him. Clark was shorter, she bent her knees, sliding a little off the desk. His cock moved upwards in her, bringing new sensations. But he kept falling out. He had no rhythm, almost every stroke of his cock was different, it was almost maddening.

Josh stepped in again, after Clark's brief fucking, and soon she was being rammed breathlessly against the desk. Her blouse and jacket were drenched with sweat

"Wait! Wait!" she called. "This isn't working. Let's move!"

Once let up, her legs were wobbly and she was panting from the sexual energy in the room. Josh pulled his pants up from around his knees, he was still wearing his shoes. Clark had discarded his shoes to slip out of his pants. He was naked from the waist down, except for black socks. Sometimes, she thought, her eyes passing over them, there's no way to look good having sex.

Her clothes were driving her crazy, and they were already tangled up in her cuffs. Rather than take them off, Josh and Clark helped her push them over her head and down her forearms where they formed a big wrinkled knot around her wrists, a tangle of bra, blouse and jacket. At least it was off her now.

For a moment, she stood panting. Then Clark's hand slipped across her breast, capturing her nipple. The sensation was gentle, pleasurable, a relief from the heady pounding, she swayed, leaning back against the edge of the desk, enjoying it. Without a word, with no sound from any of them, Josh joined, fondling her other breast. Their free hands began to move over her body, roving and possessive.

Two sets of fingertips probed at her pussy, sliding in and out, sometimes against each other, stoking or pushing against her clit, without any coordination. It was deeply pleasurable, but so strange.

Perversions and Infidelities / Page 55

She had a flash of a video of starfish at high speed underwater, slowly crawling all over each other, both full of meticulous intent, but utterly unaware of each other. The hands parted, touched, moved away, explored, each on their own journey.

Josh lowered his head to suck on her nipple, she was intimately familiar with the way he did it, the teasing tongue, the scraping nibbles. Clark followed suit, and she had two mouths on her nipples, a delicious experience. Except that Clark's style was different, biting lightly, alternating probing and sucking.

She closed her eyes trying to follow the sensations, swaying as she did. But she couldn't, there were too many touches, too many things going on in too many places, sensations and kinds of sensation, different experiences. She couldn't track it all.

So she just gave up and simply experienced it, surrendered to the pleasure of the touches, the licks, the nibbles, the random explorations of her body. No longer trying to follow it or focus on who was doing what, but simply letting it happen, she experienced it as a new kind of pleasure. She allowed herself to float on it.

"Okay," she whispered. "This is good. This is great, let's keep doing this for a while."

She allowed them to lean her backwards, lifting and supporting her until she was laying on her back on the desk, her bound wrists above her head, hanging down one side, her knees bent and legs spread, heels perching on the other side.

She closed her eyes and floated, allowing them to touch her, to explore her. The image of the starfish relentlessly crawling all over each other, full of mindless, oblivious purpose came to her again.

Someone kissed her, and she simply welcomed it, letting a tongue slide into her mouth, meeting it with her own, all part of the endless sensation as other hands explored her, her nipple was pulled, fingers slid inside her. Then another mouth on hers, different, but she welcomed it as well, feeling as it kissed her. A second mouth briefly on her nipple, and then it was between her legs, hands griping her thighs, while other hands fondled her breasts.

She was helpless again, as she'd been on the Credenza, drenched in oblivion. But this was different. On the Credenza there'd been possession and surrender, submission and taking, until she'd swirled down to some dark state of total relinquishment, had given up everything to a master, become property, become owned.

This was different. Here she wasn't owned but utterly free. She'd become an object again, with no will of her own, but instead of property possessed, she was worshiped, drenched in an ever changing, ever flowing tide of sensation. It just built and built, ebbed and flowed. When the orgasm came she was simply experiencing, not chasing, not anticipating. When it overtook her, it was completely unexpected, and absolutely wonderful, as were the next ones.

She had the feeling that they were entranced with her, consumed by her body and their explorations. The orgasms drawn from her were wondrous to them, and so they did everything they could to prolong it.

Eventually, there was a shift. She felt her body being hauled forward, her head closer to the edge of the altar that had been a desk. Her legs were parted, hands spreading her knees wide. She opened her eyes, and Clark was looming over her, fully naked, his pale body freckled around the shoulders, his erection proud in a glistening condom. She noted his pubic hair was blond too. Looking closer, she saw he had chest hair, so sparse and pale that you wouldn't notice it was there.

"Is it okay?" he asked. "Can I?"

It had annoyed her. But there was something sweet about his tentativeness. He was the odd man out. Josh and her had fucked so many times, they knew each other, their preferences and boundaries. They were comfortable. But Clark was feeling his way, terrified of making a mistake, navigating a tightrope.

She smiled up at him, gave a little jerk of her head, and spread her knees just a little further.

"Come and fuck me," she invited.

He slid forward, balancing himself unsteadily on one hand, trying to guide his cock to her. It poked at the inside of here thigh. She wanted to reach down, to help him draw it in, to touch him. But her wrists were trapped. Instead, she pulled her knees back and rolled her ass forward a little. He found her, she felt a push between her legs. He threw his other hand out, hovering over her on both now, and pushed.

It was easier getting fucked this time with him. Everyones the same height laying down. She was still flying from the sensual bath of their hands and mouths, but there hadn't been much penetration. His cock felt good in her, different from Josh's, thicker, straighter. She laid back, lifting her legs until the thrusting felt just right. His pumping was more regular this time, he had a rhythm and a pace. She mewed and moaned, feeling herself floating towards another orgasm.

But before she could reach it, he leaped ahead, thrusting hard into her suddenly and making her gasp. His expression above her was that of a man falling off a mountain. He thrust convulsively, wildly. His cock inside her moved weightlessly, rushing but not pushing.

"Cum baby cum," she told him, she wasn't there and she could tell she wouldn't make it. But he was already past the point of no return. With three frenzied thrusts, he pushed deep into her, went stiff and then limp, panting.

His weight settled on her, which was all right at first, but his body was heavy, and his weight pressed her down. She couldn't do anything about his weight except jerk her bound wrists, frustrated with the cuffs.

"I'm sorry," he whispered in her ear. "I was too fast."

"It's all right," she told him. "You were fine."

Ideally, she thought, he'd have lasted until she could come, and it would have been nice if he could get off her and not crush her flat. But she still felt the residue of that deep empathy that had led her to welcome him into her body, and so she was moved to kindness.

Finally, he got off her so that she could breathe. Josh mounted up on the desk, but she put a stockinged foot on his chest, halting him.

"Get me out of these fucking handcuffs," she told him. Her shoulders were already aching, and her back was starting. "And let's do it someplace else."

Josh hopped off and found the keys and soon, she was out, and free of both the cuffs and the tangled sodden bundle that her clothes had become. It was a mess. Her wrists were raw, but being out of the fucking things was bliss. At that moment, she couldn't see the appeal of the damned things at all.

There was an old blue couch up against the wall, solid steel frame, torn fake leather upholstery in modern style. It looked like it had been stolen from a failing airport. They moved the party there.

"I want to be on top," she said, mainly because she didn't want to be on her back again, or taken from behind. She pushed Josh gently back until he was sitting and straddled him. Clark, his cock thoroughly deflated, but condom still dangling, sat beside them, watching. That struck her as funny.

Josh held his cock straight, as she balanced with one hand on his shoulder, and positioned herself over him, gently sinking down on him until he was buried in her.

She reached over, pulled the condom from Clark's deflated cock and tossed it away. It was just too ridiculous hanging off him.

"Sorry," Clark apologized.

"No worries," she assured him.

"Make sure you pick that up later though," Josh warned. "We don't want people finding used condoms in the office."

Way to ruin the mood, she thought at him, but held her tongue. Instead, she focused on riding him, feeling comfortable with his familiar presence inside her, feeling his hands creep up to her breasts, or cradle her hips. This wasn't so different from straddling him on the couch in her apartment. The weird part was Clark sitting on the couch beside them, smiling and just politely watching. Not weird good, but not weird bad, just... weird.

"Clark," she said, working rhythmically on Josh, "come stand behind me."

Shyly, he obeyed, standing carefully neutral, a foot or so behind her, keeping careful distance. At first, she didn't understand, but then realized it was some gay paranoia thing, that if he came too close, he might have some body contact with the man fucking her.

"Come a little closer," she said, "put your hands on me."

Obediently, reluctantly he approached an inch or two, but he reached out to put his hands on her shoulders. She was surprised by how much she enjoyed his touch, the intimacy of the human contact. Reaching up, she put her hands on top of his, as she rode, and gently drew them down, pulling him closer until his hands were on top of Josh's on her breasts, and she could feel him against her back. Sandwiched loosely between the two men, she felt an intimacy, a safety that went beyond sexual.

"You know what I loved," she told them. "It was when you were both touching me at once, touching and kissing. It felt so good, it felt special."

Josh's hands slithered away, finding other parts of her body to caress as Clark's hands moved around her breasts. They're getting the idea. When she leaned back, she began rocking, her back pressing against Clark's chest, and he didn't yield. It felt so satisfying to her, as if it was meant to be this way.

"Kiss me," she demanded of Clark, twisting around towards him. He bent forward, their bodies twisted against each other, his hands clutching her breasts hard, as if to steady himself. Their lips met, brushed against each other, found again and clamped together.

Riding one man and kissing another was wildly exciting, both their hands all over her was wildly exciting, and suddenly, she felt it, appearing almost out of nowhere, having quietly built up, her orgasm came roaring. She gasped, breaking the kiss, and pounded herself onto Josh's cock more and more ferociously, even as she felt the lightning bursting out below, crawling up her spine.

It was too intense, she couldn't breathe. Suddenly her body went spastic, refusing to obey her. Her fingers sank into Josh's shoulders, fingernails like claws. She gasped but no air would come. The orgasm swept over her and her body went rigid. Muscles tightening up, she rose up off his cock involuntarily, not wanting to, wanting him deep, but rising involuntarily as if drawn upward, until only the head of his cock was still in her.

That's when she felt it, the spray between her legs, like a firehose, an intense moment when her stomach was tensing so hard it hurt, and the spray burst from between her legs. She was vaguely aware of Josh's surprised yell, of Clark holding her thrashing body steady.

Then the rigidity passed, she could breathe again, sucking up great lung-fulls of air. Trembling muscles failed and she sank down hard on Josh's cock. Immediately, the white noise burst in her head, she felt her stomach tensing and another spray between her legs as she twisted. Then suddenly, she couldn't stand it anymore.

"Stop! Stop!" she gasped. "No more! Stop!"

Body hyper-acute, she struggled off Josh's cock and pushed both of them away from her, flopping on the couch, wild eyed, lungs panting uncontrollably.

Clark reached out to her, and she slapped his hand away.

"Holy shit!" she said.

Something more was called for.

"Holy shit!" she repeated.

She waited, feeling her body settle down. An aftershock hit her, and her body spasmed, making her shake, bending her forward, her thighs trembling.

"I'm okay," she told them, her staring eyes not really seeing them. She waved her hand randomly in the air, careful to keep her legs splayed, as if the simple pressure of closing her thighs would trigger another spray.

"I'm okay. It's okay. I'm just coming down."

Panting.

"I'll be all right."

"You squirted," Josh said. "I didn't know you squirted."

She gulped air, trying to focus.

"It never happened before," she lied.

Suddenly, she found herself desperately wanting intimacy.

"Hold me, both of you, hold me."

But the minute they touched her it was too much, it was overwhelming and she pushed them away.

"No no no! Hands. Just don't touch me. Hold my hands."

The two men ended up on opposite sides of the couch, with her in the middle, holding her hands in theirs, as if she was a sexual Madonna. She waited for the feelings to recede. Finally, she tried a word.

"Wow!"

Success. Try some more words.

"That was good!" She thought it was an understatement, but now she was sure she could manage rational conversation. She swallowed.

"Are you all right?" Clark asked.

"Me? Oh yeah," she said. "Totally fine. Let's just sit here a while? Okay?"

She listened to her steadying heartbeat, and held up a hand arm's length, studying her fingers. Vision good. Fingers numb. Toes? Numb. Lips? Numb. Body? Like rubber. She could live with that.

Out of the blue, staring off at nothing, Josh spoke. "Best! Christmas! Ever!"

For a second she had no idea what he was talking about. But then, just as she got it, Clark spoke.

"God bless us every one!"

And that was all it took, they burst into giddy giggling and laughter. She laughed until her sides hurt.

"I think we're done," she said finally. "I don't think we can top that. I don't think I could stand it."

Her head swiveled loosely, bearing on Josh.

"Hey Sweety," she asked. "Did you come?"

"Not quite."

"Oh." That was disappointing. She couldn't imagine letting anything near her pussy for at least a week. "Let me come down, I can give you a blow job."

"It's okay."

She nodded, glad to be let off the hook.

"All right, next time. I'll make it up to you."

Clark moved to let go her hand, she clamped down on it.

"No."

But it was over. When she could move, and was willing to let them go, Clark started putting on clothes, and then Josh. She was still wobbly, and they were solicitous of her.

The skirt was fine, she climbed back into that and her shoes. The blouse and jacket were a mess, buttons missing from the blouse, the shoulder ripped on the jacket. They'd need trips to the dry cleaner and a seamstress to be salvageable. Instead, she borrowed one of Clark's T-shirts from his locker.

She checked a mirror, her hair was a mess. She didn't give a fuck.

They both walked her out to her car in the parking lot.

"Sorry," Clark said again. He was apologetic.

She understood, he'd been hair trigger, over-excited, had come too fast. But she didn't mind. They all knew Clark was the weakest link, but she didn't hold it against him. Her first time with Josh had been five minutes.

"You did fine," she assured him.

He hesitated.

"Do you think we'll do it again?"

"No."

She thought of her procession through the mall in handcuffs. Absolutely drained of sexual energy, she couldn't understand it, it seemed ridiculous. She could remember the feeling of excitement and power, but couldn't feel it at the moment.

"I don't think I can set foot in this Mall again. Not without everyone calling out the National Guard. That's burned."

She had no plans for a threesome again. But then, she had a second thought. Maybe don't rule it out entirely. She needed to process the experience, the good and the bad, what worked and what didn't. It had been intense and overwhelming, and she needed to absorb it before she could think about it.

Could she do it again? Could it be better? Would Clark be more relaxed and confident now that he'd had experience, avoid some of the mistakes, focus on what really worked. This had been something of an experiment. They hadn't really known what they were doing, just improvising.

So... maybe?

"Maybe," she said out loud.

"Question," Josh said. "All that stuff about Santeria and Christmas? Where did that come from?"

She nodded. They'd charted out a much more elaborate role-play, but Clark's presence had thrown things off, so she'd short circuited and gone straight to sex. It had been a good choice, she thought.

She shrugged.

"I just improvised. Was it too hokey?"

"No, it was great. Just threw me got s loop for a minute."

"It worked out," she agreed.

They arrived at her car.

"Are you safe to drive?" Josh asked, worried.

She held her hand out to see if it was steady. No tremors. Good enough.

"Yeah."

She hugged Josh, and then Clark, got in her car and went home.

Nothing ever quite matched that adventure, although she had many other adventures.

She and Josh eventually drifted apart. There was an age difference, and except for sex, they had little in common. Josh started to see a girl, it got more serious, and so she faded from his life.

But that was all right. There were no hard feelings on either side.

She'd found herself, her bolder, better self. There were other lovers, other adventures. Her life proceeded along its previous path, but better, with more energy and confidence. She was more successful in her career, happier in her life.

There were two incidents of note.

Once about a year later, in a restaurant, she noticed a group of girls were staring at her, whispering and pointing. It took her a second to recognize Helen from the Jewelers at the Mall. Their eyes met, the girl stared at her with something like terror.

She smiled her best shark-like smile, nodded and lifted a wine glass as if in toast to the girl. Then she simply returned to her meal, unaccountably but deeply satisfied.

The second incident was years later. She was walking down the street, and suddenly, in front of her was Josh. He was a little older and sported a beard, but it was him. He was walking hand in hand with a girl.

For a moment, they both halted, Josh visibly awkward. They made small talk of no consequence.

Then abruptly, she stepped forward and hugged him.

"Thank you," she said. "For being there. You were a good friend. You were what I needed back then, and I'll always appreciate you."

There was a moment's hesitation, and he returned the hug.

After, they separated. She smiled at the woman (girlfriend?).

"Take good care of him."

And walked on, her footsteps light and confident, into the rest of her life.

In the end, she lived happily ever after.

The End

STACY

Stacy was on the verge of buying her first vibrator when the Manchesters walked in.

She blushed and quickly stepped back around a display. They hadn't seen her. She put the vibrator up on a different shelf and peaked around the corner.

Yes, it was the Manchesters. Barney and Betty. From the neighborhood. They were notorious prudes and gossips. Friendly and outgoing, but there was an arch judgemental quality to Betty. It was hard to explain, there was no softness to Betty, no ambiguity. If she visited your home, she would glance around once, and you knew you'd been judged and found wanting as a housekeeper. Discussing the day's issues with them, they were merciless in their skewering of the famous and wayward.

Barney and Betty Manchester was the last couple you wanted to run across while buying a Flexi-Mate 200, waterproof, 3 AAA batteries, seven speeds unit, for thirty-nine ninety nine. She could just imagine Betty's harsh look assessing the thing, and then that focused glare as Stacy's vagina shrivelled up.

No. They couldn't see her here. Why were they here? What did they want?

She looked around. The shop was long and narrow. There was no way she could leave without going past them. That would be unbearable. Barney and Betty skewering her, there would be a horribly awkward conversation.

Retreat, she thought. She eased further back into the store, among the anal toys, keeping them as far away from those as she could. Anal toys were the worst, each one weirder looking than the last.

At the back of the store were the peep shows.

She licked her lips, heart pounding.

She stepped towards it. There was a gate, a coin vendor. She blushed hot, her stomach doing cartwheels. Okay, she had to buy tokens before she could go in. With trembling hands, she pushed a bill into the vendor machine, collected the tokens it spit out, and slipped past the gate.

She found herself in an L shaped hall, rows of doors on either side, marked as vacant or occupied by green or red lights above them.

What do I do now? She asked herself. A door opened, a man stepped out, looking at her in vague surprise. Panicked and not wanting any interaction, she grabbed the first door with a red light and slipped inside.

Stacy found herself in a small room, just a bit larger than a phone booth. There was a place to sit down, a padded cushion on the seat. She sat and folded her purse over her knees.

Now what?

As her eyes adjusted to the dim light, she could see on the wall opposite her a flat screen TV.

There was a sound outside. Someone going into the next booth?

Stacy waited a couple of moments. From other booths, there were sounds of sex, electronically modulated sighs and moans. She knew that other people were watching porn in the booths. She wasn't innocent, she knew what a peep show was. She'd never seen the point of it. Porn was accessible enough online or through DVD's that you could enjoy it at home, so why go to a peep show? But she supposed that some people couldn't see it at home. Or maybe they just liked coming here.

She waited.

How long were the Manchester's going to be? What were they doing here? Shopping? Buying sex toys? Or lingerie? She hoped it wasn't lingerie, she could imagine Betty taking her time, trying things out, preening in the mirror. That wouldn't be quick. That would be excruciating.

She waited.

Motivated by boredom more than anything, she took out one of the tokens and put a coin in the slot. The flat screen flared to life, and suddenly, there was a tattooed woman with painfully artificial breasts, harshly sucking a heavy venous cock. It was beyond ugly. Quickly she flicked the channel selector: Two skanky women making out. Again: Another woman with a dildo. Again: Two men. She flicked through all the dozen channels, they were all completely appalling: ugly people having ugly sex, the images flat and creepy, all tattoos and pores and artificiality. Finally, she settled on a snowy pattern and left it there until the token expired.

No, she didn't see the appeal of this at all.

As her vision adjusted she noticed a darker spot on the wall in front of her, underneath the flat screen. There was another on the wall beside her. She explored it with her finger. A hole? Odd. She ran her fingertip around the bevelled edge, smooth to the touch. What was it? Had they had something installed there and took it out? She shrugged. Whatever. She squirmed in her seat, checked her phone. She'd been here only a couple of minutes.

So how long would they be? She decided she'd give them ten or fifteen minutes. Surely they couldn't be much longer than that.

Unless they were shopping for lingerie...

She mouthed a silent prayer, folded her arms and settled down to wait.

That's when she noticed the cock.

She should have jumped when she saw it, but she didn't. Rather, she was just mildly surprised. It was simply a pale erection, sticking out of the wall, near the hole she'd explored. Just there. Not doing anything. Just kind of ... there, erect, a set of testicles hanging down from its base. It seemed so ordinary, so neutral, that at first, she had no reaction at all. She just looked at it, with the feeling that it had been there all along, and somehow, she'd just failed to notice it.

Her first fleeting thought was that it wasn't real. That it was one of those realistic dildos with a suction cup base. Maybe someone had left it behind? Forgotten it attached to the wall? Or maybe all the booths had them.

She stared at it, the dim light giving its paleness a soft phosphorescent glow. It bobbed softly, like a bit of seaweed in an undersea current. There was something quite bizarre about a male member without the male attached. On its own, it was kind of intriguing.

Stacy reached out a hand to touch it, feeling warm skin, rigid flesh. It seemed to pulse. She flung her hand away, shocked. It lurched, bobbing suddenly as if called to life.

Glory hole! She thought. That's a glory hole. She wasn't a virgin, she'd heard of glory holes. She vaguely understood what they were and how they worked. She'd always assumed that they were a fixture of gay bathhouses and remote truck stops. Holes in plywood gouged out for nasty little interactions.

She felt momentarily stupid. Of course, it's a glory hole, that's a real cock, and there's a man on the other side of the booth sticking it through. Her heart was racing. What the fuck? She picked up her purse and stood up, impelled by the need to get the hell out of here.

And what? Walk out of the Peep shows straight into Barney and Betty? She could imagine Betty's eyes lasering into her, the glance at the red doorway to the peep shows, the knowing looks they would exchange. And gods, what if they asked about it - asked what she'd been doing in there? That would be awful. No matter what she said, there'd be judgement, god knows what they would think. She could imagine it.

Reluctantly, she sat down.

Beside her, the hard cock bobbed. She glanced at it. Even knowing what it was, it was still surreal and disembodied. There was a complete lack of threat.

She heard a mumble. It came again. From the other booth, from whoever was on the other side.

"What?" She whispered, ducking her head a little towards the gently bouncing erection.

"Suck it," the voice whispered back. The erection waggled. It was almost as if it was talking.

"No," she said instinctively.

"Suck it," the voice whispered.

"No," she said, scandalized, "I'm not putting that thing in my mouth!"

"Come on."

"No way!"

"Please," the voice was wheedling.

"Forget it!"

"Just suck it."

"Uh huh," she said firmly, "not touching it."

It was, she decided, the most surreal conversation she had ever had. Talking to a disembodied voice, while a pale erection floated and bobbed in front of her. She liked the erection more than the voice - it was just there, demanding nothing, seeking nothing, it reminded her of some deep sea creature, just hanging in the abyss, minding its own business.

"Come on," the voice said, "I need to get off. Suck it."

"No," she said firmly.

There was silence.

The voice no longer wheedled, begged, pleaded, demanded. It was just her and the pale erection.

She sort of liked looking at it. Normally, with sex, you never really got to simply look at a cock. It was always in motion, grinding against you, pushing in. Even when it was in your face, you were sucking it. It was never just there.

In the low light, it looked very pale, almost white. As her eyes adjusted, she could see the shape of veins, the lumpiness along the straight shaft. The foreskin that covered the head, giving the glans a sort of indistinct look, with just the prepuce peeking out. The balls hung underneath. She definitely liked it better than the wheedling demanding voice mumbling from the other side of the wall.

As cocks go, she thought, it looked all right. Good looking, for a cock. There was an odd thought. What were the standards for cocks, apart from size? Was there an aesthetic? Were there good looking cocks and ugly cocks? What were the standards? How was cock beauty determined?

He wasn't withdrawing. Whoever he was, he was determined.

"Come on," the voice said, after a few minutes of silence. The erection bobbed up and down to emphasize the point. "Don't be a bitch."

"No," she said, "And calling me a bitch isn't going to make me want to."

Pause.

"Sorry," the voice said.

It was such a strange conversation.

"Apology accepted," she replied.

The erection still wasn't going away.

"Can I ask a question?" the voice asked.

She thought about it, before finally deciding to allow it.

"Sure."

"If you don't want to play, why are you here?"

Stacy rolled her eyes. It had been a mistake to allow a question, any question.

"It's complicated."

"Complicated?"

She didn't respond.

The erection bobbed slowly, there was something hypnotic about it. It was like watching fish in a fish tank, it was almost relaxing.

Eventually, the voice came again.

"If you won't suck, how about you jerk it off."

For a second, it was like a foreign language. All the words were there, but it made no sense to her. She had to take a moment to parse it all out. Jerk it off? He meant masturbate it.

"Come on," the voice wheedled, "at least finish me."

Finish him? She hadn't even started. They weren't doing anything. But there it was, right in front of her. Just bobbing gently in the soft light, weirdly alluring, tempting, despite the annoyance of the voice.

She was kind of intrigued by the idea of touching it.

And maybe it would shut up the stupid voice.

"Well," she said, "I won't suck it..."

But she reached out and tentatively wrapped her hand around the shaft. There was a muffled moan of pleasure.

She curled her fingers around it experimentally, feeling it against her fingertips. It was hard, definitely hard, she could feel the rigidity. It was hotter than she thought it would be. She could feel a slight

pulse. It moved back and forth gently, and she let her hand move
with it.

She leaned closer until it was inches from her face. She loosed her
grip, moved her hand back and forth, up to the glans and then back.
It was very smooth, like velvet. She didn't remember cocks being this
smooth before. Did he use a moisturizer? She pulled the foreskin
back, watching the glans swell as it expanded. Opening her hand
further, she cradled the head in a loose cage of her fingers, pushing
the base of her palm till it slid against the bottom of the glans,
flattening a bead of precum and feeling its slickness drawn out.

He probably wouldn't last long, she thought, if her palm was
already painted with a slick slimy bead.

She stroked further back, enjoying the velvet smoothness of him,
the warmth of the erection. She let her fingernails curl down,
cupping his scrotum. Smooth, again like velvet. She could feel the
balls, round and pulpy in their firmness, inside the sack.

No hair. She'd never seen that before. The scrotum was absolutely
smooth.

"Lick my balls," the voice ordered.

She ignored it.

She explored the fascinating smoothness of him. No hair at all!
Balanced the testicles in her palm. Wait, further in, she felt a little
stubble. He shaved, that was it! He'd shaved down there. She'd heard
of women shaving of course. She trimmed herself. But a shaved male?
That was kind of cool.

She let her hand roll up back to the head, began to jerk him
slowly, skinning back the foreskin with each movement, gratified by
the way it swelled with each movement.

"Spit on it," the voice came. That boggled her. Spit on it? Was
that some fetish? Did he want to be degraded? Spit on his dick? But
the voice murmured again, and after a seconds incomprehension, she
realized that it was probably just to make it wet, lubrication.

She spit in her hand. And then a moment later, with a kind of
excited boldness, she spit right on the cock, watching her bubbly
saliva trickle down it. She grasped it and stroked firmly. There we go.

She was vaguely surprised to find she was sort of enjoying herself.
It was kind of naughty and transgressive. Sleazy. But there was no
feeling of risk, of threat, of things being out of control. It felt
harmless. She'd never played with a cock in this way before. Every
other time, there'd always been such an overwhelming sense of her
lovers, their bodies, their maleness and desires. Here, it was just her
and the erection. It was almost like petting a cat.

Her hand, her fingertips, were wet, but it was her own spit. Not
so bad. It overwhelmed the slimy slickness of the precum. She leaned
forward, her butt lifting up off the seat. Smiling privately, though no

one could see, she bent her head towards it so the glans was just inches from her lips. She pursed, sucked her cheeks in, and spat on it, feeling a weird kind of superiority. Maybe it was just lubrication for him, but she kind of got off on it. She enjoyed spitting on men's cocks. Who knew? That'll show it. She spat again.

With her other hand, she reached for the scrotum. She decided again she definitely liked shaved men. She pulled on his balls, tickled them with her fingernails. There was a slight pull and push, she could feel him shifting his weight, pressing his crotch further against the plywood. Go ahead and struggle she thought, I'm in charge.

Despite herself, she was smiling. Playing with the cock.... not his cock... he wasn't around, it was just 'the' cock, an indefinite article. It was just fun. Like it was a toy. She didn't feel aroused, not especially. She might be a little wet, she thought, but the sort of wet you might get from seeing a hot guy on the bus, just sort of a mild free floating thing. Basically, it was just fun, naughty transgressive fun.

She was very close to it, using both hands. When it seemed he might come, when she could tell from the soft moans and the urgent pushing from the wall, from its hardening, she would back off, her grip going loose, her motions slow. Then as it seemed to pass, her grip would tighten, her motions speeding until she could tell it was coming up to the edge again.

Abruptly, seized by a daring impulse, she took it in her mouth, pulling back the foreskin all the way, wrapping her lips tight against the glans, lapping the prepuce hard against her tongue, squeezing it a little with her jaws. It surged and swelled instantly, quickly she took her mouth off and then it was ejaculating, gobs of semen shooting with surprising velocity. Semen spattered across the floor, across her knee, her hand.

The erection withdrew. She was sorry to see it go. There was the rustle of pants on the other side. The sound of a door closing.

Typical male, she thought, comes and then goes. It was kind of funny. She checked her feelings - was she disappointed? Not really. It wasn't like they were dating, and frankly, she didn't know how she'd have felt about him sticking around. Best he left. There was something weirdly empty though, from his departure. But better that he left. What? They were going to have a conversation.

She felt good about it. Okay, it was sleazy and weird. But oddly, it didn't bother her at all. It was harmless, not scary, sort of fun. She wasn't going to talk about it, this wasn't the sort of thing you shared with your friends. But... she was glad she'd done it.

She began to root through her purse, looking for a tissue.

"That was hot," a voice said.

This time, she did jump. The voice had come from the other side of the booth, the opposite wall,, the one in front of her, under the screen. For a second, she felt a flush of adrenalin, a surge of nervousness and shame, as if she'd been caught.

"Oh," she said, not knowing what else to say, "Thanks."

Her knees, which had unconsciously parted in relaxation slammed tight together like a trap closing. She felt herself blushing hot. She was glad it wasn't visible in the low light. Someone had watched her. She felt vulnerable.

Did he want one too? Would there be another demand for a blow job. Because the spell was gone, whatever mood, whatever comfort zone, whatever sense of security had lulled her into playing with a stranger's erection, it had shattered when he spoke.

He would, she thought, have done better silently presenting his erection. She might or might not have played with it, but it would have been better.

"You were watching?" she asked, with something approaching panic. Holy shit, she thought. Being watched. She felt exposed. Vulnerable.

Whoever was on the other side must have read something in her voice.

"Just a bit," the voice said. "Not much. I'm sorry. Did it bother you? I apologize."

"No, no," she said with automatic politeness, "it's all right." But it wasn't. She could feel her body turned away slightly, defensively. The movement shifted the ejaculate on her knees.

"Really, I'm sorry. I didn't want to make you feel uncomfortable. You were just so amazing, you really handled that."

Was he making a pun?

"Thanks... I think," she said. It was weird receiving compliments in this situation. What's the etiquette for glory holes? She scrambled in her purse. She couldn't find any tissues.

"Do you have any Kleenex," she asked the voice.

"Sure."

There was the sense of movement, and then white tissues were floating in the dark hole opposite her. She grabbed them.

"Thanks."

Thank gods they were clean and soft. That would have been too disgusting if they'd been stiff or crusty. She dabbed at her knees, wiped her fingers and awkwardly dropped one on the floor to push it around with her heel. No way was she going to bend forward to wipe semen off the floor, not with a stranger watching her.

"You have some on your blouse," the voice said.

She blushed.

"Where?"

She found it and wiped.

"Thanks," she said.

She leaned back in her seat, staring at the black hole in the wall. She couldn't see a face, she couldn't see anything. Just blackness. She knew that there was a man on the other side, kneeling so he could look at her.

Yes, that was definitely creepy.

She thought about leaving. Wasn't sure. What if he left at the same time? Should she negotiate some kind of departure arrangement?

"Are you a tranny," the voice asked.

"What?"

"Tranny... Transvestite... Shemale..."

"Oh," she said. "No, I'm a woman."

"Cool."

Pause.

"Do you get a lot of transvestites here," she asked, to break the silence.

"Some."

Do you come around here a lot? She wanted to ask. That seemed so cliché, she didn't dare say it.

"If you're not a tranny, can I see your pussy?"

"What?" She asked incredulous.

The voice repeated the request.

"Absolutely not," she said, scandalized.

"Sorry," the voice said quickly.

There were a few heartbeats pause.

"I'm a real woman, but I'm not going to show you my pussy," she said. "That's right out. Not going to happen. Forget it."

Silence.

Nothing.

Had he gone away?

She hadn't heard him leave.

"Are you still there?" she asked finally.

"Yes."

"You are watching me."

"Does that bother you? I'm sorry."

"It's okay..." again with automatic politeness. She caught herself. "No. No, I don't know how I feel about it."

"Should I go away?"

A part of her wanted to say yes. That would bring an end to it. Close it down. Move on. She didn't.

"I don't know," she said, finally. She chewed her lip.

"Is that your thing?" she asked. "Do you like to watch?"

Did that sound harsh? Judgmental?

"Not really, I come here to get my cock sucked."

She nodded.

"I just heard you, and I decided to look."

"Okay."

"You're really beautiful," the voice said. "I mean, amazingly beautiful. At first I thought you were a tranny, but you looked a lot better."

"So you watched me."

"You were amazing. Sometimes you'd smile, it was just... beatific."

Odd word, at least for the context. The corners of her mouth quirked, and she found herself relaxing a little.

"Beatific, huh?"

"Yes."

"Thanks."

"Have you ever done this before?"

She laughed.

"What do you think?"

"I don't know. You were just amazing. Sexy and sweet. You were ... It was like you were a sculptor, with your hands, the way you touched and stroked And you seemed to be having fun, you were playful, smiling. There were moments, it looked like you were going to laugh. And then out put your mouth on it..."

"You saw a lot..."

"Sorry."

"It's okay," and she surprised herself with how sincerely she said it. She'd relaxed again, the surge adrenalin had passed. Even her knees, she noted, were no longer locked together.

"I've never done this before, you know," she told the voice. But he wouldn't know. "I mean, I'm not a virgin. I've played with them in bed. But I've never been in a place like this."

"You have amazing hand technique."

She laughed a little.

"I don't know. I've never done that, like that before, that ... hand technique... It just seemed, I dunno."

"You've never been at a peep show."

"No."

"No glory hole?"

"Never."

The next question, took her by surprise.

"How do you feel?"

She smiled, it flickered away, returned as a half-smile. She looked up at the top of the booth. Slid forward an inch on her seat. Crossed her legs, then uncrossed.

"I don't know," she said. She was glad, on some level, that he'd asked though. "Not bad, I guess. It wasn't anything I was expecting. It was just a ... A moment, I suppose. It was interesting."

She shrugged.

"You came here to get your cock sucked. You haven't asked me for a blow job."

"Would you?"

"No way."

"Hand job?"

"Nope."

"Okay."

His acceptance reassured her. She liked that he wanted. But she also liked that he would accept a 'no' without being a bitch about it.. The other voice had been annoying, demanding, like a spoiled child. But this one was respectful, they were having a real conversation. Impulsively, she wished she'd jerked this one off instead. She decided that, whoever he was, she liked him.

"Do you get blown a lot here?" She asked, genuinely curious. When would she ever get the chance to ask questions like this?

"Not always."

"Not always?" she asked. "So sometimes?"

"Not every time, it's hit or miss."

"I see," she replied. "And when it happens.... its men?"

"Often," the voice replied. "Sometimes trannies.... Sometimes a woman."

She was intrigued by the admission of bisexuality. But there were so many questions.

"Women come here?"

"Not often."

She nodded to that.

"Do you..."

"No."

"So you just receive them? Not give them."

"I guess."

"And if not, you watch?"

"I don't really watch most of the time, this was pretty unique." The voice paused. "I don't usually have conversations through a glory hole either."

She nodded.

Silence.

On impulse, she undid a button on her blouse.

"Still watching?" She asked.

"Yes."

"Then watch this," she said. She slowly unbuttoned her blouse, very conscious of being watched, very conscious of putting on a show. She opened the blouse with sensuous movements, her legs parting almost without her awareness. She leaned back against the wall, cupped her bra in her hands, her fingers stiff and straight and then curling to the swell of her breast.

She stared at the dark circle, knowing that someone was staring back. Was he holding his breath? Eyes wide as saucers.

She smiled.

One hand crept down, to the clasp of her bra, thumb and forefinger released it. She felt the loosening, and took a deep breath allowing the bra to part, exposing bare skin, bare cleavage. She heard his intake of breath and it pleased her immensely.

She slowly pulled her cups away.

"Wow!"

"See," she said, "I'm a real woman."

"You're gorgeous," the voice whispered hoarsely.

"You're hard," she guessed, by the sound of his voice.

"Yes."

I could tell him, she thought, I could tell him to stand up and put his cock through the hole. He would do it. He would do whatever I tell him. There was a smug feeling to that. Power. Satisfaction. Sexiness. She felt sexy, she had never felt so sexy.

She straightened up and arched her back to show off her breasts, cupped them for him. She shifted her shoulders slightly, to the left, then the right, showing off. She bent forward, letting him appreciate the sway.

"Your nipples are hard," the voice said.

"Yes," she said, she couldn't keep the smile away, that quiet sexy smile. She couldn't keep the smile out of her voice. She reached up, pinching them.

Where are you going with this? Some part of her asked herself. There was a small physical shrug as she caressed her breasts. I don't know, she answered. Why does it have to go anywhere? Why do I have to second guess everything? Why not just let it go... Wherever.

"Can I suck them?" The voice asked. Her smile froze.

"No," she said, "I won't let you in."

No, definitely not.

Whatever vibe she was on, whatever mood of sexiness and wantonness, it was entirely dependent on the privacy of this booth. On him being a voice, not even a face. On her being safe behind the door. When he had a face, when he was in, the spell would break, it wouldn't be safe, it wouldn't be sexy. It would just be sleazy.

So no.

"No, I didn't mean that," the voice said. "Just put your nipple to the glory hole, so I could kiss it..."

"Oh..." she said. That was different. Still... It was a little scary. But a little exciting. Her better instinct was not to do it. The thought of a complete stranger's mouth on her nipple, wet and sucking... It was weird, equal parts creepy and sexy.

No, best not to.

Perversions and Infidelities / Page 77

"No teeth okay," she said.

"No teeth."

"And no grabbing."

"Right."

"I don't even know... I mean... maybe no sucking, just kiss, okay... and if I pull away or say stop..."

"Yes... Absolutely."

She stared at the hole, leaning forward, rubbing her thumbs against her nipples. She bit her lip.

I should not do this.

"All right," she said.

She was going to do it.

Heart pounding, she stood, took the step over and knelt in front of the glory hole. With two hands framing it, she lifted her left breast. Her heart's pounding redoubled, her mouth was dry, stomach had the hint of butterflies. She knew if she was not on her knees, if she had been standing, they would have been trembling.

She pressed her breast against the glory hole, feeling the beveled edge all around.

She waited.

The first sensation was soft fingertips, probing, pressing, stroking lightly, the touches gentle and feathery as a butterfly's wing. Then just a light sensation against her nipple. A kiss. Another. Tiny wet lashes, the tip of his tongue, circling her the aureole, and all the time, the light finger touches stroking, teasing, probing. Her nipple hardened. Lips closed around the nub, sucking lightly.

"You are good," she whispered, surprised.

And he was. He was very good. Very very good. She felt the light scraping of teeth, but didn't mind, it made her arch her back slightly. Fingertips, and lips, and teeth and tongue, this endless sweet circle of sucking and suckling, kissing and stroking and teasing and never quite biting. She'd never felt anything like it before, had never had her nipple, her breast stroked and worshipped like this before.

Stacy found that she was aroused. Not the fun, naughty thrill of doing the hand job, not the wanton showiness when she'd exposed herself. She was wet, and she could feel herself wet, feel her clit throbbing and sensitive.

She adjusted her position slightly, spreading her knees apart. The mouth and fingers on the other side hesitated.

"It's all right," she reassured it. The mouth, the lips, the fingers, those wonderful sensations returned.

Very carefully, she pulled her skirt up, slipped a hand between her legs. It was very sneaky. She didn't want to let him, however he was, that mouth on the other side so splendidly playing with her breast, know that she was touching herself, how aroused she was.

Stacy knelt there stroking her pussy and just feeling the unspeakable delight of having her breast played with so exquisitely. At times she murmured to encourage, asked a little harder, a little softer, more tongue. He must have heard her because on the other side, he did what she asked, guided by her words, her responses.

Eventually, she shifted position, pulling her breast away, offering the other breast to wonderful worship. While she did this, she pulled her panties aside, to touch herself more intimately.

After a while, she pulled away completely, panting lightly.

"That was amazing," she whispered. "That was just amazing. That was unbelievable...."

In the darkness on the other side, she could just make out the shape of a face, shadowed features.

She leaned forward, pursing her lips. The face moved. She closed her eyes, letting the glory hole rim rest against her brow and chin. She felt lips brush hers, pushed out to the feathery contact, there was a light kiss, lips touching, opening, tentative touch of tongue.

Then it was over.

"Wow," she said. "Have you done this before?"

"No," the voice said, "never kissed through a glory hole, or sucked nipples this way."

"Virgin, uh?" She teased.

"I want to do more..."

She felt fingertips brushing her cheek and pulled away.

"I want you..." she stopped to appraise her thoughts. "I want you to feel something."

Stacy stood up and hiked her skirt to her waist. She pressed her body flat against the wall, trying to position herself in front of the glory hole, parting her legs.

"I want you to feel me."

Fingertips against her panties, lightly exploring. The feeling almost made her swoon.

"Do you feel me," she whispered. "See, I'm not a tranny. That's a real woman."

His words whatever they were, were muffled. But it didn't matter. She felt his fingers. He could feel her lips, her clit through her panties, could feel how wet her panties were. She loved the feeling of it, those fingers sliding up and down, making a furrow in her panties. She was almost breathless.

The fingers pulled at her panties, loosening them, sliding up against her bared labia. She hadn't intended that, hadn't intended to allow that. But she didn't pull away, she savoured the feeling instead. If anything she got even wetter. She tried to grind against the fingers. She moaned softly. When they pressed between her lips, she spread her legs a little wider to let them enter.

It was delirious, and she let it go on and on, riding on his fingertips.

Finally, she stepped back. The fingers slipping from her. She looked down in time to see a bodiless hand disappearing back into the hole.

"I want to fuck you." The voice was strangled.

"What?"

"Turn around and put your butt against the glory hole, bend forward, and then I'll put my cock…"

The thought of it was a heady rush, her stomach went butterflies with both need and nervousness. She shook her head.

"No." She whispered. "No. But…."

She paused.

"Put your cock through, I want to suck it. For real."

Stacy did. She wanted to suck it, she felt this wild mixture of affection and arousal, of adventure and sensuality. Her nipples still tingled and she was dripping. Fucking was just a step, a small step too far. But she wanted to suck this stranger's cock, to make him feel ecstatic pleasure. She wanted him in her mouth, to feel him, to swallow him, she wanted him to come and come hard and fill her mouth.

She slid to her knees and his erection was there. Different from the other one, this one curving upwards slightly, circumcised, with an elegantly shaped helmet head. She reached for his balls, feeling short hair. She licked them, and found herself wishing they were shaved, but buried the thought in the desire to give him pleasure. She took his head into her mouth and then let her lips slide along his shaft.

He came quickly, in bare minutes. His orgasm was explosive in her mouth, she could feel the intensity, the trembling that seized him, and it gratified her. He kept him in her mouth, until he slipped wetly out.

"Thanks," the voice was hoarse. Gasping.

She got off her knees, retreated to her seat. Wantonly, she let her legs spread, her skirt pulled up. One hand reached down and pulled the panties aside, exposing her pussy. Her breasts were still hanging out of her undone blouse and unfastened bra.

"My pleasure," she purred, stroking herself. Could she come? Would she come just playing with herself and being watched? She felt like she was glowing.

There was an erection poking through the other hole. Had someone been watching? She didn't mind. Nothing could cut through the glow. She reached for it, curled her fingers around it. It was larger, spongier rather than rigid, with the head a small cap in its girth.

The voice said something. Something about the usual time that he came. Wanting to see her again. She nodded.

Silence. Was he still there? Was he watching?

"Watch this," she said, and took the other cock in her mouth.

She sucked it wantonly, reaching down to touch herself, to play with her breasts, to spread her lips wide and roll a finger around her clitoris. Sometimes she'd lift her head, still grasping it firmly, stroking the strange erection as she stared boldly at the other hole. Was he there? She wanted him there. She wanted to be watched. Especially, she wanted him, whoever he was, to watch her.

Stacy bobbed her head around the strange cock, as much into performing for her watcher, as for the recipient's pleasure. 'Her watcher' she felt oddly possessive. She wallowed as much of the length as she could. She pulled her head off, spit on it several times. She squeezed it and pumped it with her fist, glancing again at the other hole. Yes, she was being watched, she was sure he was there. She clutched her breast, spread her legs wider, and dived on taking it in her mouth, almost seizing the head in her teeth. The owner moaned loudly.

His ejaculation too was fast, although not thick. A simple swallow and it was done. She leaned back in her seat, legs splayed. Released the now softening cock.

An erection pushed through from the other glory hole.

Was this him? She wasn't sure. Was he hard again?

"Did you like that?" She asked.

But she wasn't sure if the muffled voice was the voice she had gotten to know. It didn't sound like him, but she couldn't be sure.

She stood, pressed herself against the wall, took the cock in her hand. It felt... different? Larger? The curve more pronounced? Not the same person? Had she performed wantonly for a stranger?

She found she didn't care. She was dripping wet, in a state of complete wanton sensuality. Stacy felt buoyant, weightless, breathless, full of possibilities and urges.

Abruptly, she pushed the cock gently back through the hole. She lifted her skirt up to her hips, pulled her panties down and stepped out of them, and then backed herself to the wall, feeling the shape the glory hole against her cheeks. She bent forward and waited.

In the next instant, she gasped as she felt the hard length surge up inside her. Some part of her thought 'condom?' but she didn't really care. Some part of her felt a little bad that she was giving herself to a complete stranger, when she had just denied it to the previous inhabitant she had made a genuine connection with. But mostly, she didn't care. She wanted a cock in her, she wanted to be fucked, to know that she was being fucked. She wanted an anonymous cock. She wanted it hard and full up inside her.

Perversions and Infidelities / Page 81

The cock pounded her. She could feel the wall bending as whoever was on the other side slammed his body against it again and again, as his cock leapt up inside her, up the length of her. She cried out, bending forward, rubbing her clit, pushing back against the wall.

When the cock came, she felt it. She could feel the surge of ejaculation, the warm flood of semen. Stacy was panting hoarsely. She squeezed with her pussy, refusing to move. She was close, she was so close. A light sweat covered her body. She felt weak and powerful at the same time, depraved and wanton and full of need.

When it pulled out, she almost whimpered with loss.

But she didn't pull away. She remained in position, bent over, ass pressed against the glory hole. She wasn't thinking, she was just existing, just swimming in the moment of arousal and sex and heat, refusing to let it go. She wanted him, whoever he was, to keep on fucking her, she wasn't finished. She wanted him to enter her again. She wanted to be fingered, licked, however, he got her off. As long as he got her off.

There were vague noises of shuffling, words.

Then, yes, oh yes, pressure against her pussy again. Stacy bent forward a little more, pushed her butt harder against the wall.

And was entered. A cock, hot and hard and urgent. Thick. She could feel the thickness, it made her cry out a little. Not so deep.

Stacy knew that this was someone else, that she was being fucked by another complete stranger. By a stranger that knew her only as a wet cunt pressed against a glory hole - no face, no breasts, no legs, her entire existence, her entire dimension to him was simply a cunt freshly fucked, dripping wet, oozing semen.

"Cunt," she said out loud, the primal baseness of the word surging through her, "fuck that cunt. Fuck it hard."

She revelled in it. This was sex, this was the ultimate reduction of sex, pure sex, distilled sex, sex as a cunt and a cock and naked purified lust, fucking squared, fucking cubed, fucking infinity, with the messy human dimension of ambiguity and nuance, choice and anticipation vanished. Cunt. Cock. Fuck. The universe reduced to primal flesh.

It fucked her hard, pulling out all the way and then ramming in, each time making her squeal with its thickness, stretching her. It didn't reach up inside as far, not to the good spots. But its thickness was a pleasure all its own.

It had more control, sometimes halting, making her fuck herself onto it, a further wantonness that she revelled in. Sometimes there was a mutual rhythm, pounding onto each other. Sometimes it teased her, pulling back, until only by pushing hard up against the wall, squirming her ass back and forth, she could just feel the head of it. But then it would slam in. making her gasp loudly.

The orgasm came finally, breathlessly, as her fingers pushed hard on her clit, the cock pushed spreading her cunt open inside her. She came, panting and gasping. A moment or two later, whoever he was, came. She didn't feel an ejaculation inside her, just knew it from the way he pumped, the sound he made.

Had he been wearing a condom? She had no idea. She knew she would care, that at some point further down, she would care an awful lot. But right now, right at the moment, if she had an opinion, she would not have wanted a condom. She would have wanted him coming inside her, wanted to know that two strangers had come in her, to have the semen of two complete strangers dripping from her.

The cock withdrew. She turned, flopped back on her seat, her legs akimbo, her pussy exposed. Wantonly, she reached down, opened her labia. She dipped a finger into the wetness, and smiled at the hole.

A cock appeared beside her. She took it in her mouth, because she wanted to, because she didn't care. She was sated, she'd finally come and it was sooo good.

But she wanted, she still wanted. This one was skinny, with a mushroom head, the balls were so hairy as to be black and she practically yanked on them. She nibbled with her teeth, took advantage of it size to push her face all the way down until she almost gagged. It ejaculated, the semen was thick and sour, she swallowed as quickly as she could, but could still smell it on her breath, almost feel its tingly pungency.

That was it, she found that she had reached some threshold of satisfaction. The cock vanished. Was someone watching her through the other hole? She stared with a kind of satisfied indifference.

After five minutes, she fastened her bra and then did her blouse up.

She bent forward to pick up her panties off the floor. She thought about putting them on, but changed her mind and stuck them in her purse.

A cock slid through the glory hole in front of her. She stared at it for a second, reached up and stroked it, feeling the skin, the shape of the head, the thickness of it. It was dusky, not pale. Was this a black man? An Arab? Some olive Mediterranean complexion? That might have intrigued her. Then she let it go.

"NO," she said flatly. "I'm finished."

It withdrew. That pleased her.

Stacy spent another couple of minutes tidying herself up and then stepped out of the booth.

It would have been nice if it had been an empty hall. But there were a couple of men standing down the hall. Waiting for her. She looked at them, and then looked away. Thankfully, none of them tried to speak to her. She would have been mortified.

Stacy left the peep show gallery, blinking slightly in the brighter lights of the open store. The whole experience seemed unreal, as if being inside the booth had been another world, as if she'd been a different person. As she stepped back into the real world, she found herself almost shocked by her actions. Had that really been her? Had she done all those things? It seemed almost unreal, the surreal conversations, the escalating boldness. There had been a feeling of complete safety, of anonymity, and it had... what? Simply freed her to do anything, to follow any impulse, to experiment and just act. Every step she'd taken in there had led her willingly to the next step.

Stacy felt that perhaps she should feel guilty or ashamed. But again, it was like the booth had been another world, a place of perfect safety, and no rules. There was no guilt, no shame, the worst she could muster was astonishment.

She would never ever do it again though.

Unless she wanted to.

But definitely not.

Never.

Next time?

She checked her phone. She'd been in there an hour and a half. Had it been so long? Her 'Flex-Mate' wasn't where she left it, someone had probably picked it up and put it back. She grabbed another one from the display shelf.

No sign of Barney and Betty. Good. She paid for the Flex-Mate at the front desk.

The clerk was a punk girl, piercings through her nose and lip, tattoo on her forearm, a short buzz haircut. Stacy wondered if she sucked cocks too? Or if she preferred women? She was still buzzing with sexual curiosity and excitement.

And that was it. Onto the street, on her way home. Even as she walked, the experience bubbled up through her. No regrets, no recriminations. She was already getting wet. She knew that she would relive the experience tonight through her Flex-Mate.

* * *

Barney and Betty watched the video clips on Betty's phone. The clips were in low light format, the images gray and slightly fuzzy.

But Stacy's features were clearly visible, the way she wantonly spread her legs, a momentary sheen from her wetness. Then more clips from another angle, Stacy bent over, grunting and shaking as she was rammed again and again from behind, pushing her ass hard against the wall desperate to get as much cock into her as she could manage.

"I had no idea she was such a slut," Barney said, "she always seemed so straitlaced."

Perversions and Infidelities / Page 84

Betty's hand was on his erection, teasing it with manicured fingernails.

He was hard again, watching the phone, remembering the feel of Stacy around it.

"I guess," Betty said, "everyone's full of surprises."

The End

CATFISH

"You're married?"

I looked down at the man I straddled. My heart was dropping through my stomach. This awful, horrible sinking feeling. I felt adrift, unmoored, like I'd been sitting on top of a house of cards tumbling down.

I climbed off him, standing, wobbling on black thigh high fetish boots that I'd bought specially for our rendezvous. I pushed my spandex miniskirt back down my hips as low as it would go, which wasn't much. I was regretting not wearing panties.

"Come on Kate," Jay protested. His face was smeared with my glossy red lipstick. "No! I'm not married."

"Bullshit!" I snapped. I was angry, this beautiful sexy fantasy, had gone to shit, and now I was stuffing my breasts back into a tiny bustier, while his exposed cock wilted.

My face burned, I felt so stupid. Weeks of texting back and forth, the phone calls, the endless flirting, the dirty talk, the excitement I'd felt every time I saw his name on my screen, all of it turned out to be a stupid joke. I was humiliated.

"How did you know?" he asked, his face a mask of panic, as he was pulling up his trousers.

And just like that, it got worse.

I could have been wrong, I wanted to be wrong. I wanted him to deny and explain and we could get back on track. I'd apologize for my psychotic episode, and then we'd carry on.

"Jesus Christ!" I swore. "You're such an asshole."

"I don't... it's not a big deal. Look, it's complicated."

I wasn't buying it. Mainly, I was kicking myself. Months of flirting and sexting, long phone calls, heartfelt conversations, phone sex, opening up to each other. We had shared fantasies. I had exposed myself, sending naughty pictures, telling him things I'd never shared with anyone. I felt so betrayed.

"Not a big deal?" I snapped. I had dressed up for him! I'd bought lingerie, and hooker fetish boots. We'd planned this... this adventure. The fucker! "Not a big deal, but somehow you never mentioned it? You wear a fucking wedding ring!"

Unconsciously he moved his hand to cover it, feeling its absence.

"Tan line, Jay!" I snapped.

It had been perfect. I'd been straddling him, his pulling his hands onto me. I'd looked down, and noticed something odd, and then it all snapped into place.

"I can see the tan line. If you've got a tan line for your wedding ring that tells me you're pretty committed."

"All right," he admitted. "But it's complicated. It has nothing to do with this..."

"Sure, it's always complicated," I snarled. "That's why you lied."

I felt stupid, which was what made me angry. If I'd have known, maybe it would have been different. I'm not a slut or anything. But people's lives are complicated, and maybe it would have been all right, maybe it would have been normal, or acceptable. Maybe the marriage was dead and I wouldn't have been treading on the wrong side. Or maybe I'd be up for a little discrete fling with a married man that harmed no one.

But he hadn't told me.

He hadn't been honest.

I'd been looking forward to him coming to town for weeks, we'd been talking about it, planning it. I'd shopped carefully, building my outfit, building towards this night. The thigh high fetish boots, all shiny and black had been the final touch. I'd showed up at his hotel door, looking like sex incarnate. When he opened it, when we finally met in person, I could see the wonderful astonishment on his face, the way his heart skipped a beat, his jaw dropped.

We'd made it to the couch, kissing passionately. I'd straddled him, miniskirt up around my hips, exposing my lack of panties. His cock pulled out of his pants hard and hot in my hands, our bare genitals lightly brushing each other, his hands on my boobs...and I'd noticed the tan line.

I wouldn't have even noticed, but I'd read about it the day before at the hair stylist, "Tips on spotting a married player."

And the bottom dropped out of my world.

Played for a fool.

That's what hurts.

You think you've got something, something real, a connection. Then you realize, you were just stupid. He played you because you were stupid. He played you because he thought you were stupid. And you fell for it.

How do you trust someone after that?

"Look," he said desperately, "it's not a big deal. We're not really together. And it's far away. Come on, we've had all this... we have a connection. Real chemistry."

How do you fuck someone who thinks you're stupid?

"Jay," I said, "if that's your name -"

"It is!"

"You catfished me. I'm sorry, we're done."

I was trembling, shaking with humiliation and embarrassment. I could still feel wetness between my legs, the sense of lightness and excitement I'd had riding the elevator, walking down the hall. But now it had turned wrong, and I had this weight in my stomach. Shame. I was blushing, my face was hot.

With as much dignity as I could muster, I turned around, grabbed my purse and walked out the door.

"Goodbye Jay," I said frostily, with as much dignity as I could muster, "it wasn't fun."

The door closed, I was in the hallway.

It was over.

I sighed. I still felt stupid and angry. I pulled my smartphone out of my purse and I deleted his contact. Another tap on the screen, months of increasingly hot text messages vanished out of the world. Fuck him.

I felt a little better. I stalked down the hotel hallway, the high heels of the fetish boots giving my stride a slightly martial quality, like I was marching instead of walking. Stomping. How do hookers walk sexy in these things? Whatever. Fuck Jay.

He didn't even have the decency to come after me. The phone didn't ring, no texts appeared, he didn't follow me out into the hallway, didn't try to explain or beg or apologize.

He could have done all those things, if he gave a shit. He could have tried to win me back. And maybe I'd have considered it. But he didn't even bother.

Fuck him.

At the Elevator, I turned around and marched back angrily. Suddenly, I was standing in front of his hotel door again. Was he watching me through the peephole? Should I knock? I didn't want to see him, but I sort of wanted to see him. It didn't feel right like this, there should be something more. But here I was dressed like a hooker, standing in front of the door of a man who had played me, angry and horny and without any idea of what to do.

"You're an asshole!" I shouted at the door.

No response. I kicked it a couple of times.

"Fuck you," I shouted. "Just fuck you, okay."

Then I marched off.

Did I feel any better?

Maybe.

Sort of.

No one was in the hallway, or the elevator. I punched parkade level. Hopefully no one would get on and I'd avoid further humiliation. I fished my compact from my purse, to check my make-up, and used a wet wipe to clean up a lipstick smear.

Go home, throw all this hooker-looking crap into the rubbish.

No, burn it!

How?

I'd figure that out. Get a box of wine, drink the whole thing and just blot this stupid night out.

The doors opened onto the parkade. And a cold breeze swept around me, up under my skirt, across bare midriff and shoulders, hardening my nipples and tickling between my thighs, and I realized, I'd been wearing my good trench coat.

After all this bullshit, I absolutely refused to drive through the city looking like a hooker.

No way.

I'd forgotten it up there.

I'd have to go back and get it.

Well, there goes my big dramatic righteous angry moment.

My face reddened and went hot.

Fuck!

Back into the elevator, back to the floor, march down the hallway. Should I knock? Fuck that. There was no way out of this without looking stupid. I didn't want to look like I'd come crawling back.

I kicked at the door. No response. I kicked harder.

"Hey asshole," I yelled at the door. "I want my coat back."

Nothing. I waited, counting off fifteen seconds.

"Hey!" I kicked the door again.

He was ignoring me. The fucking coward! God, I was so stupid, I should have known he was a cowardly passive-aggressive weasel from the start. I should have known.

I kicked it hard, leaving scuff marks.

"Hey," I yelled loudly. "Stop being a dick. I want my coat. Just give it to me, so I can fuck off out of here."

No response.

"You coward! You passive aggressive dick! Give me back my fucking coat."

The door swung open.

A complete stranger looked out at me. Some fat middle aged guy with a comb-over and an undershirt loosely tucked in his pants, bare feet.

For a moment, we stared at each other with mute incomprehension.

This wasn't Jay. Had Jay invited him over after I left? Were they together? Where was Jay? Was this a gay thing?

Then it hit me.

"Oh," I said weakly. "Wrong room."

"Right," said the man, his voice flat.

He looked tired and annoyed..

"Yeah," I said, I could feel myself shrinking by the moment, folding in on myself, a bigger and bigger idiot. "Yeah. My ... uh... my boyfriend, he left. I left I mean. I left my coat in his room... just now, not like yesterday, but you know, just a moment ago and I wanted to get it..."

He was staring, but not in a good way.

"We kind of had an argument. So I forgot."

"It's not here."

"I can see that. Sorry... did I wake you?"

The door slammed shut. The number was right. The floor was wrong. What floor was Jay on? I couldn't remember.

I pulled my phone out to check the text message with his room number.

Deleted.

Of course.

This night just kept getting better and better.

That was an expensive coat. I'd paid top dollar for it, and it was practically new.

Fuck me.

Time to quit while I was ahead. Go home. Maybe Jay would text me and we'd make arrangements to have it returned. Or maybe he'd leave it behind, and I could get it from the hotel. But mainly, go home, forget this whole Catfish episode ever happened.

As I approached the elevator again, the door opened. A heavy-set, dark haired young man stepped out. He flashed a badge.

"Hotel Detective," he said. "Ma'am I'd like you to come with me."

Fuck me.

* * *

This was my first visit to the security office. I wasn't thrilled. I kept tugging at my spandex miniskirt and wishing I'd worn panties, even a thong. We were on the third floor, which seemed to be the service floor. It had that unfinished utilitarian look, laundry carts

Perversions and Infidelities / Page 92

along the sides of the hallways waiting to go into action, light
fixtures without their plastic sheaths.

Security was a windowless room. On one wall a bank of monitors
showed shifting displays of the lobby, of hallways with people waking
down them, of the parkade. Not a lot of empty hallways.

"Not a lot of empty hallways," I said conversationally.

He looked up from a form he was filling out beside me, I noticed
he let his eyes travel across my body like I was oiled head to toe,
before he looked me in the face.

Well, why not? I sighed mentally, I was dressed the part.

"Motion sensors," he said. "The security cameras cycle through
on a random program, but if there's motion, that activates them.
Mostly it's just people going to and from their rooms."

Oh right.

Or demented hookers going from floor to floor, kicking doors
and screaming at guests. I was grateful he left that part out.

So there was a video record of my humiliation.

This just got better and better.

"I'm not a hooker," I said.

He gave me another sliding look, starting at kinky fetish heels, to
latex thigh high boots, all the way up again.

"I know what it looks like. But I'm not a hooker. Really."

"Okay," he said. I could tell he didn't believe me. "Ma'am, I don't
really care. I'm just doing my job."

"No really. I was seeing this guy."

"Uh huh."

"And we were having this thing, this really intense thing. So I
dressed up. But then I found out he catfished me and I got mad..."

"Catfished?" Careful, neutral, indifferent.

I sighed. This was pointless.

"Never mind."

I could see it now. Crazed hooker harasses guests. The police
would haul me away. I'd be stuck in jail overnight with real hookers.
Then I'd be in front of some Judge who wouldn't believe me. Jay
would be back wherever he'd come from, I couldn't even contact him
to get him to explain. And he probably wouldn't even admit
anything even if I could contact him, because that would screw up
his marriage. My picture would be in the papers, probably with video
stills of me kicking down a door. The hotel would sue me. I'd lose
my job.

Fuck me.

How do real hookers get out of these things? Promise of sex? I
eyed the Hotel Detective speculatively. His name tag read 'Mike."
Would that work? Maybe I should? He'd probably say no.

What a life.

Fuck me.

"So when do the police come?"

"Police?" he looked up more quickly this time.

Sure, I thought. Police.

"To take me to the station, and process my charge."

"You're not under arrest."

"I'm not?"

"No," he said, "I just fill out a trespass notice barring you from the premises, take your picture for future reference, and escort you from the building. That's all. Then I go to the rooms you harassed, and fill out incident reports."

"Oh!"

Suddenly, this sense of relief flushed through me. I could literally feel tension washing out of me. I felt lighter, suddenly happier. I looked at Mike with a warmer light.

"If you try to return, we'll call the police then," he assured me.

"I don't plan on coming back here for the rest of my life," I said sincerely.

"No problem then."

"I'm parked here."

"I just escort you from the building, if your car is in the parkade, you'll have to get someone to come get it for you. Or it will be towed."

"Oh," that wasn't so great. But still, a lot better off. But then again, I was going to have my picture taken, and I'd be in their files as crazy hooker girl, and they'd probably keep the footage of me kicking doors. So that kind of sucked.

Then an idea crept back in my mind, one that had emerged in fear and futility when I'd been scared and thought I was going to jail. It had felt stupid and desperate. But now that the stakes were lower... it almost seemed plausible.

I looked him over. Not bad looking, not great. Ordinary, attentive. One of these regular, unexceptional men, but not bad. Maybe I could flirt my way out. I smiled at him, not huge, that would be fake. But just a little smile. Parted my knees an inch or two. Leaned forward a little closer to him.

"Mike," I said. "Do we have to do all this? I've had a really shitty night, my boyfriend turned out to be married. I promise you, I never want to come here again. Let's just let me get my car and go home."

"I'd like to do that," he said. "But I have to follow policy."

He wouldn't look at me.

"Really? I just want to go home and forget this all ever happened."

"We'll wrap up the paperwork and have you on your way."

I leaned in a little further, just emphasizing my cleavage. Okay, maybe flirting wasn't enough. How much further? A blow job? Blow jobs were almost casual, I'd done them in high school and university, I'd done them just to get out of boring dates, or on drunken impulse. Quick, simple, done. Nothing really, for all that men were so wild about them. Barely more than a handshake to a stranger.

And with embarrassment, I remembered how I'd been willing, even wildly eager to do so much more to a different stranger who had turned out to be a total asshole.

The more I thought about it, it just seemed that this was the quickest way out.

Why not?

I leaned a little further. Scooted my chair closer to his, moving to the edge of my seat. Our knees touched.

"We don't really need paperwork, do we?" I husked.

He colored slightly, not quite willing to look at me.

"It's the job."

"Really?" I whispered. "Can't we just work it out?"

I put two fingertips on his knee, moving forward a bit, the sides of our knees brushing against each other. He stopped writing, frozen.

Carefully, watching him, I walked my two fingers up his thigh, smiling gently at him, marching them slowly towards his crotch. Unsteadily, he reached down to stop me, but he didn't pull away. Instead, he let me catch his hand and guide it between to the inside of my thigh, where I laid it against the vinyl of my fetish boot. I allowed my legs to part slowly, opening.

It was as if he was hypnotized, unable to move, letting me take command. I liked the feeling, it was empowering. I let my fingers walk step by step across his upper thigh, down towards his crotch pressing at the folds of fabric, where I could feel his cock swelling rapidly.

I felt his hand moving along the inside of the boot, the pressure on my clad thigh giving way to the touch of skin on skin. I felt a tingle of excitement, and eased my ass forward just a little more on the chair, opening as it did.

My hand cupped his crotch, I could feel his cock, like a live thing, swelling and stiffening as it fought against his underwear, to rise up. I helped guide it to its new position. It felt thick. I could feel it hardening more and more with each passing moment as I squeezed it gently.

His fingers touched my labia, bringing a little gasp from me. His eyes widened a little at the touch, the unexpected softness of my folds. My secret was out, no panties, I was completely accessible to him. I could feel him tremble with excitement, feel his blush, his sensual arousal and it excited me too. I could feel my lips part, the wetness coming back, as he probed gently, as his fingertips fluttered between my legs.

With my free hand, I pulled at my bustier, exposing my nipples. He was utterly fascinated, enraptured. I had completely captured him. There was a sensation of elation, of arousal.

"Let's just forget the paperwork," I whispered, squeezing his cock. "The picture, the notice, all of it. I promise I won't come back, ever. Just let it go... and I'll make it worth it. Deal?"

"Deal," his voice husked, as his fingertips stroked my clit, slid down between but not quite inside my lips. His hand was shaking.

"Okay,"

Victory. A weird little victory, but yes, there was this tiny feeling of triumph, of validation, of being in some weird way, in control.

"I have to lock the door," he rasped.

"Okay."

He stood up rapidly, too rapidly, slightly awkward, as his erection tented his trousers. I moved back in my chair to let him past, feeling him brush against my knees. He locked the door with clumsy, frantic motions, and then came back with that weird 'trying to be casual but also too hasty' way that men have when they're super-horny and almost falling over themselves.

"Let's do a blow job, okay?" I offered. I didn't especially want him in me after all. I hoped he didn't want more. But I wanted to get it out there, set the terms of engagement. "You'll love it."

"All right."

Good, acceptance.

Blow jobs were nothing. You don't even remember them.

He leaned back against his desk. I reached out, to undo his belt. Men's belts are tricky, they're always so tightly cinched and folded into loops. As I worked it, he reached down and finished undoing it with trembling hands for me. I unzipped him, and a second later, he was pushing his pants and boxers down his thighs. I barely had a sense of pinstriped boxers and pink cock peeking out, before it was down, and then his full erection was springing out, and hot and throbbing in my hand.

I leaned forward in the chair, but my fetish heels made the position awkward, so I slid forward, down to one knee in front of him, looking for a comfortable posture. I steadied myself, one hand against his thigh, the other wrapped around his cock, and hoped he wouldn't notice my awkwardness.

"You're going to love this," I whispered up at him, mostly to distract him.

His cock was thick, extraordinarily thick, my fingers barely wrapped around it, but oddly, the head was small and circumcised, a small cap on a wide shaft, that arched slightly. For some reason, it made me think of a musical instrument, a horn.

I thought suddenly that was where the word horny came from, because of cocks like this that looked like horns. I almost wanted to press my lips to it and try to blow air down the urethra. What sound would that make? But I thought it might hurt him.

Instead, I pressed my lips against the head, already glistening with pre-cum, and let them spread, enfolding the glans and widening to encompass the first inches of the shaft.

He groaned, and I felt this wave of pleasure and weakness ripple through his body, his struggle to hold himself up as he leaned back against the desk. I glanced up at him, with his cock in my mouth, making brief eye contact. I could taste the saltiness of his pre-cum, and rolled my tongue around the glans, making him shiver and gasp again. I loved the feel of his responses, the transparency of them, the way I could make his whole body react with just a movement of my lips, a dart of a tongue this way or that.

I kept my hand on his shaft, stroking back and forth, wary of him reaching down and trying to push my head further down. My jaws were distended with just couple of inches, and there was no way I could take that thick monster deeper without gagging. Instead, I teased the head, lifting my mouth around it, then clamping down, lapping or stroking with my tongue, trying to time it with the movement of my hand. When I felt I had my balance all right, I dared to release his thigh and cradle and tease his balls with my freed hand.

My blow jobs had always been hasty things, preludes to real sex, or warm ups, or just drunken encounters, or casual 'finish this and go away' things. But oddly, here in the moment, there was something exciting about it. Maybe it was his responsiveness, the way his body shivered and quaked with every touch, as if I was plucking a musical instrument, the sense of power it gave me. Maybe it was the transgressiveness of it all, the naughtiness, the fact that he thought I was some hooker. I felt a kind of wild weightlessness, an elation, an erotic charge, that left me wet. I could feel my clit throb, my labial lips part and entrance dilate, could feel the arousal in my own body.

I expected him to come right away, prepared to seal my lips around, and swallow. But he didn't, and after moments, I didn't want him to come. When his quaking grew too intense, I'd squeeze the base of his cock tightly, pulling his balls, lifting my mouth off of it and breathing hotly, as the desperate spasms eased off from the edge of ejaculation. It had become exciting, and I didn't want to let him go just yet, denying his orgasm was another frisson of power and excitement.

I wobbled on one knee, and grabbed his thigh to steady myself, covering it by letting my palm slide up his shirt, across his hairy belly, making it sensuous. Just slightly off balance, my mouth slid down just a little too far on his shaft, I felt a slight tickle that could become a gag, and pushed off, lifting until my lips wrapped tightly around his head. There was another fleeting taste of pre-cum. The thick curving shaft throbbed hot and urgent in my hand.

Suddenly, I wanted it. I wanted it in me. I wanted to feel the head of his cock between my legs. I wanted the thickness in me. I had these image flashes of his hands on my breasts, wrapping my thighs around that thick muscular ass. I wanted to be fucked good and hard, real, raw passionate, uninhibited sex. I wanted the sex I'd been denied with Jay. No romance, no excitement, no dancing around, none of the bullshit, with him just fucking.

I lifted my mouth off his cock, still maintaining my death grip on his shaft.

"Are you ready to fuck?" I asked huskily, as if that had been the plan all along.

"Oh yeah," he grunted.

I thought of something.

"Do you have a condom?" I asked.

"No," do you.

I felt a tiny wince.

"In my purse," I said.

Terrific. Now he'd be absolutely sure I was a hooker. Who else carries condoms in their purse? But at the same time, I didn't care, because I just wanted that cock. As he turned to grab my purse from the desk and hand it to me, I slid my mouth over his cock quickly, one more time, lashing the head with my tongue and feeling a gratifying shiver of weakness run through him.

My hands shook slightly, as I fished through my purse from a kneeling position, found a condom, tore it open and wrapped him. In the sheen of the latex, it was oddly disappointing, muted, and I had this weird fleeting regret at covering its beauty. I'd never thought of a cock as beautiful before, it had just never occurred to me to think that way, and the notion surprised me.

There was an awkward moment as I climbed to my feet, pushing my miniskirt up, and we shifted positions around, pushing papers and phone back to the other side of the desk. Then my ass was perching rough against the desk, propping myself up on elbows. I lifted my knees up. He was between my legs, one hand on his cock, attention fixed on it, the other on my hip. I wanted it so bad, I could taste it. With one hand, I reached down, brushing fingertips against his erection, drawing it to me, spreading my lips apart as I felt the touch of his head.

Then he plunged into me, the girth and thickness spreading me open wide as it surged in. I gasped loudly in sheer pleasure at feeling him, feeling the thickness of his shaft, its throbbing rigidity, the way it curved up inside me as it thrust and filled me.

I wanted to savor the feeling of him inside me, wanted to drench myself in the sensation of being filled so completely. But he didn't wait, as soon as he bottomed in me, his cock pressing deep, his balls and pubes slapping against me, he pulled back and thrust hard again, drawing another gasp from me.

He fucked hard and relentless, holding me pinned like a butterfly on the desk. I wrapped my legs around his ass again and again, and he'd buck, fucking himself free, my shiny black boots and heels kicking wildly in ecstasy. My back arched to meet each thrust, trying to work him a little deeper with each lunge, to be opened by a little more by his girth. His hands were like vises against my hips holding them in place as he fucked with everything he had.

I gasped and grunted, our bodies smashing together again and again. I could feel sweat breaking out all over my body, smell the sex in the air, I could hear the sound of his cock plunging into my drenched pussy, and over it, the sound of our breathing, our gasping, my heartbeat. I wanted it all, and I wanted more. Fucking filled my mind, it was everything, I couldn't think, it was all there was, and I wanted more. I arched my back, pressing my breasts together, offering them up again and again. Finally, I reached down and grabbed his hands from my hips, wrapping my legs tight around him, I pulled his hands to my breasts, feeling their hot weight, the pressure as his fingers clenched squeezing them tightly. My boots kicked again as I ground my clit against his body.

The hands on my breasts, the almost painful clenching was ecstatic, but my hips were too free. There wasn't the intensity of pounding, even as I tried to hold him in place. Above me, his sweat dripped from his brow onto me, his face was contorted. He saw me and yet didn't see me, wrapped in his own sexual haze. I had an impulse, I didn't want to look at his face.

"Turn me over," I said. "I want to be fucked bent over the desk."

Hands came off my breasts. His cock pulled out, there was a feeling of absence, of loss. I wanted to reach down, grab it, yank it back where it belonged. We parted, again awkwardly and hastily. For a second, I was off the desk, and standing, his hands guiding unnecessarily. Then I was bending forward onto my elbows, arching my back. I could feel his vise grip hands on my hips, on my ass. I pushed back, seeking him.

His cock couldn't find me. It thrust against my thigh, my belly. I moaned with frustration, suddenly worried that we couldn't do it in this position, that it wouldn't work. He pushed down on my ass, trying to change the angle. I understood, spreading my legs wider, to lower. As my legs spread, I could feel my lips parting, opening in wet anticipation. Almost there, I could feel the head of his cock seeking purchase. I bent my knees a little.

"Yes!" I shouted in joy, as his thick cock rammed up in me in one wild thrust, mine once again, back where it belonged. Again, I wanted to savor it, but again he thrust relentlessly. In this angle, in this position, I could push into him with every arch of my back, every thrust of his hips, and the feeling was glorious. It was as if with each thrust, his cock reared out deliciously inside of me, sending wave after wave of ecstasy.

"Not so loud," he grunted.

I had a half awareness that we were in the maintenance floor, in a security office. Who knew who was passing by outside? What they might think? Who they might tell? Or who might have keys to walk in on us?

Part of me didn't care at all, just cared about this cock rearing up in me with every thrust, the rapid waves of pleasure. Part of me knew we were transgressing, breaking rules, and that made it wilder, more intense, as if we were racing against some enemy. Some part understood it would be bad if we were caught.

"I'll try," I grunted. "But it's just so good."

Stroke his ego, I thought. But I struggled to stifle my moans. He leaned over me. I could feel his weight on my back as he pushed up into me. His vise-grip hands found my breasts again, the almost painful grips bringing hisses of pressure. Pinned now to the desk by his weight, pulled into position, my legs felt like jelly. Only the rampant thrusting of his cock holding me up and in place. Then I felt it.

"Oh god," I tried to whisper. "Oh god, it's close, it's coming, I can feel it building."

"Just do it quietly."

"I'll try!" I hissed.

My orgasm felt like a boulder rolling down a hill, it felt huge and unstoppable, an immense force coming over me. In my mind's eye, I visualized myself tied down at the base of the hill, spread eagled wide, my pussy elevated and centered to meet this overpowering, onrushing force.

Then it hit. My body went rigid, I could feel my muscles going stiff and spastic, I was hot and cold, I couldn't breathe. I could feel a hand clamped across my mouth, stifling an unending scream, and pressed both of my hands against it, pushing hard, sealing it tighter. I sucked air through my nostrils, but there wasn't enough of it. Black spots, swirled around the edge of my vision, the scream flattening against his palm.

Then it was over. I tore the palm from my mouth, clutching his hand in mind, sucking in great lungful's of air. His relentless thrusting paused, and finally, my trembling body, sweat drenched, shaking like a leaf, all my muscles turned to water, could just enjoy the feel of his cock inside me, my possession, my property.

Mine, I thought with aimless delirium, I should keep it. I should take it home with me and feed it and treat it like a pet. He didn't deserve it, he just walks around with it in his pants, suffocating it. He could never appreciate it like I do.

"Holy shit," I grunted softly.

"You okay?"

"Oh yeah, that was just intense," I replied, I was still panting, and lightheaded.

Gently, he began to move inside me. At first just a little, but each movement became more pronounced, the rocking became thrusting, this time even fiercer and more urgent. Again, I felt the waves of pleasure from his cock rearing up savagely within me, full of fury and wildness. His hands moved from my breasts to my shoulders to my hips and back, always seeking purchase, exploring, pushing my now boneless form onto his manhood.

The orgasm had left me feeling like jelly, but now I felt it starting up again, building. The boneless lassitude giving it a new feeling, a sense of the dam having broken, and pleasure building in new easier ways. By contrast, I felt the urgency in the way his body crashed against mine, the fierceness and rigidity of his touch. I realized he was trying to reach his own orgasm, trying to come, or simply finally driving towards it. Perhaps not struggling, but now on some kind of threshold, he'd become the boulder rolling down the hill towards his own shattering impact.

The feeling of it, my boneless, jelly bliss, and the wildness of his fucking, the decay of his rigid control as the energy spilled and the arousal crept up his spine set me off again, in a faster, more fluid orgasm. My legs kicked, pushing all my weight onto his cock. I grabbed one of his hands, biting into the meat of his palm to suppress another scream. This one was like floating, breathless, free fall.

And then I could breathe again.

But the feeling, the come down didn't quite happen, there was no trough, just a valley, because now he was fucking with everything he had his cock pistoning rapidly inside me, shaking me, my whole body almost flopping. I was no longer standing bent over the desk, my legs had failed completely, and his hands gripped my hips holding me in place as he thrust with every inch of power in his body, while his weight pressed me down onto his cock.

Perversions and Infidelities / Page 101

Then he went rigid, his breath coming in a strained whine. Even without looking, I could feel the tension boiling through his whole body, every fiber of his being taut and singing. I could imagine his cock swelling inside me, bursting like a balloon. I tried to focus on it, to feel how rigid it was to feel it throb extra hard, extra-large. His agonized straining, the hiss of air escaping lasted for seconds.

Then he sucked in a huge breath of air and went limp. Literally limp. He practically dropped on top of me. I could feel his hot breath panting against my ear. Feel his sweat drenched shirt against my back. He didn't crush me, he must have held himself up on his elbows. But I could still feel weight, the presence of him, as the orgasm released him, leaving him wet and vulnerable.

Oddly, I liked it. Perhaps I shouldn't have. Objectively, here was a sweat drenched, trembling stranger, a complete stranger who'd used my body like a rag doll, and was now laying on top of me, trying to catch his breath, his cock slowly deflating but still in me. But there was a strange feeling of intimacy in our mutual orgasms, in our mutual exhaustion.

Finally, after a few minutes, I grew restless.

It was time to ruin the moment.

"I guess we have a deal," I whispered under him.

He stiffened, not in a good way, but just in the manner of someone pulling himself together.

"Yeah," he said.

He got off me, standing up to pull up his boxers and his pants. I pushed myself off the desk in turn, turning around and pushing my miniskirt down, smoothing it. I only had the briefest glimpse of him tidying himself.

For a moment, I was seized with a weird longing. I wanted to see him naked. I wanted his cock in my hand again, even soft, even wet. I wanted to hold it, maybe put it in my mouth, to experience it in this state. But he was doing up his belt, and the fugitive impulse passed unfulfilled.

I tucked my breasts into my bustier, they were tender. I wondered if they might bruise. I felt achy all over but in a good way.

In my thigh high fetish boots my feet were sweaty, and the heels felt awkward. I longed to just take them off and walk barefoot. That's the thing with fetishy stuff, it looks hot, but underneath its awkward and sweaty. I couldn't though. If it was just the hotel, I'd have taken them off. But I wasn't walking barefoot in the parkade.

Besides, what would he say or think? I had an image to uphold. I certainly couldn't ruin it now that I'd burned it into his brain.

"I promise," I said, "I won't ever come back here."

"Good."

But I thought he betrayed a little regret about that. I think that there's an inevitable sadness in a really great spontaneous fuck, that you'll never see them again, never revisit that pleasure.

Or maybe it was exhaustion.

Now that our coupling was over, I was sure some part of him was wondering how much of a pain in the ass I might turn out to be, what sort of trouble I could end up making.

Now that it was over, we were both strangers again, not really wanting anything to do with each other, each full of potential risks and headaches.

I watched as he ran the forms through the shredder.

"What about the guests, incident reports? You mentioned that."

"I'll take care of it. I'll write something up."

"And the video?"

"Deleted automatically after twenty-four hours, unless there's a reason to keep it. There won't be a reason."

"Okay."

He sounded tired now.

"Listen," I asked. "Could you walk me to the Parkade? I just need to get to my car, and then I'm gone."

He stared at me for a second, and I could tell he didn't want to. He just wanted it all to be over, to move on. But he didn't have it in him to say no. Honestly, I didn't really want to ask, but I just felt so wobbly from the fucking, and the boots were uncomfortable. I felt worn out, and even if neither of us really wanted to be around the other, I didn't quite want to be alone.

We didn't talk much as he guided me to the elevator and walked me through the parkade. I suppose we said something, but words were purely perfunctory. I thought about my trench coat, but I didn't mention it, we were miles past it. My flare up with Jay felt like it belonged on another world, kicking the stranger's door was an awkward encounter on some other day.

I got in my car and drove home and flopped on the couch with a glass of wine. Sometime later, I took a shower, went to bed and fell right asleep.

The end...

* * *

Over the next few days, I tried my best not to think of that evening.

When you have an epic streak of bad judgment like that, you don't want to dwell on it. Any part of the night felt simply embarrassing, whether it was the ludicrous exercise in dressing up, falling for Jay's bullshit, that painfully awkward fight, waking up a total stranger mistakenly, or getting fucked like a cheap hooker by

Perversions and Infidelities / Page 103

another total stranger... I mean, there's no part of that I could come off looking good to myself. It was a blundering car crash of a night, best forgotten.

Some parts were hard to forget, like the finger bruises on my breasts and hips, the delicious achiness in my thighs and pussy. Badges of my serious lapse of judgment, albeit a sexually intense lapse.

Jay texted to apologize. In a calmer state, and wanting to put the matter in the past, I accepted his apology, was cordial but polite, and ended the relationship.

The trench coat never came up. He didn't mention it, and I didn't want to give him a hold over me, some basis for continuing contact, by mentioning it.

I think he floated the possibility of continuing, with the promise of his honesty. Whatever we had, it had been real and exciting in a sense, and perhaps, with the air cleared, there might be a chance?

But really, I just didn't want to.

Honestly, the whole thing had been a humiliation. I was done with being humiliated. It stung.

But you know how it is, after a while, even a sting fades. The thing with Jay, that kind of still hurt. I'd been played for a fool, and you can't ever forgive someone who makes you feel stupid.

But the encounter with Mike, the House Detective, that was a little different. I'd had agency, I'd made choices, bad ones, but I'd been in control of the situation, sort of, and the sex, as cheap and sleazy and empty as it had been, had also been intense and... Genuine?

I found myself reliving the experience, revisiting, especially alone at night with a vibrator. I embroidered the encounter, wrote new dialogue, revised the scenario. Sometimes handcuffs were involved, or a genuine arrest. Sometimes Mike was putty in my hands, and I was a femme fatale in some old movie, Basic Instinct or something, effortlessly deflecting an interrogation with poise and raw sexuality.

I guess, yes, I am a little pervy.

We all are, alone at night with our vibrators.

We were complete and utter strangers to each other, with absolutely nothing in common, and apart from our flash point of lust, no chemistry whatsoever. I couldn't see any reason for us ever to even talk to each other, nothing about him that could ever interest me, no place he'd even possibly fit into my life.

I was sure he viewed me as a cheap hooker who he'd been lucky to fuck, and luckier to evade long term consequences from our encounter. I had no intention of ever going near that hotel again. So really, there was no reason for either of us to ever want to, or even to

imagine wanting to, get in contact again. Apart from the memory of
the sex, of course.

But obviously, that's not enough.

So of course I got back in touch with him again.

* * *

It wasn't as if I just woke up and decided to do it. I didn't wildly
fling myself into a thing. Everyone in my circle considered me the
least reckless person they knew.

Good old Kate. Dependable Kate. Careful Kate. Kate was the
woman you called when you needed someone to come and pick you
up. The one who always ended up as the designated driver. Kate who
always drove the speed limit. Kate who worked at a sensible job at the
bank.

Kate who dated men as stable and reliable as she was.

Kate who dated men as dull as she was.

I think that had been the appeal of Jay. Our cyber-romance
through texts and emails was actually adventurous. We talked about
travel, about art, about life. There had been an excitement to Jay that
simply hadn't been there with most of the men in my life.

Because it had been cyber, Jay had been safe... I'd taken no risks at
all. Right up until it blew up in my face.

The fling with Mike, the Hotel Detective, had been so left field,
so out there for me. Some weird combination of recklessness and
frustration, embarrassment and tension, and just a sudden impulsive
need to play a role, be someone different.

The sex had been volcanic.

No lie. Mike had been the greatest sex of my life.

Which is kind of embarrassing to admit, because it had basically
been a quicky. The greatest sex of your life was a quicky with a
security guard who mistook you for a hooker.

God, that was pathetic.

But there it was, it had been genuinely, wildly hot.

It's hard to let something like that go.

And there was something else, something hard to explain. Mike
had seen a different side of me. A side that didn't really exist. There
was in his mind, in his memory, a Kate that was a million miles
from who I was. Maybe a cheap out of control hooker, but it was still
a vivid picture of a totally different Kate. Maybe I just wanted a
glimpse of that women, the woman in his mind's eye.

After about a week, I contacted the hotel

* * *.

"Hello, my name is Kate. My boyfriend and I stayed at your hotel
a few weeks ago, and while we were there, the Hotel Detective, I think

his name was Mike, he was so wonderfully helpful with a problem we had. I'm just following up from the trip. I was wondering if you could put me through. We were talking, and we thought I should call him and let him know how much we appreciated him."

"Hotel Detective?"

"Yes. I think his name was Mike."

"You mean security? Mike Polonia?"

"Yes, that's him. Could you put me through?"

"I'm afraid Mike's not on shift tonight."

"Perhaps his voice mail?"

"Staff Security don't have individual voicemails I'm afraid."

"Oh, well, perhaps his email?"

"We don't give out staff email, I'm sorry. But if you send an email to our general inquiries, I'll make sure to forward it to Mike."

"That would be wonderful! Thank you."

* * *

"Hello Mike. This is Kate. I hope that you remember me. I just wanted to thank you for what you did to me during my brief visit to your hotel. Unfortunately, I will not be visiting again in the foreseeable future. But I wanted to express my appreciation for all your help. Keep in touch. Kate."

I stared at the first email of my new Gmail account. A Gmail account I'd created expressly for this email. My heart was pounding.

It had been just like this when I'd phoned the hotel: Terrifying. It had been a relief to be told that he was out, I thought if they'd put me through, I might have simply hung up out of sheer embarrassment. As it was, I'd been able to fake my way, voice casual, hands shaking, kicking myself at the sheer ridiculousness of it all.

Now here I was emailing him directly, sort of. I stared at the email, changed "to me" to "for me." It was originally "for me." But it had been exciting to write it the other way. It had made me wet.

Which was sort of pathetic.

Sensible, dull Kate, getting horny over a slightly risqué reference. Still, other people would see this.

'For me' was better. Subtle. He'd know. No one else would.

There was a moment's reservation. What was I doing? How would he react? He was going to get a mash letter from the crazy hooker who'd gone up and down the hotel kicking doors and harassing guests, and then fucked him to get out of a trespass notice. Men like bold women, they don't like batshit insane ones. A message from me would not be a welcome thing. He'd think I was stalking him.

He'd probably just take one look and delete. Or maybe send a polite reply and hope I'd go away forever.

I really shouldn't do this, I told myself. The sensible thing to do would be to delete..

I pressed send.

Then I went to work at the bank, and spent the rest of the day thinking about what a mistake it was.

Anyway, odds are, he wouldn't even respond.

That evening, I got a message back. I wanted to dance!

"From Mike Polonia,

Dear Kate. Thank you for your kind words. At the Imperial, we do our best to provide first class service to clients and visitors. We were happy to service you. Mike.

PS: If you need to contact me directly, this is my personal email...."

I had to smile. He'd 'serviced' me, all right. Bold of him to put that in the email, I felt relieved, my contact hadn't been unwelcome. He didn't see me as some weird, crazy, stalker slut who would make his life hell. Or maybe he did, but he was trying to divert me down a path that wouldn't get him fired? No, he could have just ignored the whole thing.

I had his private email, which was both exciting and terrifying. We were communicating directly.

I waited a day, stewing over it, before I wrote back.

"Hello Mike. I'm glad you are willing to talk to me. I can't imagine what sort of impression you had of me, or of my stability. I'm not crazy, really. That night was a very bad night for me, and it could have been worse, except for you. I want to thank you for your patience and your sympathy. I would look forward to corresponding with you, if you are interested."

I looked it over. I liked it. A very nice letter, not too personal, didn't give too much away. Perfectly 'business formal' just like the correspondence I did for the Bank.

I chewed my lip, and added. "Oh, and by the way, the sex was amazing. Thank you for that!"

I hit send.

* * *

"I have a confession to make," I typed.

"Oh?" he texted back.

After a careful volley of emails back and forth, feeling each other out, checking for signs of insanity or instability, we'd gotten comfortable enough to embark on a live text session. I'd spoofed my phone, so he couldn't track me.

For our first text session, I was in bed, propped up against pillows, wearing a fuzzy bathrobe and big pink slippers with lizard toes - don't ask, it was a gift.

Perversions and Infidelities / Page 107

"You were right." My heart skipped a beat, my stomach felt light. I felt this sense of wild excitement, almost elation at what I was going to type next. "I was hooking. The guy was a John."

"Not really surprised." He texted back.

"You didn't believe me?" I smiled, playing at mock outrage.

"The way you were dressed, you looked like you were working the street down at Orion."

I'd heard of that, Orion was part of the local red light district. Quickly, I looked it up. Orion and Mulvey, they were cross streets.

"Yes." I typed. "I was. That's where he picked me up, at Orion and Mulvey, I usually worked there. I guess he thought I looked hot."

"You definitely looked hot."

I smiled.

"Thank you."

"If he picked you up, how come your car was in the hotel parkade?"

Fuck!

My smile vanished. I was having fun playing sexy, and now I was getting cross examined. I thought fast.

"He picked me up earlier, that's when we made the appointment... the date. Earlier on the street. I drove there myself later."

Please don't ask any more questions, I thought at him.

"So what went wrong? What happened?"

I smiled again. Okay, this was going where I wanted. I was prepared.

"The Trick, I think his name was Jay. Seemed like a nice guy, flashed a lot of money. I thought this would be a good time. Spend the night, make some cash. Have some real fun, you know. I was in the mood for some blow-out sex."

Okay, establish horny hooker mentality.

"I get to the Hotel and I walk in the room, and he's wearing nothing but a bathrobe. And he's got a micro-penis!"

"No!"

"Yes! I couldn't believe my eyes. It was as thick as my little finger, and half as long, and he's already playing with it. There's no hair down there, and I don't think it's because he shaves. He didn't even have balls, just this pair of little reddish warts. I've never seen anything like it!"

I grinned wickedly.

Fuck you, Jay.

"And then it starts to leak, and I thought he was peeing, right there in the open on the hotel carpet. But he was coming. It was just like water, like he was peeing."

"And that's it," I conclude. "He says thank you for coming, and shoves me out. I couldn't believe it. This asshole trick has me drive all across town and miss out on business, just so he can ejaculate his micro-penis right in front of me the minute I walk through the door."

Fuck you some more, Jay. I grinned wickedly.

If only that story could somehow get out.

"Did he pay you at least?"

"No!" I typed. "He stiffed me, and not in the good way. I got nothing. I think I left my coat behind. I was just so thrown, I forgot all about it. All I could think was what an asshole."

"Definitely an asshole!"

"Thanks. I was so stunned, I didn't know what to do. I just started walking away. Then I got mad and came back. The rest you caught on camera."

"I'm surprised you weren't angrier, when I met up with you."

I thought about that. I should have been angrier, yes.

"I was embarrassed to have ended up knocking on the wrong door. Poor guy, it wasn't his fault. He must have thought I was crazy. I probably woke him up. I just thought, well that's fucked, I should just get out of here. If you hadn't shown up, I would have just slunk away."

"Chalked it up to experience."

"Another one for the books. I could write a book with all the crazy stuff I've seen."

Wait! Where had that come from? What if he asked? This was the only story I had prepared.

Mike was the only outrageous sex I'd ever had.

"I'm sorry I caught you, it sounds like it would have sorted itself out. I didn't need to do anything."

I smiled and leaned back against my pillows. This was a more enjoyable subject.

"I'm not sorry. I'm not sorry at all, not even a little bit," I typed boldly. I felt this tiny little wet squeeze. Time for sexy talk.

Maybe I should send him a present? Maybe a sexy selfie? No. Not yet. The idea of taking a picture of myself felt exciting, but too dangerous. Maybe something without a face? I blushed at the thought.

"That was pretty wild." He texted.

"You mean you don't fuck wayward hookers in your offices all the time? Catch and release? I would have thought that was a perk of the job." I grinned at my cleverness.

"God no! I would get fired on the spot. You're my first."

"A virgin! I must be irresistible!"

"It was amazing," he texted. "Just amazing. It was the hottest fuck of my life."

Oh yes, I grinned. Keep on. I wanted more.

Compliment my sexual majesty, oh worshipful man!

"It was straight out of a porno, but better!"

"It was hot," I texted. I wanted to type dirty. "Very hot. I really needed a good hard fuck after that experience, and you came through. I loved getting plowed by that big hard cock of yours. I was so ready."

"How come?" he texted. "I always thought hookers didn't really enjoy sex. They faked it, you know. You were on fire."

"All real," I texted back, feeling like a sex goddess. "Some of us love our work."

"I'd love to do it again."

Here it comes. That was more than I wanted.

"Sorry," I texted. "I'm back in Chicago. But the next time I'm out your way..."

"You're not from here?"

"No," I typed. "I was just in town for a few days to party. I was just doing a little adventuring on the side."

"I'm sorry."

"Don't be!" I texted. "You were the highlight of the trip! You rocked my world! I had bruises!"

"Sorry."

"Loved them!" I thought a little. "What about your palm? Did I leave teeth marks?"

"Badge of honor."

"I love it!" I giggled a little. "Tell me: What went through your mind when I walked my fingers up your trouser..."

* * *

The text session was fun, sexy but disappointingly not nearly as explicit as it could have been. But heavy on the flirting, which was fine, since I'd established boundaries. Pretending to live in another city meant that sex, casual hookups were out of the question. But he'd hung in there anyway, probably hoping for future visits.

We talked about pictures. He asked. I invited him to send a dick pic. He was shy. He asked some questions I had to dodge, mostly about the hooker lifestyle. After we wrapped up, I signed off, reached for my vibrator, had a delicious, tidy little orgasm and slept like a baby.

The next day, I flew through work with a smile on my face.

* * *

Over the next few sessions, I broadened my character. I wasn't just a street hooker, I was an escort too, and an exotic dancer, and a burlesque performer. A free spirit who loved sex and adventure.

I was also an Arts History major, I threw that in because it seemed like a free spirit sort of thing. My real degree was Commerce, which had lead me to a position with the bank.

It was a little bit of a mistake, because it turned out he was very fond of art, and knowledgeable, so I had to dodge around the subject a bit, but he didn't seem to notice. What was the harm in a little fib like that?

He'd claimed to be a 'Hotel Detective' rather than just another security guard, after all.

We all told lies.

And I loved to travel! Something my chosen vocation in the sex industry allowed me to do. I hadn't ever actually been anywhere in real life. But this other Kate, this 'Better-Kate' I was pretending to be, she strode the world. Like a goddess

The problem was, I didn't know anything about art history, or art. Or the difference between a stripper and a burlesque artist, or an escort and a streetwalker.

I had vague ideas. You see this stuff on television. But how accurate was any of that?

I needed to do homework.

* * *

"How much do you charge?" My mouth was dry, but at least my voice hadn't cracked.

I'd driven around Orion a couple of times. The hooker had shaggy red hair that looked a little like Natasha Lyonne, and a black leather jacket festooned with chains. She'd smiled at me as I drove past. I figured I could talk to her without getting stabbed.

"Excuse me?" Her brow furrowed, she looked confused, bent down to look at me, as I sat in my car.

I hadn't taken hookers to be so polite.

"How much do you charge?" I asked, blushing deeply. "Is it by the hour? Half hour? By the act? Is that too personal a question?"

She stared at me.

"Do you want to...?"

"Oh," I said. "No. Not at all. I just I want to know?"

"Are you a cop? Is this a cop thing?"

"No." I blushed a little. I didn't want her to get hostile. "I'm not a cop."

"Are you a reporter?" Her brow furrowed. "A missionary? A social worker?"

"No, none of this. I'm just an ordinary girl. I work at a bank."

Perversions and Infidelities / Page 111

"Are you thinking of hooking?"

"No."

She frowned.

"Why are you asking?"

"I just need to know. It's kind of complicated, it's a personal thing."

She didn't look convinced. She was kind of starting to look a little hostile.

"I just want to ask a few questions. I'll pay!"

The hooker waved, I couldn't see where. But then a man joined her.

"Is that your pimp?" I asked.

"Fuck you," she said. "He's my boyfriend."

She turned to him. "She wants to ask questions. She'll pay."

"How much?" he asked.

"What's the going rate to ask questions?" I was floundering. This had all been such a mistake.

"Why do you want to ask questions?" he asked. "What questions?"

"It's sort of complicated. It's hard to explain. Look, I'll just go."

"No," he put his hand on the car door. I felt a surge of panic. "You'll pay. Fine, let's go somewhere and talk."

Where? I was starting to get scared. But before I could say anything, he pointed at a burger place across the street.

"We'll go over there. We can talk. We'll have lunch, on you."

Public place, okay. That was safe enough. Assuming that lunch on me wasn't a weird hooker euphemism.

It was kind of complicated to explain things to them. Perhaps not so much complicated, as kind of silly. They were bemused. But we warmed up, and so I heard about prices, which really amounted to what you could get, which amounted to what street you worked, what time of day, what acts were involved. And from there it drifted into other aspects of life, a practical matter of fact tutorial that included complaining about ill-fitting boots, or runs in stockings.

Then, as the conversation turned to threesomes and exotic arrangements, I felt a hand on my thigh, and got cold feet.

On the way home, I stopped at the bookstore and bought "Art History for Dummies."

I had homework to do.

* * *

"So the girlfriend experience..." Mike was saying, "Is you just go over and hang out and pretend to be a girlfriend and have sex."

"And watch television together, and talk. Girlfriend things," I concluded.

Perversions and Infidelities / Page 112

"It's weird."

"Tell me about it," I said. "I mean, I like Online Escort work, the money, I can't argue with that. But it's so much its own world. There are boards, you get reviews. But I don't know. Girlfriend experience, sure, there's money in it... but it's just weird and kind of boring. I want a sense of adventure, not scary adventure, but it's like a real experience, and I think that's almost the opposite. Am I weird?"

"It sounds like you almost prefer walking the streets."

"Sometimes, yes. There's excitement to it."

"Are you still online as an Escort?"

Ohh? Probing? I grinned wickedly.

"Not right now. I go up now and then, but I'm kind of past that. I'm dancing these days. I have a tour through the Midwest."

"There are tours?"

"Well, I call it a tour. I have a list of cities and clubs, I figure spend a week here, a week there."

"Sounds rough."

"Actually, I'm looking forward to it. The pole doesn't wait."

The only thing I knew about stripper poles was from watching YouTube videos, which featured quite a lot of fails. Poles falling over, strippers landing on their heads. Seriously, I was horrified. It amazed me that health and safety weren't all over this thing.

But I had a flyer from a strip mall that said "Housewives, learn to pole dance for your husband - first lesson free!"

And I had googled a list of strip clubs with reviews across three states. No interior photos, for obvious reasons. But I could improvise.

* * *

"Are you awake?" My voice was hushed, brimming with excitement.

"Yeah," he didn't sound sleepy or anything. His voice was eager. I loved the way his voice seemed to light up when I called him. He was always excited when I texted or wrote or called, enthralled to hear about my wild, fearless life. I fed off that.

"I'm in a hotel room bathroom," I whispered. I was in my own bathroom, because I thought the acoustics would lend credence to the story. "You will never guess who is sleeping in the next room!"

Then I told him...

Well, actually, there was no one in my bedroom. But in Better-Kate's imaginary Vegas suite, there was a world famous celebrity athlete. I whispered a name.

"No!" His astonishment thrilled me.

"Yes. Totally. He just pounded me, now he's sleeping it off. I had to sneak in here and tell you about it."

Perversions and Infidelities / Page 113

"What's he like," Mike whispered, he didn't have to, but he'd fallen into the spirit of the call. "Is he big, you know... there?"

"Huge, but not super hard. If he'd been hard, like you, like an iron bar, big as he was it might have hurt. But it was sort of like a really rigid loofah, so it filled, but sort of fit. Not circumcised. Really big head, kind of round, like a mushroom."

"Wow."

"Oh and insatiable. I thought I had an appetite. But he wore me out. He just wouldn't stop. He kept going and going, and every now and then he'd flip me over, or change positions."

"That's intense."

"Oh my god, I came so many times. It was incredible. And he's huge. He's what? Seven feet? He has to be seven feet tall. Everything looks like a toy next to him. He would pick me up like a doll. You know, when I was under him, and he was on top, my legs were spread so wide I felt like a wishbone. I looked up, and there's just this expanse of chest. I'm eye level with his nipples. He was so huge, he would have just crushed me. But he's holding himself up on his elbows as he thrusts into me, and the whole bed is shaking. I look on either side, and his biceps, his biceps! They're thicker than my thighs!"

"That's amazing."

"It was surreal. It was like being with a giant. What am I saying, he was a giant. Hold on..."

I texted a picture of my bared breasts, glistening wetly, nipples rigid. I'd used a spray bottle on them earlier, fooling around until I had just the right look.

"This is me," I whispered. "I'm still just drenched with sweat, head to toe."

"Wow. I'm surprised you aren't going back for seconds."

"He's sleeping right now, or yes, I'd be riding that pony. But he snores."

"He snores?"

"Like a room full of chain saws, it's unbelievable. Can you hear him?"

"No."

"Good. Okay. Well, it's amazing. Like no way am I going to sleep next to that. So I decided to come in here and tell you all about it."

"Tell me," Mike said. "I want every detail!"

"Okay, so here's what happened..."

* * *

There was a strange kind of satisfaction, manufacturing a fictional encounter with a famous celebrity athlete. I just added detail after detail, the taste of sweat on his skin, the way his tongue filled my mouth, the taste of his nipples. I gave vivid descriptions of his erection and scrotum, his manner of love making.

There was a kind of creative thrill to making up the story and sharing it that made it almost real. For Mike it was real, I could hear him almost panting as I described each moment, knew he was stroking his cock.

I was wet too, excited, touching myself, fully aroused, but swept up 0in the creativity of the moment. I was too caught up in the artistry of storytelling to allow an orgasm. That would come later, as I relived the conversation, some alchemy of the story, its vividness, and Mike's infectious arousal allowing me to reach several different kinds of satisfaction at once.

Instead, I closed my eyes visualizing everything, from his fingernails to the furniture of the hotel room, the feel of sweat drenched sheets against my back, the way his long frame sprawled across the bed, the feet hanging off, and just let the words flow, making up new details, my voice rising and falling with enthusiasm, as if it had really happened.

It wasn't entirely spontaneous, of course. I'd done my homework, found which teams played where, who the superstars were. Checked out photos. I'd let my imagination work, constructing a fantasy, adding detail and texture to the scenario. I needed to be accurate, in case he checked and I was caught out in a lie. Some details, of course, I could make up without fear of contradiction, such as genital descriptions or declarations of performance.

But even with all that, it was when I was talking to him, sexting, sharing, that the whole thing came alive in my mind, details piled up and spilled from my lips, and I loved every minute of it.

* * *

I was completely caught up in creating this strange fictional other life for myself, another identity that I had taken to calling Better-Kate, who sprang into existence in the gap between Mike and myself.

Better-Kate was a meticulous creation. I couldn't just lie, she had to feel real. Mike had to feel she was real.

As Better-Kate danced her way through clubs, I took pole dancing classes to get a feel for the experience - after only four classes, I quit, my muscles aching - pole dancing is hard! But I switched to Pilates, to make sure I had the right muscle tone for pictures.

I attended strip clubs a couple of times, not often, to watch the dancers, the interplay and dynamics of girls and audience. I found seats at the back, rebuffed any men who came close, but bought drinks for dancers willing to sit and chat and listened to their stories. I'm sure they were puzzled by why I was there. I'm equally sure that

Perversions and Infidelities / Page 115

if I'd told them they would have been bemused, or perhaps amused, but I didn't share.

A couple of them invited me to more private adventures, but I chickened out, as always.

The most I ever did was a couple of lap dances, mostly to take notes.

I practiced routines at home, to get a feel for them.

I even signed up for an Amateur Stripper Contest, backing out at the last minute. Because obviously, Real-Kate was kind of a chickenshit.

The club's management for the contest was understanding, I think it happened a lot, and they offered me complimentary drinks if I wanted to watch my competitors and perhaps screw up my courage. If I changed my mind once, I could change it again, after all.

But I only fled.

I looked up maps and googled street views, consulted Wikipedia and YouTube. Not just to make the illusions perfect, but to cast myself in them. To close my eyes and imagine I was actually there, struggling to envision the taste and texture, the sound of glasses clinking, and voices talking, the lingering smell of tobacco in the air, the weariness of ill-fitting heels, the coolness of metal pole or the wear of the dance floor.

It was almost as if the adventures and exploits of Better-Kate was an erotic novel that I was writing, pouring research and creativity and passion into it, for an audience of one person. One person who didn't know it was a novel, one person for whom Better-Kate was a living, breathing, larger than life, woman.

She was real for Mike, and so in a strange way, she'd become real for me.

She was this other, better version of me, living a life, enjoying a life in full glorious, saturated color, high definition, in 3D, while the real me just plodded along in my boring, old colorless, small-screen existence.

But Better-Kate was real. She had been real in that hotel security office, she'd come to life there.

I both wanted it and feared it. She fascinated me. I researched every possible aspect intensely, to bring her vividly to life, I loved her intensity, her passion. I bought lingerie for pictures of her, bought selfie sticks and tripods, studied art and porn to create stunning pictures. I photo-shopped her.

And yet, when the hooker and her boyfriend propositioned me, I'd fled. I turned down invitations from exotic dances. When the Amateur stripper night had come along, I'd chickened out. I wore lingerie and took pictures. I dressed up in sexy outfits but I never wore it outdoors. I was careful as to which pictures showed my face.

My actual sex life was dull, with dates carefully screened through a circle of friends, and encounters that were almost perfunctory and lifeless.

Real life is scary, and bruising, and we're not heroes and conquerors, instead we're all kinds of small things in it, constantly second guessing ourselves. No matter how secure we feel in life, we can just get squashed. I had a job, an apartment, a car, a bank account, a network of friends. But we're all sort of on the knife's edge. You could lose your job in a heartbeat, then you can't pay the rent, you can't pay the phone, suddenly you're homeless, your friends are looking the other way when they see you coming, you fall through the cracks and then what?

That's scary.

Playing pretend hooker was one thing. But there were women out there, desperate, impoverished, selling themselves and not enjoying it, just surviving and hanging on by their fingernails, with no prospects and no safety.

Fantasy was one thing, but reality was precarious and vicious.

Better-Kate was all about adventures, but adventures went wrong all the time. Things could blow up, it was easy to get hurt. Reality was terrifyingly dangerous.

Screw up, and Real-Kate's life could all come tumbling down. I loved Better-Kate, but I couldn't risk being her.

Real-Kate played it safe.

I could just bring her to life for Mike, my unwitting audience, inhabit her, play her, be her. Then put her away.

* * *

I almost got caught.

I was out bar hopping with some women from work, I looked up, and there was Mike, on the other side, sitting with a group of men. His gaze passed over our group without a flicker of recognition.

My blood froze and my heart started pounding. I wanted to angle my chair so that my back was to him. But at the same time I was afraid to. What if he had spotted me and was coming over. I turned away as much as I dared, and took out my compact, pretending to examine my make-up while angling the mirror to see his side of the bar.

Why should he recognize me? The one encounter I'd been dressed like a hooker with heavy make-up.

Still nothing. If he saw me, if he recognized me, our whole intricately detailed sex life would collapse like a house of cards. I would be exposed and embarrassed. I wasn't ready for that.

"Kate?" my friend Amber said. "You look pale. Are you all right?"

I smiled falsely.

"Just tired I guess."

After an excruciating twenty minutes, I made my excuses and left.
I'd become too obsessed and worried about Mike's presence and the
risk of exposure to relax. Instead, my tension had slowly ratcheted
up.

As I made my escape, Mike didn't even look in my direction.
My secret was safe.
Although, I wasn't entirely sure how I felt about that.
I'd been right there in front of him, after all.
It was a little bit insulting, if you ask me.

* * *

I was more careful after that.

The thing was, I really liked Mike. When I wasn't telling him
outrageous sex stories, we talked. We talked about everything.

We talked art, and I told him about my visits to the Louvre and
other galleries, he was genuinely knowledgeable about stuff I faked
my way through, and I genuinely loved listening to him. I'd make
notes about artists or schools he mentioned and looked them up.

We talked cooking, I gave him tips, I told him about foreign
cuisines I'd eaten all over the world. We talked about life and dreams.
He wasn't just a security guard at a hotel, he was working towards a
Master's degree in Architecture.

We told each other jokes, and after a while, we had private jokes
and references we shared between us - or that he shared with Better-
Kate.

It was simple to get him to talk about his personal life, the places
he went, the things he did, his friends, his schedule. He had no idea
that I was lying to him, so no idea that any question had an agenda.
He had no secrets from me. I could have gotten his pin numbers, if I
tried hard enough.

I knew exactly where he lived, I visited his apartment building
one day when he was at work, and stood outside his door. It wasn't
stalker-ish, I told myself, there was absolutely nothing creepy about it.
Just curious.

I did feel a little guilty sometimes. The thing was, I really liked
him. I liked him a lot. And if I made up an entire world for him, an
entire identity, a set of adventures and sexcapades? Where was the
harm in that? I knew for a fact that he'd jerked off to Better-Kate, a
lot. I had a special file of pictures. So clearly, he was enjoying. He was
definitely enjoying, and I was enjoying him enjoying.

Where was the harm? His life was just better for having Better-
Kate as his online/text/cyber friend. No harm at all.

I just felt a little squidgy sometimes, digging into his personal
life, so that I could ensure we didn't actually run into each other in

Perversions and Infidelities / Page 118

the real world, and bring it all crashing down. But it was for his own good.

And it wasn't even a hundred per cent that, I liked him, and I enjoyed learning about his life.

Sometimes, when I knew exactly where he was, at work or particularly someplace else, I'd visit some haunt of his, some place he liked to hang out. I'd sit in a corner of a gaming café, drinking a cup of tea and imagine him in the little group the next table over, animated and excited over their board game.

Or going to an art-house cinema, and watching some foreign movie he'd watched, sitting in the back row, wondering where he'd sat and if he'd been with anyone.

It wasn't creepy at all.

I wasn't a stalker. I just liked him, there was affection, and I enjoyed him talking about the life he lived, even if it was modest compared to my stories. I guess the impulse that lead me to research my stories, also sort of extended to him.

It made me feel closer to him.

* * *

"Fire?" Mike said.

"It was pretty safe," I said. "Or at least, I think it was. Over here people smoke in bars, there are all sorts of flammables everywhere. Even whisky, brandy, hard drinks they'll go up like candles. So doing a fire act on stage, no big deal. I did make sure a fire extinguisher was close by."

"I can't believe it. They let you do it?"

"In the Philippines? You'd be amazed at what they let you do. I couldn't do something like this over in North America," I agreed. "They'd shut you right down. Fire codes and everything, right? But in Manilla, it's like a different world for stripping."

"How so?"

"Less formula I think," I said thoughtfully. "Back home, it's almost ritualistic, it's all about the pole. Here it's a lot more open, a lot more diverse. It's more... I don't know if 'respected' is the right word, but the attitude is definitely different. Legitimate, maybe. Legitimate entertainment. It's more about being an entertainer, putting on a show. It's more wide open to do things. I really like it, it gives me a lot more freedom."

I'd done my homework. One of the strippers I'd chatted with at a bar had talked about dancing in Asia, and I'd picked up on that, followed up by reading online about the Manilla bar scene in obscure corners of the internet.

After the close call, I'd ghosted Mike for a couple of weeks, replying only once or twice perfunctorily. I decided to move Better-Kate out of the country for bold new adventures, just to be safe.

At the same time, I'd gone back through our correspondence and texts to get a sense of Mike's haunts. Our exchanges were our own little world between us.

"I never thought about it," he said. "I suppose I just assumed it was the same everywhere."

"It's not even the same back home," I told him. "We have stripping, and we have burlesque."

"They're not the same?"

"Oh shame on you!" I laughed. "Don't ever let a burlesque dancer hear that, they'll spank you, and not in a good way. It used to be the same, but they've gone off in different directions. I think they split in the sixties or seventies."

I made a mental note to look up the history of Burlesque.

"You do both."

"I'm multi-faceted," I told him. "But in their own way, they're both very narrow. Out here... it's more like dancing, genuine exotic dancing. There's no rules, you can do so much more. There's so much more freedom. I love it."

I paused.

"Although now that I think about it, I think I probably have more freedom and opportunity than a lot of local dancers. I'm North American, I think that by definition, that makes me exotic around here, almost a celebrity, which is weird."

"But a fire act," he asked, "how did you come up with that?"

"It wasn't that hard. Back in junior high, I used to do ballet with scarves."

"Aren't scarves flammable?"

"Funny guy. Yes they are, but part of the routine was swinging around these tennis balls in stockings."

This was true, I'd actually done this back in school, it had been a fad that lasted all of a couple of months for us. But years later, on YouTube, I could see that some women or girls had stuck with it, gaily dancing with ribbons and streamers, leaving audiences mildly entertained and mostly befuddled.

"The fire," I said. "I used to hang with buskers during the summers off when I was studying at University."

I needed to correct that.

"I was busking. Juggling, devil sticks, dancing - pop 'n lock, breaking, whatever got a crowd. I picked up some fire tricks. It's not hard when you know what you're doing."

I'd actually chatted in person with a busker who had done a fire act, part of my inspiration

Perversions and Infidelities / Page 120

"I saw a street performer blowing fire the other day, like a dragon. He juggled these flaming sticks."

"Cool!" I said. My stomach fluttered a little, and I had a cold shiver. It was probably the same guy.

For an instant, I had a Sixth Sense moment - that scene at the end of some old movie, where the guy figures something out, and all the pieces we've been seeing through the whole thing suddenly fall together. I was afraid for a moment that Mike would have that, that suddenly, he'd see all the connections and sources behind all the stories I'd told and realize it was all a con.

"There's a lot of that," I said lamely.

"I'd worry about being burned. After all you're dancing nude."

Back on track.

"I'll tell you a secret. I wear flesh colored gloves, just in case I have to grab it. I can snuff a fireball in my hand. And I smear on this fire resistant gel, like a body lotion, it makes my skin shine, so bonus. And sometimes I put a little food coloring in, to add a little extra. But you know what I have to be really careful of?"

"What?"

"My hair," I said. "That's the big worry, burning my hair."

"Like Michael Jackson."

"Yeah, I don't put flammable gunk in my hair, but still..."

And in my mind's eye, in his mind's eye, I step out onto a Dancer's stage in Manila, nude but for heels and those flesh colored gloves. I stand tall and straight, my breasts are magnificent, my nipples rigid, my skin glistens. I dance confident and commanding, my body bending back and forth. Effortlessly, with perfect control, I wield two flaming sticks like a burlesque dancer's boa, reversing the teasing. Then I swing two fireballs around and around, the crowd gasping as I step in and out, bringing cheers and applause. Finally, on my knees, I throw my head back and breathe a column of flame, as the audience roars and there's a standing ovation.

I am magnificent.

And afterwards, I get into my bathrobe, and my oversized slippers with their lizard toes, and listen to a little music, sipping a glass of boxed wine, back in my humdrum life.

I feel weirdly satisfied. Sometimes it's not even sexual, although I do masturbate constantly to the stories I tell him. Sometimes while I tell them to him, but as often before or after. It pleases me to know that he believes them, that there's this wilder, free-er, bolder version of me in his head.

Time to go to bed.

Long day at the bank tomorrow.

* * *

"Thailand," I announce, "has ruined me. Totally ruined me. I can never have Thai food again, not unless I come back here!"

"That's a long way for Take-Out," he agrees.

Better-Kate's adventures are half travelogue now. Maybe more than half. There are still exotic dance performances, or performances I've seen. I describe watching a live sex show with a statuesque woman and an extraordinarily athletic and well hung dwarf.

There are assignations with wealthy Filipino businessmen and Generals, invitations to high (but not highest) society events and private parties, private shows where sometimes I'm the performer, and sometimes the audience, but it's always exciting and transgressive. Better-Kate is sexually unconquerable and utterly fearless, free with her body in a way that transcends morals.

But there's more. I describe for him the sunrise over the Manilla skyline, the beaches of Luzon, extremes of wealth and poverty. There's an encounter with a monkey-like tarsier. A game of strip poke with billionaires where I clean them out, and finally in frustration, they simply pay me to take off my clothes. Flying over the mountains in a tiny plane.

Eventually, Better-Kate moves on, briefly stopping in Singapore. Then to Thailand and descriptions of jungles and ancient Buddhist temples, the night life of Bangkok, rude American tourists, ladyboys, the beauty of the Thai people, the exquisite food.

I always wanted to travel. And as I researched, scouring the internet and travel books, looking at pictures and videos, and putting myself in the middle of it, embroidering detail after detail, imagining taste and texture, heat and the sweat of my skin under clothes, the sounds of insects or street life, the smells... In a way, I'm there with him. Telling him, sharing it with him makes it vivid for me.

The lies make it real for both of us.

* * *

I went on a date. My life didn't stop when Better-Kate came along. I still went out with friends, I went on dates.

He was all right. His name was Tom. He worked at a law firm doing tax cases. He was sincere and mildly funny. He clings to his sense of humor, because he did tax cases, and he thought wit kept him from turning into a drone.

The date went well, we did all the usual things, dinner and drinks. The bar was too loud, so I invited him back to my place, where we made out on the couch and then took it into the bedroom.

The sex was perfectly acceptable.

In my mind, as we laid together, I reconfigured him into a taut bodied young German, not a trace of fat on his rigid, rippled frame. A casual tourist, a backpacker, in Bangkok that Better-Kate connects with, who after incandescent, wildly athletic sex, talks about mountain climbing and his ambition to make an assault on Mount Everest.

Tom and I saw each other a couple of times. But after that, the mild chemistry just sputtered out.

I didn't miss him.

* * *

We discussed whether I should get nipple piercings, going back and forth over the subject.

In her lines of work, Better-Kate should get breast implants. And honestly, I'm mildly intrigued by them.

On one of my visits to a bar, a stripper allowed me to fondle hers. There was something intriguing about their soft rigidity, the yielding firmness. There was a sense of presence there, of confidence or assertiveness that surprised me. I understood a little better why some women got them and why they liked them.

I shared these thoughts with Mike. Better-Kate feels more thoughtful than I am. She was more observant, she paid closer attention to the world, and gave it more reflection.

In a weird way, I feel shallower. But then again she's off traveling the world, seeing new places and new faces. Real life is more humdrum, full of consistency and repetition.

Better-Kate has thought about breast implants, she shared with Mike. Maybe someday. But for now, she likes her body natural. Mike concurs, he liked her body too.

The nipple piercings we discussed at more length. I'm actually intrigued by the thought of getting them for real. The idea of going to work, of going through the monotony of life, with a secret under my clothes, that's exciting to me. I think that they'd look good.

Mike agrees.

I almost do it. But then I chicken out. Because I always chicken out.

Better-Kate tells Mike she changed her mind, for now.

* * *

Dubai, I talk about sandstorms. The awful unbearable heat. The incredible wealth and opulence, and the hidden but pervasive near slavery. I reveal that the Burq Khalifa, the tallest building in the world, is not connected to water and sewer, and so every morning at five am, dozens of trucks line up to cart away sewage and deliver water for showers and baths.

I tell him about straddling a perfumed Sheikh in his limousine on a crowded street, the windows blacked of course. Coarse hands on my body, a mixture of repugnance and excitement.

Perversions and Infidelities / Page 123

I've been in a limousine in real life, at least, for my high school graduation, a bunch of us in over-ruffled dresses, drinking non-alcoholic wine, giggling about the future.

I'd have rather had the Sheikh.

* * *

"This woman, she's dressed like a nun, except that it's a fetish nun. Her habit and wimple is red latex, skin tight, strategically exposed in places. She's got piercings and little bells hanging from chains on the piercings between her legs. And there's a Dominatrix with what looks like a shock wand, and she's touching the nun with it to make the bells ring."

"That's pretty freaky," Mike responds.

I'm describing a night at a fetish club in Berlin, high on MDMA, and the gorgeous kaleidoscope of bodies of every size and shape covered in latex, leather and costumes so extreme as to be ludicrous.

"Now the next one up on stage, the next few, men and women. They're not dressed nearly as wildly as that. But they're wearing these metal plates over strategic parts of their body, like their breasts or crotch. The Dominatrix, she takes this industrial grinder, and jams it into their crotches."

"Holy shit," Mike texts.

"The shower of sparks is amazing, it just lights up the whole stage. It reaches ten feet in the air. The sub is shaking and moaning loudly. You can hear him over the sound of the grinder. He's pretending to have an orgasm. Or maybe he's actually having one, I wouldn't be surprised. After, the Dom walks around the stage waving this piece of industrial machinery over her head, and then the next one comes forward."

I pause.

"Did you get the pictures I sent you?"

"Oh yes, amazing. Did you take them?"

I laugh, prepared for the question, prepared with an answer.

"No, I would have been afraid to. There was a photographer there. He posted them online."

"What were you wearing?"

"I was pretty conservative for that crowd. Topless. I wore a Catwoman mask, my black PVC thigh highs, and a strap on with a twelve inch black dildo."

"I think I can see you in some of the pictures, in the background."

Or a woman that can pass for me. I've sent him pictures now and then, some quite explicit ones, depending on my levels of excitement or adventurousness. I've actually bought lingerie just for some

Perversions and Infidelities / Page 124

pictures, or ventured to some locations. My boldest picture was in a run-down toilet stall, giving a fake blow job to an imaginary stranger.

Other pictures from exotic locations, I stole from the internet and painstakingly learned to Photoshop myself into them.

The conversation turns to strap-ons, and I describe the night, embroidering details as always, and ramming transvestites in the basement of the club.

"I thought I was freaky! That was a whole other level."

And then later.

"I should be back in a couple of weeks. Do you want to get together?"

Oh so casually. But I've shocked myself. Where had that come from? My heart starts to race, my stomach flips with excitement, with terror and eagerness, even though I know what the answer will be.

"Sure."

The answer was just as casual, but I'm imagining his shock, the sudden instant surge of his erection. The wild, eager, heart stopping enthusiasm and elation on his side. Or am I just imagining it.

"Cool," I type. "I'll let you know."

What did I just do?

* * *

Given our strange relationship, choosing what to wear was a challenge.

All afternoon I debated. Wear something normal? After all the stories I'd told him? Fetish clubs in Germany, orgies in Amsterdam, dancing my way through Southeast Asia?

I'd sent him pictures of my vagina. Several.

Technically, they could have been anyone's vagina, and I almost used some I'd found on the internet, but in the end, I'd opted for authenticity. After all, it wasn't as if my face was in my more explicit pictures.

What to wear? The only option was to go big, and by that, I meant slutty sex goddess. At first, I opted to wear the same outfit, or lack of outfit, as I'd worn on our first encounter. Sexy, cheap, nostalgic.

Yeah, wearing it around the apartment or on the way to my car in the parkade was one thing. Out in public where people would see? Nope.

So I opted for a trench coat over it - that was what I'd worn on the way to meet Jay. A different trench coat. But I couldn't help the feeling of Deja vu.

I tried on the thigh high fetish boots and walked around experimentally. No way. They'd never been really comfortable, and each time I'd worn them, I'd gotten less willing. Instead, I opted for some very nice red, calf-length boots with slightly less torturous heels.

Naked, I checked them out in the mirror. Not bad.

I tried with the miniskirt, turning this way and that, and sucking on my lower lip. Without the vinyl boots going all the way up my thighs, there was something missing - that was such an expanse of bare flesh from calf to miniskirt. I added fishnet patterned stay ups. It worked with the miniskirt.

I tried on the bustier? I needed a little more. I had a fishnet top that would go well with the stay up stockings. I tried that. Nice, but it clashed with the bustier, I was 'overdressed slutty.' Tried it without the bustier, too much nipple action. Pasties? That was stupid. I tried a bunch of different tops, tank tops, tube tops, sequined tops, plunging necklines, really tight showing the outline of breasts and nipples, or loose and deep so you could look down my cleavage and maybe when I moved, catch a glimpse of nipple. Tops with transparent panels.

I'd accumulated a remarkable collection of slut-wear.

In the end, I chickened out and went with a plunging red tank top, with a loose fishnet over it. It was still embarrassing to be seen in public with it, but I'd wear the trench coat.

I stared at the full length mirror, boots and stay-ups, miniskirt, tank top, lots of skin. I sighed, somehow, I felt a little awkward, like a little girl dressing in grown-up clothes.

Better-Kate would have worn this so much better. Better-Kate would have just worn whatever she wanted without a thought, no second guessing, and she would have been stunning.

* * *

That afternoon he was already waiting for me when my cab arrived at Barleys, a bar on the edge of the seedy side of town. The autumn air was cool, but the patio section was still open, and he was sitting by the railing under an umbrella.

I smiled and waved back as I got out of the cab. But my stomach was doing flip flops, my heart was racing.

I'd planned an exit from the cab, the folds of the trench coat parting as I swung my leg out, the red boot and length of stocking all the way up to my thigh momentarily on display. But I forgot all that. Instead it felt like I stumbled out, gracelessly, like a clod.

It was night and day between how I actually moved, and the flamboyant grace and poise that Better-Kate radiated effortlessly.

Still, I managed to get up the stairs and into a chair opposite him, without embarrassing myself. I was excited but terrified, not of him, but of making a mess of it. I was aroused, but intimidated. I wanted to just run away. This whole thing was such a mistake, I needed to go back to text messages and emails and occasional phone calls, exotic stories and carefully staged pictures from the safety of my apartment. Right now, he was altogether too real, too three-dimensional.

He was just sitting opposite me, blushing slightly.

I should say something. I smiled and unconsciously licked my lips, tasting the gloss.

"So here we are?" I offered.

Mentally, I kicked myself for being so lame.

"Here we are," he agreed.

Oh god, after all those online exchanges, we had nothing to talk about in real life!

"Nice outfit."

"Thanks," I said, clutching the trench coat, it was practically buttoned up to my neck. I crossed my legs in a non-Sharon Stone way, which drew his attention to my legs and made me blush. Why? I'd wanted him to see my legs as I was riding over in the cab. I should unbutton the coat... But I couldn't.

The waitress came over, and I chatted with her about selections until I ordered a Shiraz red wine. He was having a beer.

"It's on me," he said quickly, before she left.

Nervous, he was nervous. His movements a little too quick. He kept glancing at my legs, and when he looked at me, I could tell he was mentally trying to see through the trench coat. Definitely nervous.

Well, that made two of us.

Oddly, talking to the waitress, the three of us interacting, had helped me regain some self-possession. I undid a button from the trench coat, just one, but it was a start. I re-crossed my legs, again in a non-Sharon Stone way, but he watched anyway.

We chatted, at first about the weather, and then about the city. I pretended not to have been here for a while. I asked him about his job and his interests. The waitress brought our drinks, and with the wine, I was almost starting to relax.

Then he asked about Thailand.

My heart skipped a beat, and for a moment, I was frozen, not sure what to say. Then, suddenly, I had the weirdest Deja vu, it was like I was twelve and in elementary school, the teacher calling on me out of the blue, and this weird elation when I realized that I absolutely had the right answer, the bestest answer!

I can do this, I thought, as I smiled and lied, visualizing photographs in my mind of an old abandoned temple up the river and embroidering details of the journey, the call of birds, the insects the suffocating heat and humidity and the decaying grandeur of the ancient stones.

In the back of my mind I made up an impromptu tryst with an androgynous but swarthy Thai tour guide, a quick unforgettable encounter up against a stone wall, surrounded by vines and parrot calls. Force of habit. I didn't tell him that part of it though.

Suddenly, I was Better-Kate, or at least I'd slipped into playing her, had grabbed onto her confidence and easy sexuality. I undid more buttons, leaned forward, shifted casually in my chair. His eyes glittered as I exposed more. Another glass of wine and he watched like a hawk as I touched lips to glass and sipped.

There were more questions, more stories, we laughed and chatted. He told his own stories, none so adventurous as mine, but these were heartfelt and genuine. His were true, and they were sweet, I enjoyed them.

I leaned back and as he tried not to look at my cleavage, I let the tip of my boot accidentally brush against his calf.

"You used to work around here," he asked. The trench coat was completely unbuttoned and open, still hanging from my shoulders because I was chicken, but still exhibitionistic. The waitress when she came back with the third glass had looked me up and down.

Every time I shifted in my seat, Mike glanced at my legs, trying to see up my skirt. I liked that. I let the miniskirt ride up so that he could see the smooth thighs above the stocking, and then pulled it down.

I turned, looking over my shoulder, feeling the sway of my breast. It's amazing how vividly aware you are of your own body when you know someone else is watching, drinking it in. Especially when you know how exciting it is for them, and you want it to be.

"Yes," I said. "Yes, I did."

I remembered my lunch with the hooker and her pimp, sorry, 'boyfriend', the hand on my knee.

"We used to all eat together at Sammy's Burgers," I said. "Slow nights, or just taking a break with the girls. We'd all laugh together."

I turned back.

"Is Sammy's still there?"

"Yes."

"Good burgers," I told him. "All the girls thought so. Homemade, you know. Nothing like it."

"We can check it out, if you're hungry," he offered.

I shrugged.

"Maybe later."

"Where did you used to work out of?"

Trick question? Was he suspicious? No, just asking. Besides, I knew this one.

"Different hotels," I replied. "The Stock, the Regency. My favourite was the Fairmont, that used to be high class, and you know, even run down, it had a mystique."

"The Georgia?"

I that was the closest one to us, just down the street. The cab had gone right past it.

"That one too."

I smiled.

"How much did you charge?"

"That would be telling," I teased, smiling at him over my wine glass. I slouched back a little, and his eyes darted to my breasts.

I should have gone with a push up bra, or maybe the bustier. Or the tight number with the transparent panel. Real-Kate couldn't help second guessing everything to death!

I pushed her down, and brought up Better-Kate to give him a smokey look, "Asking for any particular reason?"

"Just curious," he blushed deeply.

"What do you think? What's the going rate these days?" I asked.

"I don't know. A hundred?" Which was actually the going rate. I wanted to tease and ask how he knew. Maybe I could get another deep blush. But I decided not to.

"A hundred?" I let my half empty wine glass twirl slightly on my fingertips. "Surely not."

"A hundred and twenty?"

I rolled my eyes, and took another sip to cover my excitement. I couldn't believe it. It was happening. I'd been trying to think how to broach the subject, trying to figure out how to move us from here to the next step. And here it was, I couldn't believe how simple it was. Every date should be like this - just make an offer.

"A hundred and fifty?"

I finished my glass and set it down on the table, crossing and uncrossing my legs in the Sharon Stone way. I smiled at him and said one word.

"Sold."

* * *

"Cool!"

He sounded so excited and relived at once, it was kind of sweet. We'd already had sex, and since then, I'd filled him up with a hundred stories of raunchy adventures. I couldn't imagine why he might have doubted we were going to fuck.

Hell, I wanted to fuck. Sure, I'd struggled with cold feet. But seriously, it had been in my mind since I'd agreed to meet again. And at some point, after the first glass of Shiraz, I'd firmed up the decision to climb up and down him like he was made of ladders. The only challenge was how to get there.

"Money up front," I said. My nervousness had evaporated, I was playing a role, and I wanted to play it to the hilt.

"Here?"

"Sure," I said confidently. "Put it on the table."

He opened his wallet and laid out the bills. I made a show of counting it and slipped it into the trench coat pocket. There were a few other people at tables now. Had they noticed? Were they wondering? Making assumptions?

Mike paid our bill, the Waitress giving me side eyes at the way I was dressed. I smiled back, wishing I could have counted the cash in front of her. We stood together. I left the trench coat unbuttoned, aware of male glances sliding off me. My nipples were hard, my breasts swayed with each move. The miniskirt had ridden up just enough that the tops of stockings and a little bit more showed.

"So," I asked, as we walked by patrons, "where are we going to go? Your place."

"Georgia. I rented a room. It was the closest. A short walk."

I laughed. Perfect.

"Oh my, you were pretty sure of yourself, weren't you?"

Even without looking, I could tell he was blushing, and I had this weird flood of affection for him.

"I was hoping."

"Well I hope you didn't go for their hourly rate," I said.

"No, I paid for a whole night there," he said, almost apologetically. "I figured... you know."

I patted his hand.

"Good boy."

* * *

I'd never been inside the Georgia, or any of the downtown hotels that catered to indigents and prostitutes. I'd known about the Fairmont and its faded grandeur, because of a newspaper article in the Arts & Culture section. But if the Georgia had ever been classy, there was no sign of it.

The lobby was stripped of all furniture but wooden bench and a broken pay phone. You could tell it had once been expansive, but a crude retrofitted wall had been constructed, with cheap doorways, all the walls covered with too many coats of cheap paint. One of the doors said "Restaurant." The whole place had that musty dusty heaviness that you get sometime with decaying buildings, a place that's had its day long ago, and is just patiently marking time until the wrecking ball comes.

Perversions and Infidelities / Page 130

The front desk was enclosed in a glass partition, or perhaps thick Plexiglas judging by the scratches. Behind it there was a fat old man in a sweat stained shirt and muttonchop sideburns, watching a small television. He looked up at us.

I smiled and nodded at the old man as if I came here regularly. He looked me up and down with a kind of practiced appreciation, and nodded back.

"Long time," I said.

He glanced at me, indifferent, and selected a safe reply.

"Haven't seen you around in a while."

"I've been travelling," I told him.

He grunted.

That had gone perfectly.

Mike waved his key, and the man pressed a hidden button. The metal door buzzed and we went through.

"Just so you know," I said in the elevator, "I wanted to wear the exact outfit I was wearing when we met. But a heel broke."

"You look good."

"Thanks. I am wearing the same underwear."

"I don't remember you wearing underwear."

I smiled.

"Exactly."

I wasn't looking directly at him, but I was sure he blushed. My smile stretched into a grin, and I took his hand in mine.

Upstairs it was as seedy as you would expect, the carpet worn through, the walls and fixtures covered with multiple coats of paint. Our room was a bed, a bathroom, a single dresser-table and a chair. The musty odor was even stronger. How many people had fucked on that bed? The mind boggled.

I heard a noise.

"Listen," I held a hand up, motioning silence, listening hard at the wall next to the door.

As we listened, we could just barely hear the rhythmic sound of springs, a series of feminine grunts, and then very clearly, a woman's voice. "Oh god, oh yes, fuck me, now, now, now!"

I grinned.

"Someone's having fun," I whispered, as if they could hear us if we were too loud and I didn't want to interrupt them. I was glad of the distraction, I had this hesitancy, it seemed that each step left me uncertain. Here we were in the room, now what? Sure, sex, but how do you get there?

I let the trench coat slide off my shoulders as he stepped towards me. He wrapped one hand around my waist, as I caught the other one and guided it to my breast feeling his fingers splay to cup it. In my heels we were the same height, I pressed my lips to his.

The kiss felt... right. His lips were softer than I expected, almost tentative. We hadn't kissed at all that first time. His hand slid down to my bare skin and then slid back up under my tank top, pushing it upwards. The intimacy of the touch gave me this little wet shiver and I felt my heart give a little bump. We kissed harder, more passionately. His lips parted, and my tongue flickered in, lightly touching the tip of his.

His head dipped, then he was nibbling at my earlobe. I turned my head slightly, to give him better access, enjoying the way his tongue darted just below. I arched my neck, smiling with pleasure, feeling his body pressing against me as his kisses followed one after the other, down my throat, along my shoulder, making me shiver with pleasure. I loved the feel of his hands on my bare skin, the way he cupped my breast.

He went lower, bending to where my tank top had been pushed up, sliding over it to take my nipple into his mouth. I moaned slightly, and slid my fingers through his hair at the back of his head, pushing him harder onto my rigid nipple.

"Oh yes," I whispered, "suck harder."

I moaned again as his cheeks caved and I could feel the wet suction, making my nipple throb and tingle.

I was going to get my nipples pierced, I decided. Fuck Real-Kate and her chickenshit ways. I was going to get it done, even if Better-Kate had to drag Real-Kate kicking and screaming.

Disappointingly, he left my nipple. For a second, he lightly kissed the other, and went lower.

Oh my, I thought, where is this going?

Then he was kneeling in front of me. His hands, palms flat, moving slowly from thighs, to belly to breast, a sensual exploration that had me purring like a kitten. I pulled my miniskirt up to my waist and leaned back against the dresser, parting my legs and bending my knees to give him better access. I was wet with anticipation and excitement, panting slightly, almost on the edge of trembling. I knew what he wanted, and I wanted him to have it. I ran my fingers through his hair, but he needed no guidance.

"Oh my!" I whispered suddenly, my eyes opening

Oh what was that? His tongue unerringly found my clit, a single wet press, a hint of motion, and lifted, leaving nothing but lingering shock and his warm breath.

I caught my breath. It was delicious.

He reached around behind my thighs, his arms snaking forward, fingers reaching in from each side to part my lips, spreading them from my clit, pulling back on the hood. I shivered at the intimate exposure. His tongue darted in again, touching, teasing, never lingering.

"Oh my!" I said more forcefully. "Oh my! You are good!"

My clit felt like it was radiating sheer pleasure, every touch and lash of his tongue sent a shiver through me. I'd had men go down on me, but... oh wow... never like this. Mostly it had just been lapping away, a dog-like persistence until I was massaged into orgasm.

But this, this was heaven. This was ballet, my hips twitched to the touches of his tongue, it was nowhere and everywhere, triggering waves of sensation, never quite the same, but each delightful.

"Fuck!" I said. "Where did you learn this?"

He lifted his head, to speak, and almost desperately, I shoved his face back between his legs, grinding my mound against his face.

"Never mind," I said quickly. "Tell me later. Right now, just keep on doing this. Oh wow!"

I spread my legs a little wider, leaning back and reaching down to press fingers and pull against my pubic mound, exposing my clit to him that much more. His tongue slithered down between my labua, and then back again, making the insides of my thighs tremble.

I knew where he'd learned it! Of course, of course, I thought, floating on his flickering tongue. I'd told him, how to do it.

I'd laid it out, explaining, describing, fantasizing an oral sex inspired by my own masturbation laced with pornography, erotica and my own imagination fabricating endless detail.

The bastard had been taking notes all along. The fucker. The delicious, delirious fucker.

"Oh my gods," I cried out, and jammed his face against my mound, grinding for a moment, before releasing him to let his lips and tongue dance and tease. I could feel his hot moist breath down my thighs, my labia open, my vagina dilating. I wished he'd stick a finger, two fingers up inside me, that would be delirious.

He did something with his tongue, I couldn't visualize just what, but it was wet and muscular and slithered like an eel in exactly the right way.

"Yes, yes, yes!" I cried. "Exactly that, do that, do that!"

Suddenly, as the sensation repeated again and again I could feel the pleasure, the sensation coalescing into a blinding white ball between my legs, lightning crawling up my spine. I grabbed his head with both hands, my thighs both rigid and trembling like jelly, spasming open and then clamping around him, opening again. I threw my head back, my body going stiff, and just cried out with ecstasy, and just came, and came.

It faded, leaving me breathless, and panting, little spots across my vision. Suddenly, I felt drenched with sweat, and weak as a kitten, my muscles like water.

Mike rose from between my legs, arms around me, as I sat with my ass on the dresser, it was all that was holding me up.

Perversions and Infidelities / Page 133

He said something, I didn't register it.

"Okay," I breathed. "Okay, you just earned a refund. I might have to pay you. Oh, I'm taking that home with me."

"It was good?" he asked.

I grinned, cute little attention whore that he was. He played my pussy like a harp, and now he was begging for affirmation? I kissed him.

"I can live with it."

I plucked at his shirt.

"You're really overdressed," I whispered, undoing a button. I reached down with one hand, feeling him rock hard in his pants, fingers tracing the outlines of a cock I remembered so well.

"You're hardly dressed at all," he replied.

That made me giggle. I pulled off my fishnet and tank top, it was already pushed up over my breasts to my armpits. I discarded it on the floor. He stared at my breasts, not just stared, worshiped, transfixed. They hypnotized him, it was if they were miraculous. I loved it. I arched my back, thrusting them forward, wanting him to stare and stare, drinking up his arousal and attention.

"Aren't they just great!" I exulted, celebrating my amazing breasts. Why hadn't I ever noticed how terrific they were before? "Why would I need implants?"

"They're perfect," he agreed.

I reached out to his shirt, half unbuttoned and pressed my palms against his bare flesh, sliding them across, feeling his pectorals and nipples. He was hastily undoing the rest of the buttons and pulling the shirt tails out. My hands drifted lower, pulling at his belt.

I slipped off the dresser, my legs still wobbly. Oh man that had been good, I was still a little shocked by how good he'd been.

I shoved my hand into his loosened pants feeling my way across his boxers. Frustrated, I pulled back and reached again, this time fingertips gliding down bare skin thick with wiry hair. My hand curled around his bare erection and I felt it throbbing, the tip already wet and slick. The feel of it, the texture, the hardness, my own boldness thrilled me.

"Oh hello in there!" I whispered, delighted. "I remember you! Did you miss me?"

Mike pulled my miniskirt down my hips. I let it fall. We stumbled towards the bed as he shrugged out of his shirt and kicked off his shoes. His pants fell clunking around his ankles, weighted down by wallet and phone and belt, while his boxers were twisted around his thighs. I kept my fingers wrapped around his cock, I didn't want to let it go.

I was almost crazed with sexual excitement, I couldn't think of anything else. I wanted him so badly. I wanted to feel him in me, I wanted him looking at me, touching me. I felt radiant, as if I was glowing, incandescent with erotic fire.

As we approached the bed, he turned me around nibbling at the back of my neck, his hands reaching around cupping my breasts, making me purr like a cat. I loved the way he touched me, I wanted him to keep touching me, exploring me forever. I took one of his hands, and slid it down my body, between my legs.

"Feel this," I husked, pressing his hand against my mound, fingers parting my labia. "I'm so wet, so fucking wet!"

Gently, he pushed me on my back. I took the cue, bending forward, climbing onto the bed, my knees at the lip, going down to my elbows as he gripped my hips. I could feel him moving behind me, almost delaying, hands lifting. I pushed my ass back towards him.

"Just a minute," he gasped. I could feel him kicking off his boxers and pants, his hand returning to my ass, pressing down to steady himself. My thighs backed against his, I could feel his erection beneath us. Steadying on one elbow, I reached for it, holding it for a second.

"Give it to me," I moaned.

"Spread wider," he husked, pushing down. My knees went wider on the bed, lowering.

Then suddenly, I felt him at my lips, a moment of probing, finding me, sliding against my clit, and then up to my entry.

Then a wonderful deep thrust! I gasped and arched my back to accept it deeper.

"Oh yes!" I cried out.

His hands had locked on my hips, holding me in place, as he started to pound with powerful thrusts. Slightly off balance on only one elbow, my face hit the bed for an instant until I could get both arms under me, my thighs spreading wider, feeling him deeper. I arched my back, mewing with pleasure. I made guttural noises of sheer pleasure, loving the feel of his hands, the tension that radiated off him, the cock hard and hot and wildly rigid pistoning rapidly in me. I felt like a rag doll on his cock, my body flung this way and that with each thrust, sensitive to every movement, the swing of my breasts, the flex of thighs and elbow and back, the toss of my hair. With him behind me, invisible, it felt almost like I was in my own world, alone and experiencing a sexual earthquake.

Wild intense thrusting gave way to more measured strokes, steadily increasing in speed and intensity, the strokes shortening even as the thrusts became harder. His hands on my hips were like iron, fingers digging into my flesh. He loosed me, reaching out to grab my shoulder and pull me harder onto his rock-hard erection. His free hand sliding down my sweat drenched back.

I flashed on our previous fuck, the way he'd gripped my hips and thrust into me from behind, the sensations and memory so vivid that the two experiences seemed to merge together, bringing a renewed visceral intensity. Had the last few months happened? Mike's cock rigid and pumping seemed so intense, so real, so permanent and immediate. All I knew was that I wanted it, I wanted it forever, even inside me now it wasn't enough.

"More," I screamed. "More cock! Harder! Fuck me harder!"

This seemed to set him off, his grip on my shoulder past my neck tightening. His other hand dug into my ass, it was as if he was physically pulling me back onto his cock with each forward thrust. My ass smacked against his hips with a series of rapid wet slapping sounds, almost stinging as if he was spanking me. Animalistic grunts poured out from behind me, becoming deeper and coarser.

It was too intense, my second orgasm felt like it poured over me, like a flood, an intense wave and release. I cried out, my body going stiff. My face hit the bed again, back arching and I slid forward stiffening, slipping from his grip. There was an almost painful combination of regret and relief as I felt his cock slipping out of me as I went rigid, it was too much, too intense, and yet not enough, I didn't want to let it go.

I felt him climbing onto the bed on top of me, his weight settling over me like a flesh blanket, hairy and sweaty and welcome. I reveled in it, wanting to pull him further over me. I could feel his erection against my ass cheek, ready and waiting.

Mike let me catch my breath. I twisted under him, and he rolled off, the two of us, side by side in bed.

I loved looking at him, his plain unassuming face, bursting with humanity. I reached out to stroke his arm, drawing fingertips from there to hairy chest. Hair on his arms, his chest, wiry and undisciplined. He'd be hopeless as a man-scaping case, I thought. But then, that was him all over, a little thick, a little heavy, muscles like slabs covered with a layer of fat. His body was a million miles away from the gym sculpted men I'd dated, their body hair carefully pruned, sprayed, body-washed and exfoliated.

There was something so viscerally authentic to him that overcame his apparent ordinariness. I couldn't stop looking at him. I wanted to touch him, and keep touching him all over, to feel him on my fingertips and palms. I wanted to turn him over to look at his ass, to explore every inch of him. I wanted to lick him like an ice cream cone, every bit of him.

"Pretty intense, uh?" he was breathless. His eyes were luminous, staring at me. I grabbed his hand, and drew it to my breast.

"Oh yeah, just feel that," I replied. "My heart is just pounding."

His eyes shifted down from my gaze to my breasts. I lifted one knee, exposing myself, letting him look, wanting him to look, to see me. I wanted to feel his gaze, the lust and fascination in it.

My hand slid down towards his erection. I felt slick rubber. Glancing down, I saw a condom. Right, I thought. I'd felt it back when I'd reached under on the bed, but it had been so quick, and I'd been so impassioned, I hadn't really registered it.

I toyed with his erection, letting my fingers crawl down its length, until my palm was splayed, cradling full hairy testicles.

"I didn't even notice you put it on," I said.

"Yeah," he agreed.

"You're clean right?" I asked, plucking at the base of the rubber, rolling it back a little. "I want to feel you. The real you. I want to feel this naked."

"You sure?"

I'd gone on birth control pills for a month just for this meeting, just in case. I was absolutely sure.

"Oh yes," I whispered. I pushed him onto his back and rose up on one elbow, pulling on the condom, stretching the rubber out as it clung to his erection. It came off with a tiny wet noise, and then his raw cock was in my hand, slimy with condom sweat, but full and glorious, and mine. I wrapped my fingers around his cock, feeling it throb, feeling possessive.

I'd felt this way before, I remembered, during our first time. A moment, a feeling where I hadn't just held it, but I wanted it, I wanted to possess it, to own it. A feeling like I'd taken it for my own, it belonged to me now. Mine, all mine!

It was such a strange sensation. I couldn't ever remember feeling this possessive about any of my other lovers' cocks. They'd always firmly belonged on their men, I'd had no urge to claim, no sense of wanting to own.

I stared at it, my hand sliding up and down, fascinated by his erection, acutely conscious of how unique this fascination was, and wondering why it was so. It didn't matter, I just wanted it.

I didn't just want it. I wanted it to be mine.

I dipped my head over it, taking his glans in my mouth. I tasted cock sweat and smeared pre-cum and the residue of sour latex, and licked the prepuce, triggering a shudder through his body. I loved the response, if not the taste.

"Ready to go," I asked.

I laid back, pulling his cock towards me, his body floating after. I got under him, spreading my legs, pulling my knees back up, holding him in both hands as he hovered above me. I loved looking up at him, loved him suspended above me. I looked into his face as he stared down at me, and let my gaze drift down the length of him, drinking him in.

"Wait," I whispered. "My boots."

They'd been sexy. But my feet were starting to sweat, which was less than sexy. And I was afraid of the heels tearing the sheets.

"Take them off for me," I husked, holding my legs straight up in the air.

"Sure," he leaned back on his haunches, his erection standing up proudly. Tentatively, he ran his hands down my left boot, found the zipper at the top of the calf and pulled it back to my ankle, pulling the boot off. He kissed my calf, and then repeated on the other one. The boots clumped on the side of the bed. I wiggled my toes, enjoying the relief.

"The stockings?" he asked.

"Sure," I replied.

"I kind of like them actually," he said.

"Then we'll leave them on."

He leaned forward, sweeping over me. I felt the bed shift with his weight, the depressions as his palms pressed down on either side of me. The way he loomed over me, his erection eager and dangling below us, excited me.

I pulled my legs higher, knees bent, spread wide for him. I could feel my lips wide, practically gaping for him. This time, I wanted to see him, I wanted to watch his cock slide into me, as if I was watching a porn film, I wanted to see, as well as feel, him entering. I guided him down, rubbing the head of his cock deliciously against my clit, feeling the shape of him stroking up along my pubic mound, and then down, finding the wetness, the dripping folds, my entrance.

"Slow this time," I whispered. "I want to feel it this time, I want to savor it."

"I'll try," he whispered above me, looking down as well.

"This is the first time for us," I whispered. "Skin to skin, bare. I want to memorize this, this intimacy."

The head of his cock pressed between my lips, opening me. I arched my back as it paused, sliding just a little further into my vagina.

"Yes," he whispered. "You feel so good. So good."

I relaxed, the arch disappearing, my knees going a little higher. He slid slowly into me with exquisite sweetness as I reveled in his progress inch by inch, until his hairy crotch was pressed flat against me, grinding against my mound, flattening my clit hood, rubbing against my clit with intimate tension. It felt so vivid, I almost felt as if I could count each curling pubic hair.

He began to pull back with exquisite slowness, I hooked my thighs around him, heels almost touching as they pressed into his ass.

"Don't go too far," I giggled. "I wouldn't want you to get lost."

"Oh don't worry," he assured me, "I'm coming right back."

His head dipped to kiss me. As we broke the kiss, his head and shoulders lifted, I felt his hips move as he kept his promise to return, sliding deep within me. I pressed my heels into his ass, to encourage him deeper, and reached up with my arms to draw him down, until our sweat covered bodies were sliding together.

We fucked like that, with me pinned like a butterfly under him, beautiful wings spread gloriously wide, penetrated deep. Long slow thrusts succeeded each other, punctuated by kisses, my hands up and down his body, feeling him, exploring him. My hips shifted, knees and legs bending and spreading, changing angles with each stroke.

We climbed into frantic hard pounding as one or the other of us neared orgasm, and then changed pace, pushing back the climax in favor of sensual exploration. I'd come twice, but I wanted more now, I wanted the intimacy of his body, the feel of his cock, I wanted to prolong it, spread it out, immerse myself in it. To treat it like wine and sip it slowly, savoring each taste, each mouthful, the intimacy of each thrust inside me, the sensation of him so deep.

The feeling felt mutual, it felt like he was drinking me in as much as I drank him, and that excited me. I reached up, ran my hands all over his body, drew him close and kissed him. I wanted to be drunk by him. I wanted him drunk on me, intoxicated. I wanted him to have me, to drown in me with an intensity that surprised me. I felt it, and felt it feeding my own fascination.

As our bodies moved against each other, our eyes met, and I remembered the first encounter, the way I'd wanted him to come into me from behind so that I didn't have to look at him. There was a flicker of shame. That thought felt so alien, the first fuck almost unreal, a kind of crude sketch of genuine intensity.

But if that was hollow and superficial, it felt as if every other fuck in my life was nothing, the other men, the blow jobs, the cocks between my legs, the hollow pace-less orgasms that seemed no more consequential than a breeze blowing through an empty room.

It felt like I was finally having sex, and it was glorious!

And it wasn't enough. I wanted more of him, I wanted him everywhere. He needed two cocks, or three, he needed six hands, all of them touching me.

I pulled him down and thrust my tongue in his mouth, wrapping my arms and legs around him as tightly as I could. In this position, his cock wasn't deep enough, even grinding together.

"Let's change," I whispered. "I want to go on top."

"Okay."

We rolled, and then I was straddling him, looking down. One of my stockings was gone and the other was down to my knee, so much for stay ups. I drew my knees together, lifting my hips above him. He held my thighs as I hovered over his erection, guiding it into place and relaxing. Moaning, I sank down on him, a sensation so different from being entered. I let my weight settle, sinking deep, pushing him up inside.

I leaned forward a bit, intimately aware of how the motion made my breasts sway, and vividly aware and enjoying the way his eyes tracked that motion.

I looked down at him, and drew his hands up until they were cupping my breasts, remembering how he'd clutched them the last time, his fingers like vises, digging in, leaving bruises.

I stared at his eyes, his pupils dilated, the sheen of sweat on his forehead. I felt the motion of his cock stiff and curving inside me as I rocked on it, the feel of the worn hotel sheets against my knees and toes. Putting my palm flat against his chest, I wallowed in the texture of his skin, the curling hairs mashed flat, the sweat, the firmness of muscle beneath the slight layer of fat, the bone beneath the muscle, the faintest throb of a heartbeat. Our breaths came in tandem, rasping and measured. Sweat trickled down my spine, dried on my forearms. I could smell him, and us, the rich scent of our bodies and breath, of our sweat and exertions and arousal.

It was all so intensely vivid in a way I'd never experienced. I could practically count his pores, and they delighted me, every bit of him delighted me.

Why?

I had spent so many weeks and months, telling stories, researching and seeking out details to make it sound real, embroidering, searching imagining and manufacturing cascade of images, scents, sounds, touches, describing them, making them vivid to make them real. And now, here, beyond fantasy, actually doing it, it carried over into a sort of sensual awareness, a hyper-awareness, a vividness that translated into hungry intensity.

Leaning over, I pushed my breasts against his hand as I ground my hip in a circle, feeling him move inside me. I splayed another palm on his chest, exploring him.

"The moment I saw you," I whispered. "Out there in the hallway of that hotel, I wanted you. I forgot everything else. I just wanted you. From the very first moment, I knew I had to fuck you."

Mike's eyes widened, he almost seemed to glow. His hips seemed to lift and I could feel his curving erection stiffen inside me.

"Really," he gasped.

"Oh yes," I lied, not really knowing why I was lying, but needing him to hear it, to feel it. To feel special, to feel desired. I wanted it to be true. If passion could make it true, then it was. It felt like I had wanted him my entire life, and had just never known until I'd finally had him.

I leaned forward, planting elbows on his chest, bending to kiss him deeply, even as my hips lifted until barely more than the head of his cock remained between my lips.

Then I slammed down wildly and rode him, picking up the pace steadily. My fingernails raked down his chest again and again, leaving red scratches that excited me even more. I remembered my bruises from the last time, the bruises I would have from his grip, and now I was leaving my own marks on him, my own legacy on his body. The thought aroused me wildly, it thrilled me.

It was another claim, another possession, and the more of him I had, the more I wanted. I wanted to mark him, fuck him, to swallow him down every inch, and I drove my hips down harder and harder again and again. Lifting high until he was barely in and then crashing down all the way with wild abandon.

His hands gripped my breasts so tight the fingers sank in and I loved it. He'd switch his hands to my hips, and I'd put them back on my breasts. I touched him, explored him, running hands along his arms. Once, he fell out, because of my hunger to kiss him deeply. He held his cock steady, so I could push myself onto it. The hunger for each other kept on building.

Then his hips lifted, for an instant, my knees were off the bed, I swayed. His hands shifted to a death grip on my thighs, holding me in place, pulling me further down onto him. I swore I could feel his cock pulsing inside me, swelling. His body was rigid, sweat breaking out, flushed and radiating heat, his face a mask of strain.

Again, his hips lifted me up off the bed, but this time I was ready, rising up with him even higher, lifting myself above him, feeling him slide from me, and then grinding down as hard as I could.

Mike was approaching orgasm. I could see it in his face like an oncoming train, huge and relentless and unstoppable. It excited me, I wanted him to come more than anything. I needed him to explode, to see his face, to watch him go white light and his mind explode into a million brilliant shards of pleasure.

"Come on, baby," I grunted. But he was beyond hearing me. Instead, I ground on top of him, lifting and sinking, faster and faster, leaning forward, his death grip on my hips holding me in place as he writhed and surged under me. I grabbed my own breasts, squeezing them, pulling so hard on my nipples it was almost painful.

Then I felt him surge up inside me, I swear I could feel him ejaculating up inside me, a sensation I'd never felt with any other man, a sensation I would never have believed. But I was feeling it. Under me, his body seemed to radiate with tension, going explosively rigid, I felt a wave of body heat bursting from him.

I ground my clit hard against him, feeling him so deep, pushing my long delayed orgasm, until I could feel it rolling over me. Lightning crawled up my spine, and I pushed and arched convulsively on him, even as he spurted inside me, hitting my peak even as he passed his, fucking myself to bliss as his semen seeped down between us.

Then I collapsed on top of him, unable to do more than pant. At that angle, his cock was barely half in me. I felt a sense of deprivation as his erection weakened and it fell out, but I was too weak and exhausted to do anything about it.

For long moments, we didn't do anything but pant breathlessly. My heart was racing, and I could feel his own thudding away. He lifted arms to hold me, but we were both so sweat drenched that they just slid along my body.

Finally, when I could breathe, I rolled off him, and we cuddled together. My hand slid down, wrapping around his cock, now deflated, slimy with our juices, and still I felt a surge of possessiveness.

"Wow," he said finally.

"Yep," I replied. "You definitely earned that refund."

"That was great."

I squeezed his cock. No life there, not yet. I still liked holding it. I was definitely possessive.

"Just so you know," I teased. "This is mine now. I'm taking it with me. We'll travel the world together. You can do what you want. We'll send you postcards."

"I don't know," he replied. "It's kind of attached."

"Really?" I said. "That's such a shame. I guess I'll have to come back and visit it. Lots."

"What about me?"

I pretended to think about it.

"I guess you're okay too."

He laughed.

"I have to say," he said, "the first time I met you that was the wildest, craziest sex of my life."

Ditto, I thought, and smiled.

"But this," he finished. "This drives a truck through that. This was mind blowing. This was amazing. Thank you so much."

I put on a pretend frown.

"What?" I asked. "You think we're finished? You paid for the whole night, remember?"

"What about my refund?"

"Well, if I'm paying you," I teased, "then I definitely want to get my money's worth. We're just getting started."

I spread my legs and guided his hand to my soaking crotch.

"Down boy," I joked. "You've got work to do. Round two, coming up. Get that tongue in gear."

And damn, if he didn't do it!

I was thrilled. Men never went down after they came! But he didn't even hesitate. Even wet as I was, even dripping semen, albeit his own semen, his head bobbed enthusiastically between my thighs.

Pounded as I was, I thought I might not feel anything, but his lips and tongue were as fresh and inventive as before, Laying in a soft bed was a lot more comfortable, and soon enough I was screaming and pulling out his hair.

Then I returned the favor with a ravenous possessive enthusiasm, and when he was fully at attention, round two.

And later on that night, round three.

* * *

Much later, I cuddled up against him as he slept, and I watched the sky lighten with dawn. I was thinking about what to do next.

I wanted to tell him the truth. To say: "My name is Kate, I work at an entry level position as a clerk at a bank, and I live in an apartment and watch Netflix. The most exciting thing I do in real life is order a Frappuccino at Starbucks. This me you think you know? I made her all up."

Except I couldn't imagine saying it.

The Kate that existed in his mind, Better-Kate, was so much more exciting, so much more vivid, so much more full of life than my drab existence. How could he ever trade that in? What would he think of me, if he knew every single thing about me was a lie?

But for better or worse, I should tell him. I needed to come clean, to start over.

I didn't want to.

The thing was, I loved Better-Kate. I loved the idea of her, the adventurous free spirit. I loved researching for her, studying art history, talking to prostitutes and dancers and street performers, seeking out pictures and details of places I'd never been, and making them come alive. Fantasizing trysts and adventures.

This night, wasn't me. This was Better-Kate.

This was me playing the role of Better-Kate, as I'd played her through emails and texts and whispered telephone conversations. I reveled in her, wallowed in her confidence and wanton sensuousness, this was just another performance, slipping her on like an identity, inhabiting her personality.

Perversions and Infidelities / Page 143

And it was the best night of my life, the boldest night, and the bravest. It was the best sex I'd ever had, wild, traumatic, addictive life changing sex.

Give that up?

Let that go?

I didn't want to let her go.

And really, she was the only Kate he knew.

Whatever we did, whatever we had, she was the center. If I gave her up, there wouldn't be an 'us.' Just two strangers in awkward wreckage of lies, there wasn't any possibility of a future. We could only exist together through the lie of Better-Kate.

I remembered from my research the story of an Indonesian monkey trap. It was simple, leave a glass bottle out in the jungle with a piece of fruit inside. The monkey comes along, sees the fruit and easily reaches inside to get the fruit. But once the fruit is in his fist, it's too big to get through the neck of the bottle. It could free itself easily, by releasing the fruit. It wants the fruit too badly to let go, and so it's trapped unwilling to surrender its desire.

Suddenly, I understood how the monkey felt.

I couldn't stop being Better-Kate, I couldn't let her go.

Instead, I'd go back and live my boring life, and she'd travel the world having adventures, and every now and then, she'd come back here, drawn back to Mike, and they'd get together and have amazing sex.

They'd fall in love.

They'd already fallen in love, I admitted.

Mike and Better-Kate's relationship would continue, deepening, becoming more intimate, a thing of longing and hunger and moments of exquisite satisfaction. But Better-Kate could only ever be a passing visitor in his life.

I thought of Jay and how I'd been catfished, how hurt and humiliated I'd been. How devastating it had been to find that the person I'd thought I'd known, that I'd lusted for was a lie.

I watched Mike sleeping beside me, and yes, I'd fallen in love. I wanted to cherish and protect him. I could never hurt him, the way Jay had hurt me. I couldn't bear the thought of him humiliated and devastated by the discovery that the amazing woman he loved was just a lie told by a mousy bank clerk.

He could never be allowed to meet the real me.

I was the catfish now, and I couldn't let go.

I'd set my own hook.

And the catfish was caught.

The End

RED DRESS

She has been sitting in the hotel lounge for almost an hour, waiting for a complete stranger to rent her body and fuck her.

Nursing her third glass of wine, trying not to smudge her lipstick, she resists the urge to check her phone for the time, for messages, for anything but this mindless waiting. This was such a stupid idea, she thinks, with a mixture of shame and embarrassment. She should go to the washroom, she thinks suddenly, check her make up, then come back and if nothing happens in fifteen minutes, she'll leave.

But it wouldn't be to check her make-up, not really. It would be to look at herself in a mirror, at a pointlessly gym-tightened body, at full breasts, at a sexy, curve hugging, red dress with a deeply plunging neckline, a dress that made her feel sexy and slutty and wanton.

She vividly remembers finding the dress in the store, being attracted by its daring. Much more daring than she was used to. She recalls the excitement of putting it on in the store, and seeing herself as this provocative, vampish figure.

And she remembers wearing it for her husband. The way his eyes slid off it, as if it was oiled. Looking, and then looking away. The nervous smile. The hesitant chuckle.

"Don't you think it's a little much," he'd said.

"But I want to look sexy for you," she'd told him.

"You are sexy," he'd said. "You don't need the dress for that. You don't need to show it off. I've seen you naked lots of times."

So she'd laughed with him, and put the dress away, come to bed naked, and laid under him as he'd laboured over her. But on some level, deep down, she felt disappointed.

He wouldn't even look at her in the dress.

It was as if he had become so comfortable with her, so used to her as a wife, as a mother, as a person who had shared years, that he was embarrassed to see her as a sexy being. They had seen each other naked so many times, thousands of times. Explored each other's bodies. Slept together, cuddling, woken up. They had become ordinary to each other, casual, when she was with him it was okay that her tits were starting to sag, or it was okay with him that his gut was starting to grow.

But where was the magic? Where was the electricity? There'd been a time when knowing he was hard was enough to make her wet. When all he had to do was look at her to get hard. When they would simply look at each other and they would get hungry. Where had that hunger gone?

She felt so ordinary, so dull, so leaden. She didn't want to be that. She felt like so much was passing her by. That there was a whole world of sex and life and excitement that she'd missed out on.

Her husband was the first man she'd been serious about. She hadn't been a virgin when she met him. There'd been crushes and romances, and dates, had sucked a few cocks, spread her legs. Once in college, she'd dated a black man but it hadn't gone further than a grope. Sometimes, alone with herself in the bathtub, she'd wished it had gone further, closed her eyes and fantasized and touched herself.

Maybe it was the dress that made her a whore, she thought. A wannabe whore anyway.

After that disastrous night, the next day, she'd resolved to take it back. But instead, she put it on again, looked at herself in the full length mirror. She'd pulled the hem up slowly, exposing knees, then thighs, then her pubic thatch and are vagina.

She was still hot?

Yes.

Had pinched her nipple, then clutched her breast, squeezing it, imagining an eager masculine hand, grabbing her this way. Someone who wanted her, someone who lusted for her, a mouth that devoured, a body that shook with hunger, a cock hard and relentless.... She had gotten a chair, and sat in front of the mirror, pussy exposed, and brought herself to fierce orgasm.

The dress did not go back to the shop.

She didn't wear it again, not right away. What would be the point? There would have been something pathetic about doing it again. Dressing up like a slut, to do what... Finger yourself for the mirror? She had some pride.

She wanted someone to see her in that dress. To look at her and get hard. To think about fucking her. To want to fuck her. To see her as more than a wife of seventeen years, as more than a mother, as more than a naked body that you woke up to or went to sleep next to after a thousand nights. She wanted to be mysterious again, desirable, exciting.

So the dress hung in the closet, and sometimes she took it out
and looked at it. And she thought about wearing it. To the mall? To
shopping? No. On a stroll? No. Maybe some night alone, order a
pizza and wear it when the pizza boy came.... she laughed at that
impulse. There was no place in her life where she could wear it, where
she could dress up and be slutty. It was a knowledge that was almost
painful.

Which was where the idea to become a hooker had entered her
thoughts.

Or perhaps it had always been there. She had never known a
prostitute. There'd been whispered rumours about that girl in
university, the one in English Lit, who had dropped out, or been
expelled, the stories were vague.... that she'd been seen working the
streets. That was as close as she'd ever come.

But she admired the idea. Sex had been so complicated in high
school and university. A matter of unspoken negotiations, of looks,
and flirtation, dates, and stages - first base, second, home run, where
every aspect and facet had been such a project, from figuring out
where to do it, or how far to go, to the endless baggage of the
aftermath: Would he talk about me? What should I say about him?
Should I keep it secret, or brag about it? Are we dating? Do I want to
date him? What if people think I'm a slut?

Prostitution seemed so elegantly simple in comparison - a
proposition, if acceptance an exchange of money.... And then
fucking. And then each gone their separate ways. It was all the
baggage and complications shorn away, stripped away, just sex and
nothing but sex.

Of course, it was a horrible thing she knew. Prostitutes were
beaten and robbed, there were diseases, arrests, it was a degrading,
dangerous lifestyle.

But still.... Just sex and nothing but sex.

Oh god, that appealed to her.

That world of excitement and being excited and exciting that had
slipped away from her. That was what seemed so compelling.

Was it so wrong to want to be desired? To be desirable? To feel
special?

Her slutty dress was still a dress, still classy. Not something a
streetwalker would wear.

Being a streetwalker didn't really appeal to her. It was too gritty,
too nasty. She envisioned something higher class, a hotel room with
clean pristine sheets and fine furnishings. An escort? That seemed too
complicated, too elaborate. It was the simplicity.

A Hotel Prostitute? Was there a name for that? A sexily dressed
woman who would hang out in a hotel lounge, wait to be picked up.
Relaxation and elegance and dressing sexy, she envisioned old

movies, the flare of a cupped match, lighting a cigarette for her, smoky voices whispering over martini's.... and then a walk to the elevator... And then....

Ridiculous of course, she didn't smoke, and anyway, smoking had been banned from hotels and bars. And they'd probably throw you out anyway.

It was utterly unrealistic, a fantasy built out of scenes from old half remembered movies, vague and nebulous. A fantasy, disconnected from reality.

The dress would be perfect for that.

The idea wouldn't go away.

She'd have her rational moments, when she'd think it was a stupid idea. That it was a good way to get raped or beaten, or pick up a disease. And the sex would probably be terrible, the sort of man who paid for it was likely some one-minute wonder.

But it kept coming back.

Because, as stupid an idea as it was.... It would still be doing something. It would be being something, being sexy. As opposed to this place of dull and dulling comfort that her life was become, of being sexless, of losing that part of herself.

There came a day, when she realized she was no longer playing with the idea, that she was going to do it. If only for one night, one adventure, just so that she could know she had done it.

That, is how she came to be sitting in the hotel lounge, dressed in her form fitting red dress, the fabric clinging to her curves, her nipples hard, wearing high heels and black stockings and a garter belt, but no panties. Her lipstick glistened, her make-up perfect, red hair loosely spilled around her shoulders.

Waiting for a man to make her a wanton.

* * *

Rejection hurts.

There's a particular shame, a humiliation that comes from putting yourself out, from offering yourself, you heart, your soul, your pussy... And finding no takers. It gets in deep, burrows down and eats away. You've just offered yourself up... and no one wants you?

No one cares.

It's the sort of shame and humiliation that sends people home with each other at the end of the night sometime, that pain of being so afraid of being unwanted, undesired, that you will do anything, take anyone. It's the pain that makes you order drink after drink, hoping that intoxication will numb the awful humiliation of being you.

How long had she been thinking of this? Months. How long planning? Weeks. The patient arrangement of a night to herself? The covert shopping expeditions for stockings and garter belt? Days. Carefully doing hair and make-up? Hours. She had shaved her pussy for this! Special bought razor and moisturizer, long, long minutes, gingerly checking for stray hairs!

And nothing!

The first fifteen minutes in the hotel lounge had been terrifying. Terror of being asked to leave. Terror of someone coming up and taking her for what she was pretending to be. Terrified of being laughed at. Terrified of being a dumpy middle aged woman in a shapeless red dress clinging to the delusion that she was still a sexual being. Her stomach had been full of butterflies, her heart had pounded, she had stuttered when ordering her red wine. Had taken huge swallows, almost gulping it down. That first fifteen minutes, she'd almost bolted a half dozen times.

It had been an exquisite, exciting terror, waiting for something to happen, her nerves keyed to fever pitch.

And nothing.

The second fifteen minutes, she had relaxed. The first glass of wine entered her system, providing a pleasant warmth, a sense of relaxation. She took a deep breath, allowed herself to look around the lounge. She'd ordered a second glass of wine, checked her make up a couple of times to make sure it was perfect. She looked good. She looked hot. Her nipples were visibly hard, insistent through the red fabric of her dress. Her cleavage looked great, she crossed her legs, exposing a flash of thigh above the stocking, and then uncrossed them.

"Soon..." she thought, "something will happen, and she'll start on her adventure." Butterflies rose again in her stomach at the thought, and she smiled.

And nothing.

The next fifteen minutes. Unrealistic to think anything would happen right away. This was a slow thing. Yes, that was it. Checked her make-up again. Touched up lipstick. Wait for the right man. How did real hookers do it? Did they walk up to prospects? Make eye contact. Glancing around the hotel lounge. Not wanting to make eye contact with certain men, too old, too young, balding and fat, a punk, geriatric, dull. An attractive man... he's with a girl. Another man, decent, his eyes linger upon her.... she looks away, looks back, not quite sure how to make eye contact, smiles, thinks 'come here and buy me a drink...' But he leaves. In her belly, the worms slowly coil and twist, devouring the butterflies.

And nothing.

Another drink? Yes please. Checking make-up twice. A trip to the bathroom. Do I look hot? Yes, yes, I'm hot. Waiting. Fidgeting. What if no one comes? What if I've dressed up like a fool, humiliated myself. Who am I fooling? I'm a middle aged housewife, maybe I'm really as dry and sexless as I'm afraid of being. I should just walk away, end this now. Her stomach is nothing but worms, and she's afraid of the things they whisper. She thinks of checking her make-up, but she's checked it too many times. She wants to check the time but doesn't want to know what it will say. She wants to go to the bathroom but doesn't want to look in the mirror.

"Excuse me," a man says, startled she looks up, "Are you waiting for someone?"

She hasn't noticed him approach. He's short, perhaps an inch shorter than her, even shorter while she's wearing her heels. Early middle age, no signs of gray in his hair, but not much of it. Male pattern balding is well advanced. He's not fat, exactly, but he's thick, heavy set. Thick brows, and a pug nose, it would be generous to call him average.

Here it is, the moment caught up to her, and she didn't realize it. She's startled, tongue tied. He's not her ideal, not even close to it. If she had time to think of it, she would reject him. But she's off guard, and her response is honest.

"No," she replies, "I'm not waiting for anyone in particular."

He takes this as encouragement.

"May I buy you a drink?"

Is he oblivious to the half full glass she has already? It doesn't matter, she decides. He's hitting on me.

She feels like she's standing on a ledge, on the cusp. He's not the man she wanted, although she didn't really have any idea of what she wanted. A stranger. Definitely not looking like him, he wasn't anywhere in the profile. But he's here.

So what now? Say 'no', end it, go home, burn the dress, garter belt in the trash, throw away the razor and just be.... dull, and sexless, and hollow?

Or go forward? With this guy??? But she's come so far.

In the end, something, even if it's not the something you had in mind, is better than nothing, even if the nothing is familiar. Or maybe it's because the nothing is so tediously familiar that she decides.

"Yes, you may."

She tries to smile at him. It's nervous and friendly, not the alluring smile he had hoped for, not the alluring smile she wanted to give. She feels awkward and clumsy, in her fantasy, she was poised and graceful..

He wonders what she's doing here, he wonders who she is. She looks hot. He dreams of getting lucky. He has no idea.

He sits, there's a drink, but she doesn't touch it. They make small talk. He's a salesman of some sort. He talks a little about his life. She wonders how much of it is true. He tells her she's very beautiful, and she smiles. It's genuine. He compliments her dress, she crosses her legs, the tip of her shoe brushes his pants, but it doesn't seem to her that he notices.

Finally, he asks: "What is it that you do?"

It's what she's been waiting for, there's a script in her head. She's rehearsed this in her mind.

"I'm working," she says simply, and smiles.

"What kind of work?"

He doesn't get it. She keeps her smile on. But inside she freezes, butterflies and worms flutter and twist in her stomach. She doesn't want to say it out loud. She doesn't want to say the words. They're suddenly too obvious, too vulgar, too awkward. What if he's an undercover cop, or hotel security? Maybe she should quit now, while she's ahead. Walk away. In the end, she compromises.

"I'm working," she repeats.

And then he gets it.

"Oh," he says. She watches him, there's a moment of indecision. He'd half expected this actually. It would have been nice for a hotel chat in a bar with a regular girl, but that almost never happened, and the odds were a million to one against it going anywhere. But this... She can almost see him settling into comfort... It's a sure thing now, if the price is right.

"How much?" he asks.

She frowns. "I don't discuss business out here."

Honestly, she doesn't know how much to charge. What are the going rates? She's here to get picked up and fucked. She's nervous talking money out here, she's read up a little, and that seems to be how it works - if she names a price in public, she can be arrested.

Her breath catches in her throat. This is the big step.

"If you're interested, we can talk about things in your room."

He's uncertain. Not a good idea to invite a whore to your room without working out the terms. What if she wants too much? What if she decides to demand payment even if he doesn't want to? What if she starts a fight or something? That's not a good place, too much an go wrong. Better to work things out before you get there.

"I dunno," he said. "I don't know if I can afford you. I'm not a rich man. I don't have a lot of money on me. Just..."

He's about to name a figure. She puts a hand on his.

"Let's just go up and talk about it there," she says. To his eyes, she looks calm and reassuring, very much in control, very sophisticated. He decides he trusts her.

Inside, she's nearly close to panic, wanting out of this excruciating half moment - go forward or walk away, but do not stay in this moment.

"Okay," he concedes.

She stands first, and knows as she does that it's a mistake. She should have waited for him to stand, and offer his hand. Her legs are wobbly, like water, and her heart is starting to pound. Worst of all, she's made herself look eager and hasty.

He admires her body, the curves of her body. For the first time, he notices her stockinged legs, notices her nipples hardness is visible through the fabric. He enjoys the cleavage. He stands, and they walk out together.

With each step, she feels like she's falling into an abyss. It's happening, she's doing it. She's changed her mind, she needs to quit, to stop, to run away. But she just keeps walking. She feels herself trembling, can he see it? Is she blushing?

All he sees is class, she's got it. She's out of his league, he knows it.

They make it to the elevator. Will he grope her in there? She wonders. Does she want him to? But they're not alone in the elevator. So they ride in silence. She finds she can't look at him.

She's wet.

She's excited.

She feels alive.

* * *

They are standing in front of the hotel room door. The number is on the door, 612, impersonal and indifferent.

She's trembling, she can feel it in her whole body. She's excited, she's terrified. On the other side of that door, this strange, relatively unattractive man is going to fuck her. So much for marriage vows, so much for the dry chastity of her married life, so much for normality. Does she really want to do this? Isn't the safety of dullness so much more alluring?

But the door opens, and she walks through, as much through inertia as choice. She's come this far after all, and all the decisions that lead up to this are weighing down on her, pushing her.

But she does choose. For all her indecision, there is a resolution. She's enjoyed the way he's looked at her body, the stolen glances. She's aroused. She is wet, and there's a tingling deep down, a throbbing in her pussy, she hasn't felt for a long time: Anticipation.

Perversions and Infidelities / Page 157

That lost feeling, anticipation, the sense of excitement, of
uncertainty, that feeling of wanting that's somehow slipped out of
her marriage, dribbled away, evaporated.

She feels it. It's a good feeling.

It decides her.

Once through, he comes in after her, the door closes. There's the
rush of adrenalin. If things are going to go wrong and horrible, this
is where they'll start. But there's a sense of relief, of relaxation. She
has committed, has been committed, the door is closed and now
she's somewhere private and privacy is its own kind of safety, and
more than that... It's all decided.

"Nothing left to do," she thinks, "but get fucked."

The thought is as exhilarating as it is terrifying. So much in those
little words.

It really was that simple, she marvels - offer, acceptance, money
and sex. How elemental, how breathtaking, it cuts away so much
bullshit that it's almost liberating. She wonders why all woman are
not whores, why everyone doesn't do this.

He sits on the edge of the bed. She wishes he wouldn't. Him
sitting, her in heels, she's much taller than he is, she can see the top
of his bald spot, and he's very plainly what he is, a not particularly
attractive, pudgy, balding, middle aged man.

But then, what is she? She wonders. What does he see? A middle-
aged woman, gone to seed, desperate to recapture some lost identify?

In point of fact, he sees something glamorous, some movie star of
old, all poise and grace and sensuality. He's happy to be sitting,
because he's eye level with her cleavage. He thinks about telling her
how beautiful she is, but she's probably heard it a thousand times, so
he simply sits and looks at her.

He's blind to her insecurity.

But her insecurities don't matter, she's decided she's going
through with it. Even if the sex is just a quick couple of minutes. She
imagines him drooling and vacant eyed, coming the minute his cock
enters her.

It doesn't matter.

At least she'll have done something!

At least she will have lived!

"How much?" he asks.

She doesn't know how much to ask for. Instinctively, she knows
that fifty or twenty are far too little, an insult. That would lead to
awkward things. But five hundred? A thousand? He doesn't look like
he has that sort of money.

"What do you think?" she asks, trying to appear calm and in
control. She leans against the dresser. Her legs parted slightly. One
hand pulls up the hem of her dress casually, exposing more

stockinged leg. She's trying for classy but sexy, not wanton. Available... desirable, but not cheap.

"A hundred," he offers. He knows she'll want more. But it's a safe number to start with.

"All right," she says, surprising him.

She doesn't really care about the money. That's not what it is about for her.

He stands, not quite understanding her slight smile of approval, and reaches for his wallet. He opens it carefully, trying to conceal it from her, pulls a series of bills. Three twenties, three tens, some rumpled fives. She takes it, drops it into her purse.

He has bought me, she thinks to herself. I'm bought and paid for. He's bought my body, it's his. The thoughts have a delirious excitement that makes her heart pound hard and fast against her ribs.

In her fantasies, in her mental rehearsals, she's undressed slowly, she's stripped for the man who bought her, exhibited and exposed herself. But her knees are wobbly, her adrenalin is running, she can hear her pulse pounding in her ears, and there's not quite enough air in the room. She's nervous.

So she pulls the dress up over her head, taking it off in one smooth move marred only by a tiny bit of awkwardness around the elbow, and lays it on the dresser with casual care.

She stands there naked in heels and stocking and garter belt, naked in front of a complete stranger, naked in front of a man who, besides her husband, is now the only man who has seen her naked in decades. There's a free floating excitement to it. A joy, an exhilaration. Part of her wants to say 'look at me!'

And he looks. He stares at her breasts, at her long legs, at her gym toned belly, at her shoulders and thighs and her shaved pussy, and wet pussy lips, and she loves it, she loves being looked at, she loves the look in his eyes, because no one has looked at her that way in such a long time, and she's hot. She is affirmed as hot.

"This is what you've bought," she says, the words sound awkward in her ears, not like she rehearsed. "Do you like it?"

"Oh yes," he says. She's a little disappointed he doesn't say more. She's fishing for compliments... It's been such a long time.

"So what do you do?" he asks.

He steps toward her, she steps forward to him. She's pressing her breasts against his chest. His hand cups her ass, slides long the back of her tailbone, confirms what his eyes have told him.

She's not even wearing panties! Fuck, she's hot!

"Anything you want," she whispers. It sounds better. "Everything."

She hesitates.

"As long as it's not rough or creepy."

Perversions and Infidelities / Page 159

She hates having to put a qualifier on it, but she doesn't want to open the door to something going horribly wrong... What if 'everything' to him includes whipping her with a belt?

"I'm yours to play with," her voice is husky.

His hand reaches up to squeeze her breast, it's full and natural. His grip is firm, he takes a big handful, his palm just short of her nipple, and lifts and squeezes, there's hunger in his touch,, his fingers digging in, trapping her nipple and pinching between ring and index finger.

Her pussy goes wetter. Has she ever been grabbed like this? Her husband's touch on her breast is gentle, caressing. This is almost rough, it's eager, it's hungry, and it's deliriously exciting.

"Nice tits," he says, and she loves hearing it. "Natural."

He pushes his face to her, and to his surprise, she doesn't turn her cheek. Whores don't like to mouth kiss, he knows. But he likes it, likes the feel of a woman's lips. He kisses her and she returns it. He kisses more passionately and is gratified by her mouth opening. He pushes against her, pressing his face, slobbering in her mouth, but even the slobbering is exciting to her, it's all about hunger and desire and she loves his eagerness, the way his hands roam across her body. He kisses her hard, as he draws her towards the bed. His hand reaches between her legs, her lips are already parted, drenched as he draws the edge of his hand up.

"Fuck," he grunts, breaking the kiss, "you're dripping wet."

She doesn't know what to say to that. It's vulgar, but an exciting vulgarity. She lets him kiss her again. Her legs won't support her any more, lets him sit her on the bed. Her legs spread wantonly. He's the first man to touch her pussy, other than her husband, in so long. His touch is electric. Exciting. She wants him to touch her there, to put his fingers in her, to play with her clit. She wants to spread her legs wide for him like a wanton whore. She wants his hands all over her body. How long has it been since she's felt this desire? How long has it been since she's felt desired?

He breaks the kiss, standing in front of her. She looks up at him. She prefers her sitting, him standing, its much better. He looms over her now, his ordinariness transformed into potent maleness, his thickness is mass and strength. He starts to unbutton his shirt.

She almost offers to help him undress. In some fantasies and rehearsals she does. But her legs won't support her, and she's so excited she's not sure she'd say the words right. She watches the shirt unbutton, there's a hairy chest, hairier than her husband, the shape of him revealed as he undresses is so different. She wants him to fuck her. She can see the bulge in his pants. There's something exciting about his matter of fact masculine stripping, the undoing of the belt, unzipping the fly, the pants dropping.

She reaches between her legs to touch herself, fingers delving into wetness, making a circle around her clit. She's smiling and not even realizing she's smiling. She's enjoying this stranger get naked in front of her.

He steps awkwardly out of his pants, one leg at a time. His boxers are the last to go. His pubic hair is thick and black, his cock resplendent and hard. She wants to stare at it, to get closer.

"Suck my cock," he says, part question, part request, part order. Will that offend her? "Please," he adds. He steps close to her. She smells his maleness now that he's naked, a subtle musk. She lays on the side of the bed, legs spread, leaning towards it, it's only inches from her face.

She's fascinated. It's not the smooth straight torpedo of her husband's cock, it curves upward, the surface laced with veins, the head a round mushroom. She reaches for it, it feels thick, hot in her hand, hotter than her husband's. Is he feverish? Or has she just gotten too used to her husband's? Maybe cocks are supposed to be hot in your hand? It throbs. She thinks she can feel the vein's pulsing.

She looks up at him, and sees him looking down over the curve of his belly, waiting for the touch of her lips. Experimentally, she licks the head, wanting to know its taste. Nuzzles it, wanting to breathe its smell, feels it against her cheek as she presses her face into his pubic hair, drowning in the sensual immediacy of him. She runs her lips against the shaft, holding it, glances up one more time and then presses her lips to it, her shiny red lipstick-stained lips, and lets her mouth open on it. She moans in her throat, a sound he doesn't hear over his own louder moan. She feels his hands slide down to her head, fingers knotting in her hair.

After a moment, he pulls her. She feels the tug on her hair, drawing her off the bed.

"On your knees," he says, he's feeling bold, she's hotter than the usual whore he thinks, she's more into it. It makes him braver. "I want you sucking my cock on your knees..."

Hesitation.

"Like a good slut." He wonders if he just went too far.

Her pussy clenches at the words, she feels boneless, filled with formless excitement. She loves the dirty way he talks, wishes he would talk more. Let's herself be pulled off the bed, pushed to her knees which she spreads wide.

"Oh yes...." She whispers, just before he slides his cock between her lips, his hips rolling as he thrusts gently into her mouth.

Her words excite him, the confirmation of her submissiveness, her enthusiasm inflames him. He tightens her grip in her hair, sliding deeper. He pushes her face down till she gags a little, and then relents allowing her off, ordering her to lick his balls, to take them into her mouth, she worships his crotch with exciting abandon. He does not see her hand between her legs.

It goes on, her squirming under him, on her knees, hair pulled, wrapped in his fingers, sucking his cock, tonguing it and licking it, swallowing balls, allowing his thrusts deeper almost to gagging, slobbering until saliva is spotting on the floor between them, drool coating her chin, his cock shining with her spit. The moments when he pulls her off it, she glimpses its wonderful dark curve, loves the way it looks shining with her spit. Eventually he's pushed it all the way down her throat, holds it there as the gag reflex comes and then passes and then comes again, as her delicate hands beat against his hips.

He lets her off, hears her panting gasping. Looks down, her hair a wreck, her make-up ruined, her eyes shining and cheeks flushed, chin streaked with drool.

"I want to fuck you now."

"Yes," she says, it's almost like someone else saying it, someone breathy and urgent and desperate, like she's standing outside her body and listening to her body say it. "Oh yes, yes, fuck me now, with your hard cock in me."

* * *

He half drags her, she half crawls up onto the bed. She feels the bed sink under his weight as he joins her. His hands are on her ass, trying to position her, but she resists rolling onto her back under him, twisting her way up onto the pillows.

He's spreading her legs, as she bends her knees, elevating for him. His body is so solid over her. His hand clutches her breast in that whole hand grab and squeeze of his. Will he leave finger marks? She squirms further up the bed, till her head is resting up, elevated on the pillows. He's trying to pull her towards him.

"This way," she gasps, "no this way... I want to see it. I want to see you going in. I want you on top of me, I want to feel you all."

If he says anything, she doesn't register it. He crawls, pushes himself up until he's kneeling between her wantonly spread legs, his cock resplendent, so hard, so fucking hard, so instantaneously automatically hard it makes her crazy, she loves the hardness of him, loves the excitement and desire in his eyes, loves his body that's about to take her.

She lifts her knees up higher and higher, spreading her legs wide, she can feel her pussy just dripping, can feel her lips opening of their own accord. His body is this endless landscape of maleness, the head and face so far above her. She runs a hand through a hairy chest. There's too much of him to take in all at once. Her attention is entirely focused on that hard cock, that wondrous pulsing erection in her hand, being drawn to her pussy.

And some part of her thinks with wild excitement, that this is the point of no return, that when that cock slides into her pussy, she really is a whore, she's been bought and sold and now claimed, that her body is now his, that years of marriage and fidelity and blandness are as ruptured as her hymen of so long ago. And she knows that she wants this more than anything she's ever wanted before. She can't wait.

She cries out with pleasure when she feels his cock against her lips. Moans with satisfaction as it slides into her. If feels thick. It feels hot. She's so wet it moves inside her like velvet on velvet.

"I'm a whore," she says wildly, and has her first orgasm, sudden as a wildfire, tearing through her. "I'm a slut! And I love it!"

"You're a good slut," he groans, thrusting into her. She hadn't asked for a condom, he wonders. Some part of him worries that she might have something, but he's loving the wet feel of her too much to wonder. Maybe she was just too excited to think of it, he thinks, not realizing how right that is.

"You're so fucking wet," he grunts, pumping hard, listening to her moan. Maybe she's just in a class usually beyond him, where sex is elegant and more satisfying, more intimate.

Her legs wrap around him momentarily, but he breaks her grip with a fierce thrust that has her arching her back in what he thinks is a faked (but it's not faked) orgasm. Her hands push at his chest, fingers running through his chest hair, and then they're around his back, pulling him so their bodies grind together his chest hair sliding against her nipples. Her legs flail.

"You're so fucking tight," he says.

She doesn't know what to say, just moans, she's almost beyond words. Her pussy rises to meet his cock, almost pushes to get him into her deeper.

What a performance for a hundred dollars, he thinks. And then he wonders if it is a performance. What if she's one of those legendary woman that does it because she loves it? That needs a cock in her so bad that if he didn't pay her, she'd pay him, that needs to get fucked, that wants it and screams for it.

What if she's not a prostitute at all, that this is some adventure for her? He dismisses that. A woman like this would find so much better than him. She's working., that's the only way a man like him will ever have a woman like her.

"You fucking love it, don't you," he growls, lifting up on one hand to grab her breast tight. He watches her head lower, so she can stare fascinated by the cock driving piston-like into her pussy. He grabs her other breast, his weight pushing her down into the bed, squeezing her breasts so hard that the flesh balloons between his fingers. "You fucking love getting fucked you hot fucking whore."

Her eyes are wild when they look up, almost rolling, shifting between his face and the cock between her legs.

"Yes, yes, she says, I'm a hot fucking whore."

"You love being a hot fucking whore."

"I love getting fucked, because I'm such a whore, I'm a whore for fucking and I love it."

Her legs go up, scissoring around his hips locking, and her pelvis rises against him pushing his cock deeper, straining, her last words are an incoherent moan, a shriek, and he feels an explosive surging wetness drenching his crotch, realizes she's actually, genuinely coming and squirting, and it's too much for him, his erection doubles, harder and deeper, so rigid it feels like he's going to explode, and then he starts to come. Her arms wrap around him, hips grinding against his, legs scissored and locked as if she desperately wants every drop of him spent into her wet body, and he obliges, pounding her harder and harder with relentless force until he can't move.

After, he lays on top of her for a few minutes, the sweat cooling on their body, still as deep in her as he can get, feeling his cock throbbing slowly in satisfaction, milking the remaining drops of semen into her wanton pussy.

Finally he rolls over, listening to her take long shuddering breaths, one after another. He watches her touch herself, watches her hands make a spastic journey, thighs to pussy to belly to breasts and throat and back again, watches her back arch.

Eventually, he reaches over, spreading her legs open, they part easily. Pushing her fluttering spastic hand away, he slides his fingers into her wet pussy, starts to move them, and she starts to come.

He can't believe how wild she is, how freaky. He feels a stirring in his crotch. Even though he's just come, and he's nowhere hard, he wants to fuck her again. He wonders if he can get hard again. Most whores its pop and lock, once you fill the condom they're out the door. Even if you don't fill the condom, they'll only go so long. But this one, this woman with the sex drive of a nineteen year old porn star...

"I'm not done," he says, tentatively, then more boldly. "We're not done. I want to ... I'm going to fuck you again." There's no refusal, just the roll of her hips as she grinds down on his fingers, is that a nod as she gasps and arches her back. He guides her hand to his deflated cock, feels her squeezing it in her fingers. He strokes her clit hard, making her gasp and writhe, displaying her submission.

He pulls her, grabbing her hair, and pulling her gently towards his crotch.

"Suck my cock..." he orders, the word "...whore," spoken more tentatively but somehow effective.

Her mouth settles on his limp cock, and she works it eagerly. He positions her so he can finger her pussy as she does.

"That's it, suck my cock, bitch. Suck it, get it good and hard, I want to fuck you again...." He hesitates. "I want to fuck your ass..."

She doesn't quite like the word 'bitch, but she's in the zone and it can't break her mood. She moans and swallows as her response, there's no sign of refusal, her hips lifting to his fingers. She wants his touch, even as she takes him in her mouth. He feels his cock start to harden.

* * *

With his erection gone, she has no difficulty taking all of him into her mouth, pushing her face up against his pubic mound, the coarse hair rasping against her skin. She can even stretch her jaws wide and slide her tongue out against his balls. She presses her hands against his meaty, hairy thighs, savoring the maleness of him, all the imperfections adding up to a potent masculinity.

His fingers are in her and sometimes she stops enjoy the feel, the orgasms he triggers as well as the almost orgasms he misses. His fingers are clumsy, sometimes they pinch, but she loves the feeling of being handled. Why couldn't her husband touch her like this, with this hunger, this eagerness.

One wet finger probes her asshole, pushing rudely in, making her gasp.

She's not sure about that, she's never done it. She's read about it, but never tried it. There's a moment of ... not panic, but trepidation, uncertainty. She doesn't know if she wants to do it, more she doesn't know if she can't. He's come, isn't that enough?

His cock throbs against her tongue, she feels it a little firmer, a little larger, the beginning of swelling. The smell of sex is potent. She decides not to think of it, to focus on his cock, on the fingers in her, on the slickness of their bodies, on the feel of him.

He pushes his finger in and out of her ass, using her own lubrication to wet it. It's almost uncomfortable. Not quite, but getting there, if he's rough. If he pushes harder, or another finger, then it will be uncomfortable, it will hurt, and she'll tell him to stop.

She almost doesn't hear him, he has to say it twice.

"Stick your finger up my ass."

Awkwardly she complies. They're lying on the bed together, on their sides in a sort of sixty-nine, but she has to twist to get her arm around to push a finger up his ass.

It's hot inside him, surprising her, and she can feel an artery throb against her finger inside his colon. He twists trying to make the position easier. His cock swells slowly.

"He's getting hard again," she thinks with excitement, she's doing this to him, making it happen. It's an affirmation of the power of her sexuality, her desirability. She feels validated.

Or maybe he just likes a finger in his ass. She's vague on the subject, some men like it, something to do with a prostate? Whatever. If she can make men hard so easily just by shoving a finger up their bums, maybe she should just go around shoving her finger up their bums. Try it on her husband?

He withdraws his finger from her ass, surrendering and giving himself over to her, allowing her to finger his butt deeper.

Eventually, he pushes her onto her back, crawls over her, her until his genitals are over her mouth, she opens wide, sixty-nining him. He pulls her legs back until they are almost under his arms, in his elbows. Her pussy is directly under her face, he licks it, spits into it.

With a free hand, he pulls and jerks until he's in position to push a finger up her ass again. This time more slowly, a series of thrusts, and then once in the motion is smoother, easier. The spit of his mouth, and lubrication from her pussy runs down in trickles between her ass cheeks, and she's acutely aware of it.

His cock hardens, his weight on her is stifling, she squirms, pushes, and he allows her off. They roll over, until she's straddling him, going down on his cock. Her legs are splayed wide across his chest. His fingers are in her pussy, and in her ass, the movement drives her wild. She arches her back to let him do what he's doing, pushing and pushing until it drives her to a squealing orgasm that leaves her collapsing.

He's rock hard now. His cock throbbing like a cobra, shining with her dripping spit.

She's panting. Calming.

"I don't know," she says, her voice is cracked, she clears her throat, "I don't know about fucking me in the ass."

"I'll pay you more," he says, he consciously names a ridiculous number, perhaps it will tap her submissive side again, "I'll give you another twenty."

She doesn't pick up on it, the number goes right past her. If she had registered it, she might be insulted. But it's the act itself that fills her thoughts. "I've never done it, that's all. I don't know if I can..."

"No, it's okay," he lies, "I've done it a lot. I'm really good at it. I know what to do."

She thinks about it. At the beginning, she wouldn't have thought at all. She'd have been out the door in a flash. She would have screamed if she needed to.

But the woman lying in the bed right now, and the woman who had walked through that door are two different people. She's relaxed, filled with satisfaction, in the glow of orgasms. She has a complete stranger's semen in her, has felt his hands all over her body, sucked his cock on her knees and loved it. Her heart is still pounding, and she's still dripping.

She feels alive. She feels wanted. She feels confident. She wants to hold that feeling a little longer.

"Fifty," he says. But really, it's not the money.

"What if it hurts?" She asks, but there's no force to the question.

"If it hurts, we won't do it," he says, which reassures her.

She's surprised by how she finds herself trusting him. But maybe, when you're naked with someone, and they make you come, maybe some kind of trust, some openness, is instinctive. Regardless of whether it's wise. She reflects on this.

"But you took two fingers," he is cajoling.

"Two?" She's surprised. It wasn't bad at all. Two fingers? Interesting. Intriguing. Tempting.

"Almost three...." he says.

He did buy her, she thinks to herself. She sold herself, he owns her. She did say 'anything.'

"You did say anything," he says, almost as if he's reading her mind.

She pauses for a long moment, thinking it over.

"Okay," she says.

He hadn't expected her to say yes.

"But if it starts to hurt, you stop. We stop, okay."

"Sure, of course," he reassures her, not sure that if it gets to that point that he will, or that he will be able to.

She reaches for his cock, curls her hand around it. Such a dirty thing, she thinks. She's never done it with her husband, not in all the years of her marriage. Never done it at all. She's heard of it, of course. And heard that some women like it. But she's never done it. Because they never try anything, because in her marriage, she's dull.

And now, she's sold herself, she's giving her last cherry up to a stranger who bought her. It's a strange feeling, but it makes her cunt tighten. There's some awful, wonderful place she's in, a new world of sex and abandon. She slides a condom down over it. She's remembered condoms.

It's the hardness of his cock, this desire of his to have her, to possess her. It's the intensity that arouses her, the fact that he desperately wants her, wants to have her this way. After so many years of being ordinary, she loves the thought of being wanted, of being desired, of being hungered for.... She wants to be devoured.

"Okay," she says, finally, "How do we do this? Where do you want me?"

* * *

He positions her on all fours on the bed, ass up in the air, legs spread, pushing her head down until her face is on a pillow. She looks absolutely wanton like this, she can feel her pussy gape open, feel a thin thread of semen or pussy juice spool down.

"Is there enough lubrication," she says suddenly. His finger is rough against her anus.

"I need lubrication," she insists.

She realizes she has it, she brought it, just in case. She hadn't entirely trusted herself to be wet, or wet enough, if something actually happened. She's glad she was careful.

"I've got some in my purse," she tells him. He mumbles something. "Just go in my purse, and get it. It's okay."

She feels the bed shift as he gets off the bed, walks over to the dresser. She probably shouldn't let him go through her purse, she thinks. Truthfully, he's a little shocked that she gave him license to enter her purse, even with regular women, that's sacrosanct. For a prostitute? He has the irrational sense that maybe she actually likes him, that he's not just a john. He's not sure where to put that or what to make of it.

He finds it easily and returns. The lubrication is smeared over her ass cheeks, its cold. She gives a little gasp. He finds her anus, works it in, the finger enters, withdraws, and in again.

"Two fingers," he says from behind her.

"Right now?" she asks. "You have two fingers in me?"

It doesn't feel so bad.

She feels a pushing, a stretching, feels herself tighten instinctively, pushes. And then she consciously relaxes, feels the pushing return. That goes on for a minute or two.

"Three fingers," he says. "You're ready."

The bed shifts as he positions himself, a finger... (Two fingers?) pull out, but here's still one in her.

"I'm going to fuck your pussy first, to get my cock all wet, okay...." He tells her. "Then, when we've got it going good, I'm going to put it in your ass... I'll be careful."

She wonders why at first. After all, he's got her lubricant. He can drench his condom with it.

But then she knows why, he just likes having his cock in her, fucking her pussy. She moans a little as he thrusts in, hands tight on her hips. She likes it too.

Perversions and Infidelities / Page 168

"I love it," she grunts, "your cock in my cunt."

"You're going to love it in your ass," he tells her, fucking her with growing intensity. She makes no response, just arches her back.

He fucks harder and harder, his cock stiffening with each thrust, pushing her to one near orgasm after another, never quite over. Her hand flails, trying to get underneath to reach her pussy. A touch, a stroke of her clit at the right moment... she is so close. It won't take much..

He slows, stops. He's so hard in her, the shape of him is so explicit, she thinks she can feel every vein of his cock, every ridge and ripple of his erection, in her pussy, even through the condom. His fingers flex against her ass.

"Its show time, Babe," he says.

"Okay." She's got the butterflies back, nervous, excited, wanting to go through with it. "Slow okay? And you'll stop if it hurts?"

"Sure," he says. She's not sure if she likes the way he says it.

She feels his hands pulling her cheeks apart. Feels the head of his cock against her asshole, the weight of it pressing. Her heart starts to pound.

"Here goes."

At first, there's pressure, not like the fingers, this is much thicker, a pushing against her whole body. She feels her face pushed into the pillow. And then the head pushes in, she can feel it, being opened in this strange way, the sense of stretching, of motion. Her body tightens up involuntarily.

"Stop," she says.

He stops.

But he doesn't take it out. He just stops pushing.

They can quit now, she thinks. But they've just started. She doesn't quite want to quit just yet. Consciously, she squeezes and then tries to relax. She takes a deep breath.

He takes this as a signal.

"It's okay," he whispers, "you're doing good. You're doing so good, just relax okay. It's going to be so good."

She's breathing hard.

"Give me a minute," she asks.

She tries to reach back there with her mind, squeezing, consciously relaxing. She feels him moving again, sliding forward. Then tightens involuntarily. He stops, waits her out, and slides in again. She exhales deeply, emptying her lungs. She feels her body pushed forward again, realizes his thighs are pressing tight against her ass cheeks, knows it an instant before he says it.

"I'm in," he says, "All the way in, right up deep in your ass," he says.

"Wow," she says. Easier than she expected. She wasn't sure what to expect. He's inside her, she feels him deep, feels him in a way she's never felt anyone before. Not pleasurable, not awful, just strange. She can feel her sphincter tighten, her bowels flex, trying to expel him, but of course she can't. She wonders if it's supposed to be pleasurable.

"Popped your cherry babe," he says, the idea excites him, "for fifty dollars."

He doesn't believe it though, he thinks this is just some theatre she's playing. If he knew, if he really knew, he'd ejaculate instantly.

The words sink into her.

"You popped my cherry," she repeats. Not to the man she loves, not to the man she spent her life with. To some stranger. Sold it. But there's no guilt, just a strange liberation.

He starts to pull back, holding her hips in place. And then move forward. The fucking is slow at first, almost gentle. She moans softly. The pace picks up. The more it goes, the easier it seems to get, her body relaxes accepting it even as he fucks harder and harder. There's a weird pleasure, a wild pleasure, hot inside her body, she gasps and moans, clutching the sheets, pulling from the bed and winding them in her fists. She can feel sweat trickling along the center of her back, from her elevated ass down her spine to the back of her neck.

"Oh god," she moans, "oh god oh god oh god" her words are guttural, the syllables losing meaning. She can feel the slap of his hips against her ass, pushing her hard down on the bed.

"Take it bitch, take it up the ass," he spits in her ear, but she's not registering. She's so close nothing registers but the feeling. And then it's almost there.

His orgasm hits with such force he slams her into the bed. He comes, and his noise is a roar and it almost hurts he's fucking into her ass so violently, he goes stiff. But she's not quite there. She's close.

"Don't stop," she cries out, "fuck you, don't stop don't stop."

He resumes thrusting hard, three times, four, five and then her orgasm rolls over her.

When it's over, when she can think again, his cock is out of her. She's drenched. Sweat, cum, squirt. Her hair is plastered to her forehead, and she's still panting trying to catch her breath.

"Wow," she says.

She's done, she thinks. Even if he's hard again, she's had it. Physically, sexually, emotionally, she's fulfilled.

"You're a hot bitch," he whispers.

"Don't call me bitch."

She let it pass in the heat of the moment, but not this time. Not again.

There's a pause.

"Okay," he says.

"Slut, whore, sexy, hot," she said, "that's all good. But not bitch, I don't like it."

"Got it."

He nods.

Just having him accepting a rule. It gives her confidence, a feel of security.

She feels him lifting off her body, moving up on the bed, crawling on all fours. A moment where he pulls the condom off, throwing it over the side of the bed. He pauses near her head, his fingers in her hair once again. He never quite pulls her hair hard, she notices, it's never quite rough. He just seems to like her hair.

She lifts her head. She's discovered, she thinks, she likes her hair pulled a little. Not hard, but just to kind of guide her. She likes the feel of it. Her husband never pulled her hair. She didn't think she would like it, but there's something wild about it, something lustful.

What would her husband do if she asked him to?

"What?" She asks.

"ATM, Babe," he says. "Clean me up."

"What?"

Automatic teller machine, she wonders? What's he talking about?

"Ass to mouth."

Her automatic reaction would normally be that it was disgusting and to flatly refuse. But she's been through a lot in the last hour.

She gazes at his cock. No longer hard. She's had it in her mouth twice now. He's circumcised, she's glad of that now, a foreskin would be disgusting. But it looks clean, no streaks, no foreign matter. He'd worn a condom. There's a faint smell of rubber, of sweat. But it's not vile. On impulse she opens her mouth.

The cock slips in. It tastes like it did before, with an aftertaste of latex now. She rolls her tongue on it, goes deep and then lets it drop from her lips.

That's enough she thinks, a gesture.

He allows himself to relax, falling on his back on the exposed mattress, past her head.

"That was amazing."

Yes, she agrees, definitely: It was amazing.

She's glad she's done this, she thinks.

She doesn't know if she'll ever do it again, but she's glad.

She's lived.

* * *

They relax for a while, probably no more than minutes. She takes stock. Her body is drenched with sweat, she probably stinks of it. Her stockings cling wet against her thighs, one half off where the garter belt clips tore loose. There's a ladder in one stocking, she can feel it. And her waist is red and raw where the garter belt was rubbing. She wants out of them. She asks for a shower.

She takes her purse and dress into the shower, and locks the door. She doesn't particularly want company. The shower is hot and refreshing, she stands in it for ten minutes, enjoying it, revelling in the hot needles of water on her skin. It brings her a lucid clarity. The glow is still there, the satisfaction, but she's thinking clearly.

In the cold light of reason, she's astonished at what she's done, the recklessness of it, the risks she's taken. Where did that come from? When did she get so brave? So stupid? It turned out well, amazingly well, she'll never forget this, or regret it.

But really, she was lucky.

It needs to be a onetime thing.

She dries off, fixes her hair, there's a minimal application of make-up. The stockings and garter belt, damp from sweat and sex go into the purse, she can't stand to wear them again. She wriggles her toes before slipping into her shoes.

She takes a deep breath before stepping out into the room.

He's there of course. Fully dressed. The shirt is unbuttoned. Some part of her wants to run her hand through the exposed matt of chest hair.

"Hey," he says, "That was pretty good. I was thinking, I hit down pretty often. I'd like to look you up again."

She stops.

Thinks it over. This was amazing. If she sees him again, it's not like picking up a stranger. She knows he's safe. One more time to play at being a prostitute? Or a few... He is safe. She makes a snap decision.

"Okay."

"Can I have your number?"

She gives it to him, texts only, watching as he programs it into his phone.

As he does so, he speaks.

"You know, it's hard to find a girl as hot as you. I have some friends, they're really nice guys. I wouldn't mind passing your number."

Her pussy clenches, she feels a tingle, the butterflies starting up, an excitement.

"I don't know. I'm pretty busy."

"Well, yeah, sure," he says, "But you know, if you're available..."

The thought unfolds in her mind. Strangers contacting her. Fucking. The simplicity of it. Contact, agree, pay, fuck. Surely not as risky as meeting someone in a bar. They'd come with references.

Passed on by men she's had, that she knows, vouched for in a sense both ways - she's hot, they're safe.

A secret life as a hooker. Housewife on one side, gardens and Capri pants and school shopping... But a secret life of lingerie and desire, hotel rooms and hard cocks and sweaty wanton sex with men she doesn't have to have a fucking relationship with. Men filled with elemental desire, their cocks hard and wild simply from the wanting of her....

"Yes," she says, "pass it around, but carefully. Okay? Only safe guys. Clean ones. Only contact me by text. Outcall only, nowhere cheap, and if I'm not available, I'm not available."

She's proud of the tough way she says it. Like a real veteran. Like a real woman, in control. Deep down, she's getting wet again. She will make sure she's available. Not always, but she'll find ways to fit it in her life. The wheels are already turning, manufacturing excuses, dates, excursions...

"Sometimes we like to get together for parties..." He says.

"Parties?"

"Bachelor parties, you know, stuff like that. Guys get together..."

Gangbangs she thinks.

The idea sparkles and sizzles in her mind.

"You do that kind of thing?"

The possibility, a room full of men, hard cocks, naked bodies, just for her, one after the other, or two or three at a time, in her mouth, her pussy, combinations, sweat, the reek of sex, of total abandon.

The thought gives her butterflies. She wants to jump with enthusiasm.

"Sure," she says with forced casualness, "I'm a whore."

Her phone vibrates. She looks at it. The number is unfamiliar.

She looks up at him. A test text. He just wants to be sure it's not a bum number. She holds up her phone so he can see.

There's little more to talk about. He doesn't offer to walk her to the elevator or any such gesture. She leaves, the door closes behind her.

At the elevator, she smiles.

The smile grows and grows, and she smiles all the way home...

The End

ABOUT THE AUTHOR

Eve St. Albert is private and discrete, full of secrets and satisfactions.

After many adventures, this is her first book. But it might not be her last...

Coming Soon....

PERVERSIONS & INFIDELITIES, DEUX
The Pleasures of Transgression

* * *

PERVERSIONS & INFIDELITIES, TROIS
Women Finding Power and Pleasure

* * *

WILD WHORES
A Novel of the Street